Death

From

Desire

Thank you for your support !

Mark R. Bedman

Death From

Desire

Crime Thrillers

Mark R Beckner

Becknerbooks Publishing

First Edition: September 2021

ISBN: 978-1-7369607-2-1 (paperback)

Credits

Sally Beckner - Copy review and editing

Writing companion - Roxy

This book is dedicated to our five grandkids:

Emma Hipsher
Bryson Hipsher
Dexton Hipsher
Gavin Beckner
Hailey Beckner

PREFACE

Now retired after 36 years of policing in Boulder, Colorado, I've turned my attention to writing fictional crime thrillers. My first foray into writing fiction resulted in my first book, **Behind The Lies**, a book of three crime dramas that received high reviews. I immensely enjoyed the research and effort it took to write the first book. Once I found readers enjoyed the stories, I was encouraged to continue writing. It keeps me busy in my spare time and allows me to use my knowledge and criminal investigation experience in a completely new way.

These stories are written for entertainment with a sense of realism. While none of the stories were born from actual crimes I investigated, ideas for each were cultivated from situations I am familiar with, followed, investigated, or supervised. Studying real-life crime provides more than enough ideas for fictional stories. As with all my stories, I hope you enjoy the dramatic journey to solving the crime thrillers presented in this book.

Please visit my website for additional information.

becknerbooks.com
or email
becknerbooks@gmail.com

Table of Contents

Deadly Desires

Amarillo Billy

Amarillo Billy Continued...

Deadly

Desires

Chapter 1

Tyler and Miranda were sitting outside enjoying their lattes at one of the many beachside cafes on Miami Beach. It was a beautiful Tuesday morning. The sun was glistening off the rolling waves as they soaked it all in and watched seagulls circling above. Tyler was having some difficulty finishing his latte, as he had not been feeling well in recent days.

"Why not?" asked Tyler, as he felt the cool ocean breeze against his cheek.

"You knew the rules, Tyler," responded Miranda.

"Yes, but things can change. We have a wonderful thing going here. I think I'm falling in love with you."

"Tyler, that's not an option. I made that perfectly clear. I'm not in love with you, and I have no interest in a permanent relationship. This was purely for enjoyment and as an escape. I thought you understood that."

"Yes, I did," sighed Tyler, "but I need you now. Who else can I turn to? You have fulfilled my life like no one else. We can continue to see each other, right?"

"Look, I've got a meeting to attend. Why don't you come over tonight, and we can discuss this over something stronger than coffee? Maybe we can agree on an arrangement."

"I would like that. What time?"

"Why don't you come over after work at seven o'clock. I'll have some margaritas ready."

"Thank you. I'll see you then."

Tyler Vincent had a successful law practice in Miami, Florida, with his law partner, Tony Rialto. They had built their success in defending employers and corporations against plaintiff lawsuits over various grievances, ranging from discrimination claims to product liability claims. Vincent had recently won a big case defending a chemical company against a plaintiff family who had sued over allegations that its insecticide had contributed to their son's cancer. Vincent had convinced the jury there was no connection between the use of the product and cancer, so long as the product was used correctly. The company was so pleased with the outcome, they paid Vincent an attractive bonus in addition to his regular fee.

Not only was Vincent a successful attorney, but he was quite handsome as well. He was 35 years old and stood at 6'-2", and weighed approximately 200 lbs. He had brown hair, brown eyes, and a chiseled chin. He would often take time away from the office to jog for thirty to forty minutes several times a week to stay fit. Vincent sometimes believed his good looks and verbal skills helped him win over jurors, especially the women. His suits were always tailor-made and quite expensive.

Miranda Castaneda recently filled a void in Tyler Vincent's life. He had been seeking excitement, passion, and companionship when he met Miranda Castaneda five months ago. Miranda was a beautiful woman of Cuban descent. She had long, dark hair, big chocolate brown eyes, a well-proportioned body, and long slender legs. She was also very charming. She was just the type of woman he had been dreaming about, and the sex with Miranda was highly satisfying. He had not had sex like that in years. Tyler found himself falling in love. Unfortunately for Tyler, Miranda did not feel the same way. He was hoping he could change her mind, or at least continue their relationship.

After Miranda left Tyler at the beach café, he returned to his office in downtown Miami. His feeling of illness was getting stronger, and he felt the urge to vomit. He went to his private bathroom and emptied his breakfast into the toilet. He immediately felt some relief, but continued to have sharp pains in his lower back. He had been having symptoms for about seven days, and today seemed to be the worst. *If this doesn't get better soon,* he thought, *I will need to see a doctor.* Tyler took pain medication, removed his shoes, and laid down on his office couch. He soon fell asleep. When he awoke, it was already 2:00 pm. The medication and sleep seemed to help. He ate a leftover muffin from the office kitchen and then finished some paperwork before leaving the office.

At 7:00 pm, Tyler arrived at Miranda's well-maintained and elegantly decorated home in Coconut Grove. Miranda opened the door for him as he strode up the walkway.

"Hello, Tyler," greeted Miranda.

"Hi, it's so good to see you," said Tyler, as he gave her a big hug.

"How are you feeling?"

"Better. I took some medication and had a nap. That helped some, but I've only had a muffin since this morning."

"Would you like me to fix you something?"

"No, I better not eat anything else."

"Well, I hope you can still join me for a couple of margaritas. I've got them all blended up already."

"Yes, they might help me sleep later tonight."

Miranda led Tyler to the back patio, which bordered a small, landscaped pond with a waterfall. Several Koi fish swam in circles around the pond. They sat in red cushioned chairs with a small, round metal table between them. Miranda handed Tyler a frozen margarita fresh from the blender, with a slice of lime attached to the rim. Tyler took a long sip, and the icy refreshing drink helped quench his thirst and remove the dryness from his mouth.

"Miranda," started Tyler, "you know how much I enjoy your companionship. I hope we can continue to see each other."

"I don't know," said Miranda in a soft voice. "You know my position about getting too involved."

"Yes, I know, and I'm sorry if I scared you this morning. I do love you, but I can respect your wishes. I just want to keep seeing you."

"If you are sure," said Miranda, "that you can keep our relationship strictly as one of just friends, with benefits, of course."

"It's not what I prefer, but yes, if that means we can keep seeing each other."

"Alright, then we can keep our friendship. But I want to be clear. I am not interested in anything permanent and certainly not in getting married. Been there, done that."

"Yes, I know where you stand. Thank you, Miranda. You are all I have right now."

"I know. Now let me refill your drink for you. You must have been thirsty."

"They taste good." Tyler knew he probably shouldn't be drinking alcohol with his recent stomach issues, but he thought the alcohol might help reduce his back pain.

Miranda got up and went inside to fill their glasses. Tyler stared into the pond and watched the fish swim around as he thought about his future. So much was about to change. He was relieved that he would at least still have Miranda as a girlfriend. Miranda returned to the patio and handed Tyler another full margarita. They continued to chat while sipping their drinks. Tyler finished his second drink and felt a bit dizzy. *Miranda must have put a little extra tequila in these drinks,* thought Tyler. He was also starting to get nauseous again.

"It's probably about time for you to get going," suggested Miranda.

"I was hoping to spend the night here."

"That would be nice, but I have some paperwork to do tonight and need to be at work early tomorrow. I need my rest. How about Saturday night?"

"Well, alright," said a disappointed Tyler. "But I'll be thinking about you."

"I'll be thinking about you as well," responded Miranda with a mischievous grin.

Tyler gave Miranda a goodnight kiss and headed out the door. He could feel the pain in his back flaring up again. It felt like a muscle cramp that he could not get rid of. As he drove home, he continued to feel nauseous, and his breathing became labored. *I'm going to have to see a doctor in the morning. This is more than just a simple flu bug.*

When Tyler arrived home, he parked in the garage, then struggled to get out of the car. He gingerly walked to the door and quietly entered his house. He made it to the bedroom, slipped off his outer clothing, and fell into bed.

Chapter 2

The following morning at approximately 4:00 am, the phone rang, waking Detective Rick Baez. Baez rolled over and grabbed his cell phone off the bedside table.

"Hello? Say what?"

"It's John Randle. Wake up."

"I'm awake. What do you have?" asked Baez.

"Patrol found some dead guy in his car at Stratton Park with a hose running from the exhaust pipe to the front window," advised Sergeant John Randle of the Miami-Dade Metro Police Department.

"A suicide?" asked Baez.

"Looks that way, but who knows for sure. How soon can you get there?"

"Hmm, let me see. I can be there in 40 minutes."

"Okay, I'll meet you there," responded Randle.

Baez dragged himself out of bed, quickly shaved and brushed his teeth, then looked for a clean shirt to wear. He had no more shirts hanging in his closet, so he had to sift through the enormous pile of dirty clothing in the corner of his bedroom. He found one that smelled okay and shook it to get some of the wrinkles out. Fortunately, he still had one pair of socks and underwear in his dresser drawer. He found his pants from the previous day hung over the chair by his bed. After dressing, Baez rushed to the kitchen and grabbed his coffee cup from the sink, then rinsed it out. He poured himself a cold cup of coffee from the pot he made the day before. He placed the cup in the microwave to warm the coffee. Baez stretched his five-foot, eleven-inch frame and ran a brush through his thick, dark hair. His weight was proportional to his height, but he had recently put on a few extra pounds around his mid-section. He knew he should work out more often but couldn't seem to find the time.

After downing his lukewarm coffee, he looked around for his gun and holster. He knew he set it down somewhere after getting home the previous night but could not remember where. He'd probably had a bit too much to drink the night before. He finally located the gun and holster under a t-shirt on the kitchen table. His car keys were found among some old frozen food tins on the kitchen counter.

As a single man who worked long hours, Baez found little time to clean the two-bedroom stucco bungalow he rented in the South Miami area. His home was sparsely furnished, and the only thing hanging on his wall was a Miami Dolphins poster. He also had a seventy-inch, high-definition TV to watch his football games. He had a cleaning lady come in every other week to pick up and clean the place. However, he always had to leave a big tip on the kitchen table, as she would often complain about how hard it was to always pick up after him before she could clean. The extra money seemed to satisfy her enough to keep her from quitting.

After making sure he had everything he needed, he headed out the door, got into his detective car, and drove toward the scene. He arrived 20 minutes later. Sergeant Randle met him as he exited his vehicle and told him what he currently knew.

Dispatch had received a call on a suspicious vehicle sitting in the parking lot near the basketball court in Stratton Park at approximately 3:20 am. The first officer arrived at 3:26 am and found a male subject sitting in his car. The car was running with a black plastic corrugated hose taped to the tailpipe. From there, it ran to the front driver's window. The hose was stuck in a two-inch gap at the top of the window. All the car doors were locked. The first officer broke out the window with his metal baton, pulled the male out of the car, and checked him for signs of life. He then called for medical assistance. However, the victim had been dead for too long to revive.

Baez walked toward the car, a dark blue BMW 8 Series Gran Coupe. *Nice car,* thought Baez as he got closer to the vehicle. The front driver's door was standing open, with small pieces of shattered glass on the ground, in the black leather driver's seat, and on the floorboard. The black hose was still connected to the tailpipe, with the other end now lying on the ground. The first officer had turned the car engine off. The deceased male was lying on his back, approximately fifteen feet from the car. He had been left there after paramedics attempted to bring him back to life. The male appeared to be around 50 years old, Hispanic, and well dressed in a light-blue, pinstriped button-down shirt, black dress slacks, and black dress shoes.

Randle looked at Baez. "Looks like he got all dressed up for his big exit."

"Yeah, I've seen it before," said Baez. "Some people like to look their best before killing themselves. Plus, this guy obviously had some money, so maybe he only had nice clothes. You said the car was still running when the first officer arrived?"

"Yes, that's correct."

"And then the officer broke the window and pulled the victim out?"

"Yes."

"Alright," said Baez, "get the coroner out here to take care of the body. I don't want to touch anything just in case this is not what it looks like. We also want our forensic folks to process this car."

"What are you thinking?" asked Randle.

"Nothing really, just a little strange to do this in a public park. Too easy to get discovered before the deed is complete. Of course, at three o'clock in the morning, few people are out and about in this part of town."

Several patrol officers set up crime scene tape around the car while Baez and Randle waited for the coroner to arrive. At 5:20 am, a deputy coroner, Susan Mills, showed up on the scene and began to examine the body. Baez asked her to try to locate an identification.

After carefully examining and photographing the body, Mills located and removed a wallet from the victim's right rear pants pocket. She handed it to Baez. Wearing protective gloves, Baez searched the wallet. He found $320 cash in the victim's wallet, along with a driver's license and several credit cards in the name of Dominic Lopez. Based on his driver's license, Lopez was 5'9", 175 lbs., and 52 years old.

Baez handed the driver's license to Randle. "This name is familiar to me. Does it ring a bell for you?"

Randle looked at the photo and name for several seconds. "I believe this is the Dominic Lopez who owns the string of car dealerships in Miami-Dade."

"If true, that explains the nice car and wad of cash in his pocket," responded Baez. "Even so, that's a lot of cash to have on hand. Did you know this guy?"

"Ran into him a few times when looking into thefts from his car lots or criminal mischief, that sort of thing. But I didn't know him well. He seemed like a nice guy, though. Maybe he was dealing with some personal problems."

"Maybe, or someone wasn't pleased with the color car he sold them."

Randle gave Baez a look of surprise.

"Yeah, I know, too soon to make jokes," said Baez. "Do you know if he has family?"

"I know he has two sons who help him run the dealerships."

"I'll look him up when I get back to the office."

One of the crime scene investigators (CSIs) located a cell phone in the car's front console. He placed it in a clear plastic bag and gave it to Baez. Baez stuck the phone in his jacket pocket. No suicide note was found in the car. *Maybe we will find it at his home,* thought Baez.

Before leaving the scene, Baez asked Mills to send him the report with the medical examiner's finding once the autopsy had been completed. She advised that the autopsy would take place in the afternoon, and the preliminary report would be ready the following day.

Back at the office, Baez began the process of getting background information on Dominic Lopez. Based on his research, he found that Dominic Lopez was indeed the owner of a chain of car dealerships in Miami-Dade County. He owned dealerships affiliated with several different auto manufacturers, and a couple of his lots only dealt in used cars. He was well known in the Miami area. It was easy for Baez to find public information on Lopez. Baez learned Lopez was married and had three children. Lopez's wife's name was Valerie, and they had a home in an exclusive neighborhood in Miami Beach. The address of the home matched the address listed on Lopez's driver's license. His two sons, Ricky, and Regis, both helped manage the dealership business. Lopez also had a twenty-year-old daughter by the name of Randi. He could not find information on her current whereabouts. By 7:15 am, Baez was ready to contact Mrs. Lopez to inform her of Dominic's death. Baez contacted on-call Victim's Advocate Shelly Rivers, explained the situation, and asked her to meet him in front of the Lopez residence. She said she could be there in 45 minutes.

At approximately 8:15 am, Advocate Rivers pulled up behind Baez's detective car across the street from the Lopez residence.

"Hi, Shelly, thanks for coming out so quickly," greeted Baez.

"No problem, I was already up and dressed for the day when you called."

"This may be a tough one and likely to attract a lot of media attention," cautioned Baez.

"Yes, which will make it harder on the family."

Baez knocked on the front door of the Lopez residence. The location and size of the home were indicative of the wealth Lopez had accumulated. Valerie Lopez was already dressed when she answered the front door. Baez introduced themselves and asked if they could speak to her. Valerie invited them in and led them to a sitting room. All three of them sat down.

"Mrs. Lopez," started Baez, "we have some sad news to tell you. I'm deeply sorry to have to tell you that early this morning, we found your husband Dominic deceased in Stratton Park."

"Oh, my god!" exclaimed Valerie. "What happened!?"

"We are not sure yet, but he was found sitting in his car in the park. It appears as though he committed suicide."

Valerie lowered her head and placed her hands over her face while letting out a guttural scream. Rivers got up from her chair and kneeled next to Valerie, placing her hand on her shoulder. They both allowed Valerie to sob for a few moments without saying anything.

Once she somewhat composed herself, she asked, "how did he kill himself?"

"It appears he asphyxiated himself by running a hose from the exhaust to the inside of the car. But this is just a preliminary cause of death. We won't know for sure until we get the coroner's report," advised Baez. "Do you have any idea why he may have wanted to take his own life?"

Valerie sat in silence, staring at the floor with tears running down her cheeks. Rivers pulled out some tissues and handed them to Valerie.

Baez allowed her some time before asking again. "Mrs. Lopez, anything you know may help us understand what happened."

"The kids will be devastated," sobbed Valerie. "They love their father."

"I'm sure he loved them as well. So, why would he want to kill himself?"

After a few more moments of silence, Valerie finally said, "I don't know, maybe because we were splitting up. But that was his doing."

"You were getting divorced?"

"Yes, that is what he wanted."

"If he wanted the divorce, why would he take his own life over that?"

"That's what I don't understand," replied Valerie between sobs.

"Were there any problems with the business?"

"No."

"Sorry, but I have to ask. Did you find any letter or note that might have indicated Dominic was going to do something like this?"

"No."

"Does he have a computer here at home?"

"No, but he has one at work. The only thing he has personally is an iPad."

"Would you mind if I took the iPad so that we can look to see if there is anything on it to give us some idea of why he might have done this?"

"It would probably be in his condo."

"His condo?"

"Yes. Once he decided he wanted a divorce, he moved out. He is renting a condo in Edgewater."

"How long has he been in his condo?"

"About two weeks."

"Okay, Valerie, I'll probably need to talk to you some more at a later time."

Baez turned to Rivers. "Do you have someone else coming out to help you?"

"Yes," said Rivers. "Another advocate is on the way and should be here soon."

"Great, I will need to interview all family members at some point, but can you help Mrs. Lopez with notifications of the family?"

"No problem, that's part of what we do."

"Thank you, Shelly. Mrs. Lopez, I will leave you with Shelly as I've got more follow-up to do. I will get back to you once I have more information, okay?"

"Yes," she sobbed. "Thank you."

"Oh, did Dominic have a home office here?"

"Yes."

"Do you mind if I look around Dominic's office before leaving, just to see if there may be anything that might help clear this up?"

"I don't mind. His office is down the hall on the right."

Baez then walked down the hall to Lopez's office and checked the papers on his desk. He then looked through the desk drawers, trying to find any note or letter Lopez may have left behind. Everything he found appeared to apply only to the car business. Baez could hear Rivers consoling Valerie as he left the house.

When he returned to the police department, Baez took the cell phone recovered from Lopez's vehicle and logged it into evidence with a request for digital forensics to search the phone for any possible information that could help the investigation. He then called Derek Frapke, one of the CSI's who responded to the scene and searched the victim's vehicle.

"Hey, Derek," said Baez, "did you find anything of interest in the vehicle?"

"No, not really," replied Frapke. "It seemed clean. We did find a drink glass that we collected, and we were able to get a few prints. But given the location, they will probably belong to our victim. However, while we were cleaning up, some guy walks up and tells us he saw our victim's car and another car parked next to it during the night. When he saw the police activity this morning, he thought he should say something."

"Really?" said Baez. "Did he give a time when he observed this?"

"He said it was close to two o'clock this morning. I was going to text you his information. His name is Tony Mateo. I will text you the phone number after we hang up."

"Great. What about that drink glass?"

"It had a small amount of liquid in it that smelled of alcohol. We will log it into evidence."

"Maybe he needed some liquid courage to stay put in the car. Thank you, Derek."

It was not long after hanging up when Baez received the text message with Mateo's phone number. Baez immediately called him.

"Hello, this is Detective Baez with the Metro-Dade Police Department. I'm calling about our incident today at Stratton Park."

"Yes, hi Detective," began Mateo. "I have been waiting for someone to call me."

"I understand you may have observed our victim vehicle and another vehicle in the park last night."

"Yes, that's correct."

"Why don't you just tell me what you observed."

"Sure. I was out walking my dog around two o'clock when I noticed two cars in the parking lot near the basketball court. It seemed unusual, as it is rare to see anyone there at that time of night. One of the cars was a dark BMW, and the other was a small to mid-sized white car, possibly an SUV."

"Did you see anyone?"

"Not really, but there was someone in the BMW."

"How do you know that?"

"The car was running, and the brake lights came on a couple of times while I was looking."

"Was there anyone in the white car?"

"I couldn't tell, but I don't think it was running."

"What kind of car was the white one?"

"I'm not sure. Maybe one of those small SUVs, something like that. To be honest, I was more interested in the BMW. It was a nice car."

"What else did you see?"

"Nothing. After my dog did his business, I headed back home across from the park. I just thought it was strange to see two cars at that time of night, and they were parked side by side. I walk my dog most nights and rarely see even one car."

"Mr. Mateo, you've been immensely helpful. Thank you for coming forward," concluded Baez.

Interesting, thought Baez, *now we know there were two cars in the lot at around two o'clock, and one of them belonged to Lopez. Could the other car be related somehow?*

Chapter 3

It was early morning, and Tyler Vincent was in no condition to get out of bed. He felt extremely inebriated with a pounding headache. He was groggy and had severe pain in his abdomen and chest. Vincent attempted to get up by rolling over until he felt a cold, sticky substance against his left cheek and chin. It smelled horrible. He managed to lift his head a bit and realized he had vomited sometime during the night. He was now lying in the contents from his stomach. This made him wretch, but he could only dry vomit as there was nothing left in his stomach but some acid that burned his throat. He flopped back down on his back and tried to catch his breath. He was having trouble breathing. Just then, the bedroom door flew open so quickly the doorknob slammed against the adjacent wall.

"Where the hell were you last night!" screamed Kristy Vincent, Tyler's wife.

Vincent could not answer.

"I suppose you were out screwing around again, you son of a bitch! Look at you, so drunk you vomited all over yourself. I agreed to let you stay here for a few days only if you held it together."

Vincent attempted to speak but could say nothing.

"As soon as you sober up, I want you out of here!" screamed Kristy. "By the time I get home from work, you better be gone. Go live with whoever your new girlfriend is. I just want you out of here!"

Finally, Vincent managed to softly say, "help me," between shallow breaths. However, Kristy didn't stop yelling long enough to hear it. She slammed the door shut and left for work.

***

It was close to noon, and Baez was still working at his desk when Detective Leah Mitchell walked in. Detective Mitchell was a 31-year-old African American with short, curly black hair. She was five foot ten, slender build, with well-defined muscles, especially in her legs. She was known as a tough cop. She joined the police force shortly after graduating from the University of Miami. She had attended the university on a track scholarship as a sprinter. Her specialties were the 100-meter race and the 400-meter relay race. She helped the team take the conference title during her junior year, and she could still outrun most of the younger officers on the force.

"Hi, how's it going, Leah," greeted Baez.

"Okay, still working on my homicide from last week," Mitchell responded.

"You about ready to close it out?"

"Oh yeah, not a hard one to figure out when you've got the suspect in the house with the murder weapon. What are you working on?"

"I picked up an apparent suicide from Stratton Park early this morning. Guy parked his car and ran a hose from the tailpipe to the driver's window. It didn't take long for him to die."

"Sounds like an easy clearance for your stats," suggested Mitchell.

"Maybe. There are a couple of loose ends I need to run down, and I'm still waiting on the report from the medical examiner."

"What are your concerns?"

"Have you heard the name Dominic Lopez?"

"Of course, he owns several large dealerships in town."

"Well, he's my victim, and as of right now, I haven't found a reason he would kill himself. I also have a witness who saw a second car parked next to my victim's car at around two o'clock this morning. He also had three hundred and twenty dollars in cash with him. Why have that much cash if you're going to kill yourself?"

"No family issues?"

"Only that his wife said he wanted a divorce."

"Hmmm," pondered Mitchell. "Maybe that would be a reason for the wife to commit suicide, but the husband? There has to be more to the story."

"Oh, I'm sure there is. I still have plenty of interviews with family and acquaintances to do."

"Alright, let me know if you need anything." Mitchell then laughed. "By the way, is that a new shirt?"

"Are you a comedian now?" replied Baez.

"No, but you look like you slept in that shirt."

"I got called in the middle of the night and didn't have a clean one, okay?"

"Hope you are wearing clean underwear," said Mitchell as she walked away.

"Thanks," replied Baez.

Moments later, Victim Advocate Shelly Rivers called.

"Hi, Shelly. How did things go with Mrs. Lopez?"

"As well as can be expected," she said. "Mrs. Lopez was not very forthcoming with information, but she was upset over the pending divorce."

"And just to confirm," said Baez, "it was Dominic who wanted the divorce, right?"

"Yes, she was clear about that. We stayed until both sons arrived. The daughter is a student at Florida State, so it will take a while for her to get home."

"Thank you, Shelly."

"One more thing I wanted to pass along. The oldest son, Ricky, told me that mom had received an anonymous letter a few weeks ago telling her Dominic was having an affair. He said mom was upset after getting the letter. It may explain why Dominic wanted a divorce."

"Well, now that's interesting. It puts a unique twist on the case. I'll follow up on that. Thanks again."

"You're welcome."

Baez then called both sons, Ricky, and Regis Lopez, to set up interviews. They wanted to spend the remainder of the day with their mother, but both agreed to meet with Baez the following morning. After arranging these interviews, Baez grabbed his jacket and headed out the door. He would go to the primary dealership owned by Lopez and where he kept his corporate office. The sons, Ricky, and Regis, each served as general managers at other locations. Baez wanted to find out what the employees close to Dominic Lopez may have known.

Upon arrival, Baez found the dealership had been closed for the day. A sign was posted on the door advising customers the dealership was temporarily closed due to a family emergency. Baez could see that several people were milling around in the offices. He pounded on the door and held up his badge. The assistant manager, Jimmy Hernandez, answered the door.

"Come in, Detective. I'm the Assistant Manager here."

"Thank you. I'm sorry about the loss of Dominic."

"We appreciate that."

"I was hoping I could ask you and maybe the general manager a few questions about Dominic."

"Sure, let's go into my office."

Once in the office, Hernandez closed the door. Baez wasted no time.

"Were you aware of any problems or concerns Dominic may have had that would lead him to take his own life?" asked Baez.

"The general manager, Lucas Perez, and I were talking about this before you arrived. We know he was having some marital issues."

"What type of issues?"

"He told us he was in the process of getting a divorce."

"Did he say why?"

"I don't know many details, but something about his wife always nagging at him over this and that. He also thought she spent too much money."

"Do you know if he was having an affair?"

"I don't, but Lucas might. He was closer to Dominic than I was."

"Was he depressed over the collapse of his marriage?"

"Um, not that I saw. In fact, he seemed somewhat relieved he was going to get a divorce. He appeared to be happier, if that makes sense."

"Well, you never know in these types of situations. Is it possible for me to speak with Lucas?"

"Yes, let me go get him for you."

Baez waited for several minutes before Lucas Perez entered the room and introduced himself as the General Manager who worked directly under Dominic Lopez. He also described himself as a good friend of Dominic's. Perez was 41-years-old but looked young for his age. He was visibly upset over Dominic's death.

"I'm very sorry for the loss of your friend, Lucas."

"Thank you, sir. If there is anything I can do to help, I will."

"You're already doing it, Lucas. Some of these may be difficult to answer, but they are important questions."

"I understand, Detective."

"Okay. Were you aware of Dominic having an affair?"

"He wasn't very forthcoming about that, but yes, he was seeing someone. I think he was embarrassed by it but also excited by it. He and his wife, Valerie, were not getting along so well. He thought she nagged him too much, and life had gotten boring with her. He was looking for more excitement."

"And that excitement came in the form of dating another woman?"

"Again, I don't know who, but yes, he had another woman in his life."

"Did he tell you this?"

"Not initially, but things got heated at home when his wife received a letter telling her about an affair."

"Tell me more," encouraged Baez.

"All I know is that one day she received a letter, and Dominic was upset about it. He said no one else knew, so he wondered who could have sent the letter."

"Did Dominic's sons know about the letter?"

"Yeah, because I know the younger son, Regis, was angry about it."

"Angry enough to kill dad?"

"Oh no, nothing like that. Both sons loved their dad. He was just angry because it upset mom so much. Demanded to know if it was true."

"Did Dominic admit it was true?"

"Not initially, but eventually he told his sons he was seeing someone."

"Lucas, did Dominic ever talk about or mention killing himself over all this?"

"No, and like I said, other than being upset over the letter, he seemed his usual self. He seemed to be relieved after deciding to get divorced."

"Is there anyone you can think of who might have wanted to hurt Dominic? Angry customer or something?"

"No, I can't think of anyone who would want to harm Mr. Lopez. He was friends with everyone."

"Okay, Lucas, thank you for your time."

By the time Baez returned to the office, it was almost 5:00 pm. It had been a long day, and Baez was exhausted. Detective Leah Mitchell was heading out the door.

"Have a nice evening," said Baez.

"Oh, I'm not going home," stated Mitchell. "I just got called out on an unattended death."

"No other details?" asked Baez.

"All I know is that the wife came home from work and found her husband dead in bed. At least that's what she told dispatch and the first officers on the scene."

"I'd give you a hand, but I've been up since four this morning."

"Nope, I got this. He probably had a heart attack or something. I'll see you in the morning."

"Sounds good," said Baez.

Chapter 4

At 9:30 am Thursday, Ricky Lopez, the oldest son, arrived at the Miami-Dade Metro Police Department as scheduled to meet with Detective Baez. Baez took Ricky to a witness interview room designed to make witnesses feel comfortable. The room was small but had comfortable cushioned seats, a coffee table, and a drink bar. Two large photographs of sandy beaches and the ocean were framed and hung on the wall. After introductions, offering condolences, and serving Ricky a cup of coffee, Baez got down to business.

"Why do you think your father would want to kill himself?" asked Baez.

"That's just it," responded Ricky. "I don't believe he did. He was going through some turmoil with my mom, but everything else was fine."

"What kind of turmoil?"

"He and my mom were going to get divorced, and I know he struggled with that."

Baez cocked his head. "In what way?"

"They were married for a long time, like thirty years. It was Dad who wanted the divorce, but it still made him sad. You know about the letter, right?"

"Are you talking about the letter revealing an affair?"

"Yes."

Baez pressed on. "What do you know about the letter?"

"All I know is it was sent to my mom, and someone wrote that her husband, Dominic, was having an affair with another woman."

"Who sent the letter?"

"I don't know. It wasn't signed, and the return address was fake."

"How do you know that?"

"My mom tried to drive to the address on the envelope, but there was no such address."

"Did your mom figure out who this woman was?"

"No, and dad wouldn't tell her."

"Did this make your mom angry?"

"Oh yeah, there was a lot of screaming and yelling. She even threw some things at him. Cussed him out too."

Baez leaned in closer to Ricky. "Do you think your mom might have had something to do with your dad's death?"

"No, not at all. She was mad but didn't want the divorce. She wanted to work it out."

"But your dad wasn't interested?"

"No, I think he had his mind made up. He was tired of the marriage and wanted out."

"Ricky, do you know of anyone who might have wanted to hurt your dad?"

"No. Dad was outgoing and easily made friends. I can't think of anyone who would want to hurt him, certainly not kill him."

"Anyone else your father may have confided in?"

"If anyone, probably Miguel Rodriguez. He and my dad were best friends from high school, and they did a lot together. They played golf regularly. I'm not sure, but I think Miguel may have met the other woman."

"Does Rodriguez work with your dad?"

"No, he owns a restaurant in West Miami called El Paraiso La Casa. My dad ate there all the time."

"One last question. Do you know anyone close to your dad who drives a medium-sized white car?"

"Lots of people have white cars. It's a popular color, and even Mom has one."

"Your mom has a white car?"

"Yeah, a 2020 Toyota Sienna. Why?"

"Probably nothing, but a white car was observed in the park. I'm just being thorough. Thank you for coming today. And again, sorry for your loss."

After the interview with Ricky, it was time to interview the youngest son, Regis Lopez. Regis was already waiting in the lobby when Ricky's interview was over. Regis was taken to the same witness interview room. Regis was in no mood for coffee or anything else.

"Regis, I have to ask. Why do you think your father committed suicide?"

Regis looked down at the table and said nothing for several seconds. "I don't know."

"Was he upset about the pending divorce?"

"Yes, but not to the point of killing himself. I mean, come on, he's the one who wanted the darn thing. He's the one who cheated."

"I understand this upset your mom."

"Yes, it did," snapped Regis in an angry tone.

"Can you tell me about it?"

"Nothing to tell. Mom got an anonymous letter telling her dad was having an affair, and that's when it all started."

"What started?"

"Mom being upset and angry at Dad. Hell, I was angry at Dad. Everything seemed fine until that letter came."

"Did your father admit to the affair?"

Again, Regis hesitated. "Yes, he did. When I questioned him about it, he said there was nothing wrong with mom, just that married life had gotten boring, and he needed more."

"Did he ever tell you who the woman was?"

"No."

"How angry did you get toward your father?"

"I was angry, but not angry enough to kill him, if that's what you're thinking. I love both my parents. It was simply hard to understand."

"Did your dad have a life insurance policy?"

"Yes, he did."

"Do you know for how much?"

"Why are you asking me this?"

"These are just standard questions in any death investigation, Regis. We have to cover all bases."

"He had a one-million-dollar policy."

"Is your mom the beneficiary?"

"Yes."

"Again, I have to ask. Do you know anyone who might have been angry enough at your father to want to harm him?"

"No. I'm not aware of anyone."

"One more question. Your mom was obviously angry and upset over the letter. However, she never mentioned it to me yesterday. Do you know why she would hide that?"

"She was upset. She probably didn't even think it was relevant. Now I have a question."

"What is it, Regis?"

"From your line of questioning, do you not believe my father committed suicide?"

"All indications right now are that he most likely did. However, there are a couple of things I need to sort out to be sure. I'm also waiting for the medical examiner's report."

"My mom is very torn up over this."

"I know. Sorry to have to put you through this. If you think of anything else that might be helpful, please call me. Thank you for coming."

Back in the detective work area, Baez approached Mitchell, who was intently reading a report at her desk.

"What did the unattended death turn out to be yesterday?" Baez inquired.

"Don't know yet," answered Mitchell. "Husband and wife lived together, and the wife said the husband came home drunk the night before and was extremely sick in the morning when she left for work. When she returned in the afternoon, she found him deceased in bed."

"You think it was an alcohol or drug overdose?"

"We won't know until we get the autopsy results back. But I've got to tell you, he looked horrible. And he had puked and pissed all over himself. It was disgusting."

Baez laughed. "I'm certainly glad I didn't get that one! I wondered what that smell was."

"Yeah, yeah, whatever."

"Hey, I need a favor. I'm going back to the Lopez residence this afternoon to interview the wife some more. I'd like you to come along."

"You give me crap about my case, then ask for a favor? Not very smart."

Baez stood there, looking at Mitchell with raised eyebrows.

Mitchell glanced up. "Okay, I'll go with you. Just leave me alone right now. I've got to finish up this report."

"I'll be by after lunch," said Baez as he walked away and smiled.

At 1:30 pm, Baez and Mitchell were on their way to the home of Valerie Lopez. The house was a three-story small mansion. It had tall brick walls with elongated windows on the main floor.

Vines with small yellow flowers climbed the wall of the attached garage. Palm trees and other tropical plants adorned the large front yard. The back of the house opened to a large stone patio with a large built-in gas grill. Beyond the patio was a large, heart-shaped swimming pool. Upon arrival, Baez rang the doorbell. A housekeeper answered the door and invited the detectives inside. She bypassed the sitting room and led them to the much larger living room. The living room was elegantly decorated, with fine art displayed throughout the home. Mrs. Lopez soon joined them.

"Thank you for meeting with us today, Mrs. Lopez," said Baez. "I know this is difficult, but we need to get some information from you to help us understand why your husband took his life."

Mrs. Lopez softly replied. "I understand. Shelly told me there would be more questions."

"May we call you Valerie?"

"Yes."

"Okay then, Valerie. I'd like to know why your husband wanted a divorce."

"I guess he was unhappy in the marriage," answered Valerie.

"Yes, but do you know why?"

"Once the kids left home, maybe things just weren't the same."

She is avoiding the letter and affair, thought Baez.

"Valerie, I understand you received a letter several weeks ago telling you your husband was having an affair. Is this true?"

Valerie stared at Baez. "Yes," she quietly replied.

"Why didn't you tell us this?"

"I'm not sure what it has to do with my husband's suicide."

"Well, it could be what triggered him to respond this way. Maybe he was embarrassed and emotionally upset. Maybe he didn't want to face divorce and go through the process of dividing all your property and wealth. Who was he having an affair with?"

"I have no idea."

"Really?" continued Baez, "because I think that would have been something you asked him after receiving the letter."

Now Valerie spoke much louder. "I did! I demanded to know who it was. He wouldn't tell me. He said it was ending, but he still wanted a divorce. He said the marriage had gotten stale, and he needed more. He was tired of being married. That hurt me about as much as learning about an affair."

"Valerie," said Mitchell, "who do you believe he was having an affair with?"

"I don't know who it was."

"Do you still have the letter?" asked Baez.

"Yes."

"We need to get that letter from you. It could be important."

Valerie simply nodded her head.

"What type of car do you drive?" continued Baez.

"A Toyota Sienna."

"What color?"

"Why is this important?" inquired Valerie.

"Just covering all bases, Valerie."

"It's white."

"Valerie, where were you Tuesday night and the early morning hours on Wednesday?"

"Where are you going with this, Detective?"

"Again, I'm just trying to be thorough. I know this is tough, but we have to ask these questions."

"I was home all night and all morning."

"Was anyone here with you?"

"No," snapped Valerie. "My husband had moved out. I'm here all alone."

"You didn't drive anywhere?"

"What did I just say?"

"I understand Dominic had a large life insurance policy in the amount of one million dollars. Is that correct?"

"Yes, he brought in a lot of money. He had a large policy to protect his family in the event of his death."

"I understand," assured Baez. "Are you the beneficiary?"

Again, Valerie stared at Baez and slightly shook her head. "Yeah."

"When was that policy purchased?"

Again, Valerie stared at Baez for a couple of seconds before answering. "About eight years ago."

"That means the suicide exemption no longer applies, correct?"

"I suppose," replied Valerie.

"That means you are in line to receive one million dollars, the house, and all other assets, correct?"

"I don't like the implication of these questions, Detective Baez."

"I understand. Please answer my question."

"Yes, that's correct."

"Can anyone vouch you were home all Tuesday night through Wednesday morning?"

"As I told you, I was here alone."

"Before we leave, Valerie, I would like to look at your car if that is okay."

"Why?"

"Just being very thorough in our investigation. The sooner I can eliminate possibilities, the sooner we can get to the truth."

"Do you have a warrant?"

"Nope, that's why I'm asking for permission."

Valerie didn't respond, and Baez could tell she was angry.

"Valerie," said Baez, "right now, we believe this was simply a suicide. We are waiting on autopsy results and need to be cautious in jumping to conclusions. Some people are killed, and it is staged as a suicide. Please understand."

"Alright, Detective, you may look at my car."

"Thank you. Detective Mitchell, can you think of anything else right now?" asked Baez.

"Yes," she replied. "Do you know of anyone who may have wanted to harm Dominic?"

"No, I do not."

"I still need to find Dominic's iPad," said Baez. "While I don't need it, I'd like to get your permission to enter his condo and look for that iPad or anything else that might be important."

"That's fine with me," answered Valerie in a quiet voice.

"Before we go," said Baez, "I need to get that letter from you, and we need to look at your car."

Valerie stood up. "I will go get the letter and meet you out front. The door to the garage is down the hall and through the kitchen."

"Thank you, Valerie."

Baez and Mitchell found their way to the garage, and both inspected the outside and inside of the car. Nothing seemed unusual. Baez took several photographs of the vehicle. They then opened the garage door and walked out front. Mrs. Lopez was waiting for them and handed them the letter.

"Thank you again, Valerie," said Baez. "Sorry for your loss."

Baez drove the detective car back to the police station while Mitchell read the letter out loud. The letter stated:

Mrs. Lopez,

This letter is to inform you that your husband, Dominic Lopez, has been engaging in an affair with another woman. This is a fact and can be proven should he deny it. This affair has been going on for several months. We will spare you the gritty details. How you handle this situation is totally up to you. However, should Dominic deny this fact, we will publicly expose him. We have photographs and other physical evidence of his infidelity.

Signed,

The Marriage Counselor

"That's just crazy!" exclaimed Baez. "Who would write a letter like that? And then sign it as the marriage counselor?"

Mitchell shook her head. "Wow, it gets your attention, that's for sure. Lopez may have been afraid of this getting out publicly and embarrassing his family. Maybe that was his motive for suicide."

"Maybe," said Baez. "Or, it could have been the motive for someone to kill him, like maybe one of his sons or Valerie."

"You still think she could be involved?"

"I don't know right now, but she does have a mid-size white car and will be a rich woman. I need to get the data off his phone and iPad. A nice suicide note would help."

Mitchell just grunted.

"What about your death? You got that thing wrapped up yet?" asked Baez.

"Like you, still waiting on the autopsy reports. Funny thing, my victim was also screwing around on his wife."

"Are you thinking it was something more than natural causes?"

"Nothing to indicate that right now, but the wife was pissed off. They were in the same house but sleeping in separate bedrooms. Just before leaving for work, she told him she'd had enough. He was to be out of the house by the time she got home. At least that was her story."

"Is there money involved?"

"Yeah, the husband made real good money as an attorney. And they have a beautiful house too."

"What was his name?"

"Tyler Vincent."

"Hmmm, I have heard the name before," responded Baez.

"He just won a big case involving a chemical company. You might have heard his name in the news."

Baez nodded as if to say, "maybe."

Chapter 5

Back in the bureau, Baez had a report from the medical examiner on his desk. The official cause of death for Dominic Lopez was listed as carbon monoxide asphyxiation. However, levels of barbiturates and ethyl alcohol were also found in his system. The blood alcohol content (BAC) was .04%. The level of barbiturates was not high enough to cause death. However, combined with the alcohol, it would most likely have rendered him unconscious prior to being asphyxiated from carbon monoxide.

This report left Baez with more questions. *Did Lopez self-administer the barbiturates? Did he drive to the park with alcohol in a glass or drink it elsewhere? If so, why bring an empty glass? Where was the bottle of alcohol? Bottle of pills? Who was in the white car, if anyone?*

In the background, the local news was playing on the TV monitor in the Detective Bureau. Baez overheard the name Dominic Lopez. He got up, walked over to the monitor, and turned up the volume. The local news was now reporting on the alleged suicide of Lopez. His photograph was displayed on the TV, and they showed photos of his primary dealership. Baez was shocked by what he heard next. The news reporter revealed that "according to an anonymous source," Lopez had been having an affair with an unknown woman at the time of his apparent suicide. He also said the police were still investigating.

What the hell? Thought Baez as he made a beeline to Mitchell's desk. She was not there. He then got on his cell phone and called her.

"Hello?"

"Leah, did you tell anyone about Dominic's affair?"

"No! Why are you asking me that?"

"It's on the news. They're reporting that Lopez was having an affair at the time of his death. They said it was from an anonymous source."

"Well, it didn't come from me. Remember, several people knew about it, and Valerie probably told more than a couple of friends."

"Yeah, you're probably right. I just got back the test results from the autopsy. Lopez had both alcohol and barbiturates in his system."

"Is that what killed him?"

"No, but enough to knock him out."

"So much for your simple case," teased Mitchell.

"Yeah, no kidding. See you tomorrow."

On Friday morning, Baez called Dominic's oldest son, Ricky Lopez. "Ricky, did you or Regis talk to any members of the press?"

"No," responded Ricky. "None of us have talked to the press. And my mom was not too happy about Dad's affair being spread over the news."

"Still no idea who this mystery woman is?"

"No, sir, I wish I knew."

"Do you know where I might find his iPad?"

"It's not at work, so I assume it would be at his condo."

"Okay, thank you, Ricky."

After talking with Ricky, Baez drove to the El Paraiso La Casa restaurant, where he knew he could find Miguel Rodriguez, Lopez's best friend. He had called ahead to arrange a meeting. Upon his arrival, Rodriguez invited Baez into his office and closed the door.

"Thank you for seeing me," said Baez.

"Of course," replied Rodriguez. "Dominic was my best friend. I was shocked to hear he committed suicide. It is an unfortunate situation."

"Was Dominic depressed or worried about anything?" asked Baez.

"No, he was not depressed, but he was angry over the letter sent to his wife several weeks ago. He wanted to know who sent it, as it caused a lot of discord with his wife, as you can imagine."

"Yes, I can. Did he ever find out who sent it?"

"No. The woman he was seeing denied sending it."

"Did you know her?"

"Not really, but I met her one time. Dominic had been talking about her and finally wanted me to meet her. I met him at a beachside bar, and she was with him."

"So, he was getting serious with her?" inquired Baez.

"I don't think so. For Dominic, it was just a fling, having excitement in his life. I told him it was dangerous, but he wasn't too happy being married anymore."

"Do you know her name?"

"Only as Mandy, but I don't believe that was her actual name. She was hesitant to give out too much information and would not let Dominic take her picture."

"Tell me more about that."

"At the bar, Dominic wanted me to use his phone to take a picture of him and Mandy. She refused to have her picture taken. She just came across as a little mysterious to me. Look, I wasn't happy he was having an affair, as Valerie is also a close friend. But it was none of my business."

"Can you describe her to me?"

"She was exquisite; I can tell you that. Let's see..... average height, delicate figure, long blonde hair. She had a seductive style to her. She dressed nicely, too. I remember she had a low-cut blouse on."

"White female?"

"Yes."

"And how old?"

"I'd say in her forties."

"Any more information you can give me about Mandy that might help me track her down?"

Rodriguez thought for a moment. "Yes, one time Dominic mentioned he had met her on a website."

"Website? You mean like a dating service?"

"I think so, something like that."

"Do you know anyone who might have wanted to harm Dominic?"

"No, I can't think of anyone."

"If he was happy, why would he want to commit suicide?" asked Baez.

"I don't believe he did."

"That's what it looks like right now."

"I know it does, but Dominic wasn't the type to take his own life. Other than being bored in marriage, he was happy. I believe he would have confided in me if he were depressed."

"Thank you, Miguel. You have been a big help. And sorry for your loss."

"Thank you," replied Rodriguez. "I hope you figure this out."

After leaving the restaurant, Baez checked his phone and saw he had a message from Detective Mitchell. *Call me.*

Baez called. "What's up?"

"I just got my autopsy report back on my unattended death," answered Mitchell. "More testing has to be done, but the medical examiner believes he may have been poisoned."

"No kidding," replied Baez. "Sounds like you might have a genuine case on your hands now."

"Yeah, I'm going to re-interview the wife this afternoon and would like you to come along."

"Nah, I'm going to take it easy this afternoon."

"Jackass. After I helped you with your...."

Baez cut her off. "Just joking, Leah, of course I'll help. I can pick you up in twenty minutes, and we can head over."

"Thanks, Rick, but you're still a jackass."

Baez just laughed. "See you soon."

Mitchell and Baez arrived at the Vincent home just after noon. After the death of her husband, Kristy Vincent had taken the week off from work. She knew Mitchell was coming to interview her. Mitchell answered the door wearing a Miami Marlins t-shirt and gray sweatpants. She was a stocky woman, 32 years old, with short, brown hair. It didn't appear as though she had showered or fixed her hair for the day. Kristy invited the detectives into the kitchen, where they all sat down at the table.

"I understand you have more questions?" asked Kristy.

"Yes, we do," said Mitchell. "The autopsy has been completed on Tyler, and we believe he was poisoned."

"Oh, my goodness," responded Kristy. "Poisoned how?"

"That's what we are trying to find out now."

"What was he poisoned with?"

"We won't know that until they can perform some more testing. Whatever it was, it is difficult to detect."

"Then why do they believe he was poisoned?"

"I'm not a medical examiner, but I was told the damage to several organs indicated poisoning," explained Mitchell.

Kristy looked down at the table.

"Is there anything you can think of that your husband ate or touched that could be poisonous over the last few days?"

"No, nothing."

"Okay," said Mitchell. "I understand your husband had a five-hundred-thousand-dollar life insurance policy. Is that correct?" Baez quickly gave a glance of surprise toward Mitchell.

"Why yes, in the event of his death, I would be taken care of," answered Kristy.

"When did you find out about your husband's affair?"

Kristy hesitated. "I got a letter in the mail."

Baez, who had just been listening, pivoted his head and looked directly at Kristy. "You got a letter?"

"Yes," said Kristy, as she looked back at Baez.

"From whom?"

"It was anonymous."

"Do you still have it?" continued Baez.

"Of course I still have it."

"Will you please go get it for us?"

Kristy got up and walked out of the room. Baez and Mitchell looked at each other, but neither said a word.

Kristy walked back into the kitchen with the letter and handed it to Baez. It was still in an envelope addressed to Kristy Vincent. There was a return address on Citrus Lane. He quickly removed the letter and read it.

Mrs. Vincent,

This letter is to inform you that your husband, Tyler Vincent, has been engaging in an affair with another woman. This is a fact and can be proven should he deny it. This affair has been going on for several months. We will spare you the gritty details. How you handle this situation is totally up to you. However, should Tyler deny this fact, we will publicly expose him. We have photographs and other physical evidence of his infidelity.

Signed,

The Marriage Counselor

Baez then handed the letter to Mitchell, who in turn read the letter. After looking again toward Baez, Mitchell spoke up.

"Kristy, when did you get this letter?"

"Probably four weeks ago now."

"And how did you respond?"

"I threw his ass out! That's how I responded. Then he whined and cried about having to stay in a hotel room. So, I told him he could stay in the other bedroom until he found a more permanent location. But he sure wasn't going to sleep with me anymore."

"So, you were quite angry."

"Hell yes, I was angry! He was screwing around. I wasn't about to put up with that."

"Were you going to divorce him?"

"Yes. No way I could forgive that."

"Did he want the divorce?"

"Who knows? He didn't seem too upset that I wanted one."

"What did Tyler have to eat the night before?"

"How would I know?" snapped Kristy. "He was out late and came home drunk."

"Did you talk to him that night?"

"No, I was already in bed."

"So, you didn't see him come home drunk."

"I saw him in the morning. He had vomited all over himself."

"That could have resulted from being poisoned, Kristy."

"I doubt it. He seemed to be drinking a lot lately."

"Kristy," said Baez, "how were you getting along before the letter?"

"Things weren't great, but I didn't know he was cheating on me."

"You're very angry," suggested Baez.

"Wouldn't you be?"

"Yes, I would. And maybe angry enough to make my spouse suffer a bit."

"What do you mean by that?" asked Kristy.

"Oh, I could understand wanting to put something in his food to make him suffer some."

Kristy stared at Baez. "You don't know what you are talking about."

"Maybe not, but you are going to do well with that insurance money. You wouldn't have gotten it with a divorce and then to split up all your assets."

"I did not kill my husband if that's what you're implying."

"Kristy," said Baez, "you were angry enough to poison him. Maybe you just wanted to make him sick, and you gave him too much. Accidents happen."

"No," said Kristy emphatically.

"I talked to a couple of your neighbors," interjected Mitchell. "They told me you had some loud arguments in the last couple of weeks. It sounds to me like you had a lot of anger."

"Yes, I was angry. But I did not kill my husband, and I did not poison him."

"Well then, who did, Kristy? Who was angry enough to want your husband dead?"

After a moment of silence, Kristy spoke up. "I don't know, but given his job of protecting corporations from lawsuits, I'm sure there are people out there who don't like him."

"We will look into that. Is there anything else you can tell us that might help clear this up?"

"Not that I can think of."

"I have a few more questions," said Baez. "Did you or your husband know someone by the name of Dominic Lopez?"

"No, why?"

"How about Valerie Lopez?"

"No."

"Did Tyler ever talk about anyone with that name?"

"Not that I remember."

"How about the name Mandy? Does that mean anything?"

"No. What is this, Detective?"

"Dominic Lopez died earlier this week under suspicious circumstances, and his wife received the same letter you did. Now that seems overly coincidental to me."

"Really?" Kristy thought for a moment. "I don't know what to say."

"Was Tyler seeing someone by the name of Mandy?"

"I don't know. He never told me who the woman was, but if you find out, let me know. I wouldn't mind giving her a piece of my mind. And then to write a letter like that. She had to be some kind of bitch."

"Okay, Kristy," said Mitchell, "if you think of anything else, please call right away."

Kristy nodded.

As they were walking back to the car, Baez stated, "she is quite the fireplug. Now I can see why Tyler was sneaking around."

"Oh, stop it," said Mitchell. "She has a right to be angry. Imagine if that happened to you."

"You don't think she had anything to do with the poisoning?"

"I didn't say that. Just try to be more understanding. We have nothing to tell us she did."

"Well, we have an affair, angry wife, and plenty of opportunities," pointed out Baez.

"Yes, but somehow there is a connection to our cases. We have to find the person who sent those letters."

"Roger that," said Baez.

Chapter 6

The following Monday morning, Baez took the keys recovered from Lopez and responded to the Palm Shade Condo complex in Edgewater. He contacted the on-site manager, identified himself, and informed the manager he would be searching the condo Dominic Lopez had been renting. Upon entering, Baez quickly found the iPad sitting on the kitchen table. He continued to search the condo for anything of evidentiary value, specifically looking for any letters or documents that might identify the woman known as Mandy. He was also looking for a suicide note. He could not find any such documents, but noticed the bed had not been made. He pulled back the sheet and inspected the bedding. On one pillowcase, he found a long blonde hair. Upon additional inspection, he found a second long blonde hair further down on the sheet. Baez quickly exited the condo and jogged to his car. He put the iPad in the back seat, then grabbed a pair of latex gloves and a couple of envelopes from his crime scene kit in the car's trunk.

Baez returned to the condo and carefully collected both hairs, placing each one in a separate envelope. *I'll bet this belongs to Miss Mandy,* thought Baez. Once he was finished searching and satisfied he found all he could, he left the condo and drove back to the police department. Upon his return, Baez submitted the two envelopes into evidence and dropped the iPad off to Computer Forensics. He then filled out a request form to have the iPad searched for evidence in his case. He was hoping to learn the identity of Mandy.

When Baez returned to his desk, he found a report from the computer forensics lab on the search of Lopez's cell phone sitting on top of his paperwork. The results of the report included a lengthy list of phone calls made over the past six months. Given the business Lopez was in, there were hundreds of calls listed. Most of the calls were easily identifiable and pertained to the car business. Some calls, as is usual, were listed as unknown. Baez quickly scanned the past three months of calls, looking for the name of Mandy. He also looked for any business listing that could belong to a dating service. He could not find any. Baez then looked for patterns in the calls with no names attached. To his surprise, he found one number that showed up multiple times in the last three months. He tried calling the number. All he received was a computerized voice, *I'm sorry, your call cannot be completed as dialed.*

Baez then called Steve Logan, the analyst who had provided the data from the cell phone.

"Hi, Steve, this is Baez."

"Hi, Rick, what's up?"

"Just got your report on Lopez's cell phone. A number on here shows up multiple times in the weeks leading up to his death. When I call it, I get a message that the call cannot be completed."

"Let me grab my report. What is the number you are referring to?"

Baez read back the number.

"Yep," said Logan, "that number is unlisted. Most likely a burner phone."

"Which means we can't trace it to anyone, right?"

"That's correct," replied Logan. "The only viable way is if you knew where the phone was purchased, and the buyer used a credit card. Even then, it can be tough to figure out."

"Did you find any past searches for dating services or webpages for dating services?"

"No, I found nothing like that. Most of the data was related to the automobile business."

"Alright, Steve, thanks for the help."

Damn, thought Baez. *I can't catch a break. I know there is more to this story.*

Meanwhile, Mitchell had received additional testing results on the death of Tyler Vincent. The medical examiner's report contained medical and scientific jargon, making it difficult for Mitchell to decipher. However, she understood that multiple organs had been damaged, and multiple toxic substances were found in the tissues of the organs. The heart, liver, and kidneys had suffered fatal damage from the poisonous substances glycolaldehyde, glycolic acid, glyoxylic acid, and acetone. She scanned the report until she found the conclusion.

Based on these findings, the conclusion is that the cause of death was poisoning by ethylene glycol, propylene glycol, and methanol. These are commonly found in automobile antifreeze.

Mitchell called the coroner's office for clarification. The medical examiner was not in the office, but Deputy Coroner Susan Mills was available to answer questions.

"If I am reading this report accurately, the medical examiner believes Vincent was poisoned by antifreeze?" asked Mitchell.

"Given the substances found in the body, the most likely source of the poison was antifreeze," responded Mills. "The toxic substances found in the body are the by-product of the body's metabolizing of ethylene, glycol, and methanol, the ingredients of antifreeze."

"Where in Florida do you buy antifreeze?" Mitchell asked. "The stuff we buy around here is called coolant. Is that the same thing?"

"Technically, yes. Coolant is made of the same ingredients as antifreeze but in a less concentrated form. We don't need the same level of antifreeze protection here in Florida that they do up north. It would take double the amount of coolant to kill someone. However, some people who travel back and forth use the stronger antifreeze formula. And you can order it from most places."

"Can you tell which formula was used?"

"Not for certain, but the examiner, Dr. Ballard, thought it was most likely the stronger antifreeze given the level of toxins found in the body. And keep in mind, this could have been given in small amounts over a period of time, especially if he had been sick for days."

"How certain is he with his finding?"

"Very certain," assured Mills.

"What would some of the physical symptoms have been?"

"Oh, it could be several things. Given his internal damage, he most likely would have been suffering from fatigue, lack of coordination, grogginess, nausea, vomiting, rapid breathing, abdominal or lower back pain, and rapid heartbeat, to name the most common. The poison attacks the organs of the body."

"Sounds like that's what happened to my victim. Thank you, Susan."

Mitchell sat back in her chair. *My unattended death now looks like a homicide,* she thought. *And my number one suspect is Kristy Vincent. But how does this tie into Lopez's death? Were Lopez and Vincent having an affair with the same woman?* Mitchell sat up to her computer keyboard and began typing out a search warrant for the home of Kristy Vincent.

By 1:30 pm, Mitchell had completed the search warrant affidavit and had submitted it to the District Attorney's Office for review. She then talked with Baez and filled him in on the additional information about Vincent's death. She then asked him to join her for an interview with Vincent's law partner, Tony Rialto. Baez agreed.

At 2:10 pm, they arrived at the law office of Vincent and Rialto for the interview of Vincent's law partner, Tony Rialto. Rialto was a portly fellow with a heavily receding hairline, short hair on the sides, and a well-trimmed full beard. He talked in a high-pitched voice. His suit appeared expensive but wrinkled. Baez quickly got the impression Vincent had been the public persona of the practice, while Rialto worked more behind the scenes.

"Thank you for seeing us, Tony," said Mitchell. "My condolences over the death of your partner."

"Thank you. Anything I can do to help, Detective," answered Rialto.

"As you know, we are investigating the death of Tyler and hoping you might shed some light on this case."

"I'm not sure I can help you with that, but I'll tell you what I know."

"Was there anything in his personal life that was bothering him?"

"I assume you are asking about his pending divorce. Tyler was having some marital issues. He was not happy in his marriage, so getting a divorce would not have been a terrible thing."

"Is that why he was seeking a divorce?"

"That, and probably because he had been dating another woman, and his wife found out about it."

"Did he share the details with you?"

"Some. He told me he had met another woman. He didn't talk too much about her, but when he did, I had the impression he cared about her."

"Did you ever meet her?"

"No, and I didn't want to. That was something I didn't want to get involved in."

"Did he ever mention her name?"

"He referred to her only as Sugar."

"Sugar? Was that her real name?"

"I don't believe so. He once told me she didn't want her actual name used, given that he was still married, and they were having an affair."

Baez interrupted. "Did you ever see a picture of her?"

"No," answered Rialto.

"Did Tyler ever describe her to you?"

"No, but he called her his Cuban Sugar one time. I assumed she must be Cuban."

"Did he ever call her Mandy?"

"I don't recall him ever calling her that."

Mitchell started again. "Do you know how Mrs. Vincent found out about the affair?"

"Yes, Tyler told me someone sent his wife an anonymous letter. He was upset because the sender threatened to go public if Tyler denied the affair."

"Did Tyler have any idea who sent the letter?"

"He thought Sugar must have told someone, but he said she denied it."

"Do you know anyone who might have wanted to harm Tyler?"

"Kristy told me he was sick and died in his sleep."

"Yes, but we have to investigate all unattended deaths until we can prove a cause of death."

"I understand. No, I'm not aware of anyone."

"Do you think he might have wanted to harm himself?"

"No. Why are you asking me that?"

"We have evidence he was poisoned," Mitchell informed him. "If he was depressed over his marriage, divorce, or his affair, could he have poisoned himself?"

"Poisoned?" questioned Rialto. "Damn, that throws a different light on this. No, Tyler wasn't the type to commit suicide. He was looking forward to being free from his marriage and litigating more cases like the last one."

"Do you think his wife may have poisoned him over the affair or divorce?"

Rialto paused for a few moments. "I've known Kristy for a long time. I would be surprised if she poisoned Tyler. On the other hand, she can be, excuse my language, a cranky bitch at times. I've seen enough in my time to know anything is possible. I don't think she would, but it wouldn't shock me either."

"Can you tell us a bit more about her being cranky?" asked Baez. "Did you ever see her angry?"

"Yes, she could provide a verbal beat down when she was angry. I remember one time Tyler and Kristy were having a party at their place. Tyler said something that pissed her off. I don't even remember what it was, but I remember Kristy's reaction. She gave it to him in front of everyone. I felt sorry for him."

"Would you describe her as having a temper?"

"Yeah, I think that's accurate."

"Okay," said Mitchell, "I think that about wraps it up for us unless you have anything more to add?"

"If someone did poison Tyler, I hope you find him. Let me know if I can be of any more help."

"We will," assured Mitchell. "Thank you for your time."

Driving back to the station, Baez asked Mitchell what she thought about her case.

"I don't believe Vincent poisoned himself. His wife said he had not been feeling well for about a week before his death. Would someone slowly poison himself? If you wanted to kill yourself, just drink the whole jug of antifreeze and get it over with. I'm leaning toward the wife right now. We know how angry she was, and Rialto just confirmed she has a temper. She also has motive and opportunity."

"I can't disagree," replied Baez. "Why do you always get the simple cases?"

"What are you talking about? I have a long way to go to prove the wife did it. When are you going to solve your case?"

"I can clear it right now as a suicide," laughed Baez.

"Sure, except you don't believe it was a suicide, do you?"

Baez groaned. "Unfortunately, no. He doesn't seem the type, and this anonymous letter tying our cases together has me baffled. It's way too coincidental."

"I know," agreed Mitchell. "It bothers me as well."

"Lopez made and received multiple phone calls to a burner phone number. I need to find out who he was talking to. I have a hunch it is the unknown Mandy."

"I just got word the DA approved my warrant," advised Mitchell. "I'm going to stop to pick it up, then take it to the courthouse to find a judge to review it. You coming along?"

"Under one condition," insisted Baez.

"And what is that?"

"You have dinner with me tonight. I'll even pay."

"What? Since when do you offer to buy me dinner?"

"Grace is working patrol tonight, right?"

"Yes."

"Well, I've got no one to have dinner with, and it sounds like you don't either. It gets boring having dinner alone every night, and I'm not the best cook. We can enjoy each other's company and discuss our cases. What do you think?"

"What makes you think I would enjoy your company?" laughed Mitchell.

Baez looked over at Leah, cocked his head, and smiled, "You know you love me."

"Alright, do I get to pick the place?"

"Any fast-food joint you like."

Mitchell just looked at Baez.

"Okay, you pick the place."

"O'Sullivan's," said Mitchell.

"Good Irish place, eh?"

"Yeah, I love their bangers and mash."

"O'Sullivan's it is. I'll pick you up at seven o'clock."

After stopping to pick up the warrant, Mitchell drove to the courthouse to find an available judge. Baez waited in the car while Mitchell went inside. The court clerk referred Mitchell to Judge Francisco, who had a break between hearings. Judge Francisco carefully read the affidavit.

"You think the wife poisoned her husband?" asked Francisco.

"She had the opportunity and motive. She also has a temper."

"Well, you certainly have probable cause to search the home. Good luck to you," said Francisco as he signed the search warrant.

"Thank you, Judge."

"I've got the warrant," stated Mitchell as she returned to the car. She then drove them to the home of Kristy Vincent in Coral Gables. Both detectives approached the front door. Mitchell rang the doorbell.

Kristy Vincent answered the door. She again looked haggard, wearing a pair of white spandex shorts and an orange tank top with some type of stain on the front. Mitchell could detect an odor of alcohol on Kristy's breath. Kristy allowed them in, and they sat in the living room. Baez glanced into the kitchen, where they interviewed Kristy the first time, and noticed the kitchen table was now littered with a pizza box, a newspaper, some fast-food wrappers, and what looked like documents of some type.

"What do you have to tell me this time?" asked Kristy. "Did you find the person who poisoned my husband?"

"No," answered Mitchell, "but we know he was poisoned with antifreeze."

"Antifreeze? How could he be poisoned with that?"

"It could have been mixed in his food or his drink. It has a sweet taste, so it might go unnoticed, especially in foods or drinks that are on the sweet side."

"Probably that bitch he was sleeping around with," snarled Kristy.

"Kristy," said Mitchell, "we have a search warrant. We are going to search your home for any evidence of Tyler's murder."

Kristy stared at Mitchell. "Why are you going to search my home? Why aren't you out trying to find the bitch who killed him?"

It was now apparent to Mitchell and Baez that Kristy had been drinking before their arrival.

"We have a warrant to search this house, Kristy. You will have to remain in the living room while we look around."

Baez then got on his cell phone and called the uniformed patrol officer sitting in his car a block from the Vincent residence. "You can come in now."

Approximately a minute later, the patrol officer walked through the front door. "Kristy," said Mitchell, "this officer is going to sit with you in the living room while we search your house."

"I'm not sitting here while you two dumb ass detectives rummage through my stuff. I've watched plenty of TV shows, and I know how you cops tear things apart."

Baez couldn't keep himself from letting out a little laugh.

"You think this is funny?" screamed Kristy. "I'll throw your ass out of here just like I did my husband!"

"Alright, I've had enough of you, Kristy," warned Baez. "You just sit there and shut up, or I'm going to have this officer put you in handcuffs and sit you in the patrol car out there until we are done."

The patrol officer reached behind his back to his handcuff case and pulled out the cuffs. He held them in front of his belt, waiting for Baez to give the word. Upon seeing this, Kristy realized Baez was serious, and she slumped in her chair.

"Just make it quick," snarled Kristy. "You're just wasting your time."

Mitchell and Baez then began their search. Mitchell started checking inside the house while Baez went out into the garage. Mitchell found the life insurance policy on the kitchen table. She knew they could get copies, so she simply took a photo of the papers lying on the table. She then began searching the bedrooms and office.

In the garage, Baez quickly located a half-full container of radiator coolant on a shelf. He took this as evidence. He then searched both vehicles in the garage. He could find nothing more of evidentiary value.

When he returned inside, Mitchell had collected Tyler Vincent's cell phone, a laptop computer from the office, and an iPad from the bedroom Kristy had been using. Mitchell then told Kristy she had to give up her cell phone.

"What the hell?" yelled Kristy. "I need my phone. How am I supposed to make phone calls? And that iPad is mine, not Tyler's."

Mitchell pulled out one of those limited plan cheap phones from her pocket. "This is for you to use until you get your phone and iPad back. It is already paid for the entire month, courtesy of the Miami-Dade Metro Police Department. We will get your phone back to you once we download the data."

Kristy didn't say a word, but if looks could kill, this would have been Mitchell's last day. Once the inventory was completed, Mitchell provided Kristy with a copy, and both detectives and the officer left the home.

"That was exciting," exclaimed Baez.

"The more I'm around that woman, the more I think she probably did it," said Mitchell.

"Maybe," said Baez, "but didn't you say full-strength antifreeze was faster and more effective?"

"Yes, but you can use the diluted stuff. You just need twice as much of it."

"Do you think Tyler could have had enough in one week to die and yet not notice the funny taste? If half a gallon of the good stuff will kill you, then it would take a whole gallon of this weak stuff."

"Over time, yes. He might not have felt sick right away."

It was nearly 4:30 pm when Mitchell dropped Baez off at the police parking lot.

"I'll see you in a couple hours," said Baez as he trotted off toward his car.

***

At 7:00 sharp, Baez was ringing the doorbell to Mitchell's two-bedroom townhouse. Mitchell owned the townhouse and shared it with her partner, Grace. Mitchell answered the door wearing black pants, a white blouse, and a black jacket.

"Wow, you clean up well," said Baez.

"Is that a compliment?" asked Mitchell.

"Take it however you want. Where were you making me take you again?"

Mitchell laughed. "I'm not making you do anything. You asked ME to dinner. And we are going to O'Sullivan's."

"Ah, yes. You and your bangers and mash."

At the restaurant, Baez asked for a booth near the back to have some privacy. Mitchell ordered her bangers and mash with a glass of merlot. Baez ordered shepherd's pie, a side salad, and a Corona beer.

"How does Grace like working the second shift?" asked Baez.

"She likes it, a lot of activity."

"Doesn't give the two of you much time together, with you working detectives."

"It works well for us. It gives us some alone time, and we have most weekends together."

"You ever getting married?"

"I don't know. We've talked about it, but things are good right now, and we don't want to mess it up. So many marriages end in divorce these days. What about you, any love life to speak of?"

Baez laughed. "No, I'm too caught up in my work. After Linda left me, I decided to go it alone for a while. Going through one divorce is enough."

"I can understand that. What happened between you and Linda?"

"Work," stated Baez. "I was too much into my job and worked too many hours. I think she got lonely. Our divorce was amicable, and we are still friends. I just didn't put enough effort into it. You know, that work-life balance thing."

"Are you ever sorry?"

Baez thought for a minute. "Yes, I wish I would have paid more attention to her needs. I did love her."

"Don't you find it hard to be alone all the time?"

"It gets lonely sometimes," said Baez. "And the sex life sucks."

Mitchell laughed. "What sex life?"

"Exactly!" exclaimed Baez.

"When's the last time you dated?"

"What year is it?" asked Baez, laughing. "I haven't dated much since my divorce. Relationships take time."

"You should get out more, Rick. What do you do for fun?"

Baez thought for a moment. "Once in a while, I go fishing."

"And when did you last go fishing?"

"About four years ago."

"My goodness, Rick, that's horrible. You need more in your life than work. It's not healthy."

"You're probably right, but it's hard to find the time."

"You need to make the time, Rick."

"Alright, that's enough talk about my pathetic personal life. What do you think about our Mrs. Vincent?"

"Well, she has a temper, had motive, had the opportunity, and we found coolant in her garage. Ballard will do some more tests on the stomach contents and vomit from Vincent's bed to see if he can find traces of unmetabolized antifreeze. If so, we would know he was given some the night before."

"Do you think she is lying about not seeing him the night before?"

"I don't know, but if we can prove she did, and he had recently consumed antifreeze, I think we would be close to probable cause for an arrest. What do you think?"

Just then, their food arrived, and both ordered another drink. "Mmmm, looks good," said Baez as he dug in. "How's yours?"

Mitchell waited to finish chewing before responding. "Very good." Both took some time to eat a few more bites of food before Baez responded.

"The letters bother me. I think we need to find out who Sugar or Mandy is and why she or someone else sent those letters."

"I agree," said Mitchell, "but those letters also provide a motive for an angry wife. What about your case? You said you didn't believe Lopez killed himself."

"My gut tells me no. Like I said earlier, by all accounts, Lopez wasn't the type to commit suicide, and I have yet to find anyone who didn't like the guy. Then you have the letter and the mysterious Mandy."

"What about Mrs. Lopez?"

"She had motive; the insurance money and the affair. However, it was Dominic who wanted the divorce. Valerie wanted to save the marriage. Why would she kill him? On the other hand, she has a white four-door, and no one can vouch that she was home all night."

"What's your next move?"

"I'm waiting on computer forensics to see if they come up with anything off his iPad that would lead me to his mistress. I doubt Mandy is her real name, and she might be the same person as Sugar. Did I tell you I found two long blonde hairs in Lopez's bed?"

"No, you did not. Is it Mandy's?"

"That's what I'm thinking."

Neither said much more while they finished their meals.

"That was incredibly good. Thank you, Rick," said Mitchell.

"You're welcome. Thanks for joining me for dinner. How about another merlot?"

"Sure, why not?"

After some more small talk, Baez drove Mitchell back to her townhome, arriving at 10:30 pm. "You better get some sleep," said Baez. "We might have a few long days ahead of us."

"After three wines, I think I'll sleep just fine. See you tomorrow."

Chapter 7

The next morning, Tuesday at 10:35 a.m., Mitchell received a call from the medical examiner, Dr. Ballard.

"I have some news for you," started Ballard. "I'm certain Tyler Vincent consumed a substance consistent with antifreeze in the hours just prior to his death. I found traces of unmetabolized ethylene, glycol, and methanol in the vomit from the bedsheet. This means he still had some in his stomach when he vomited."

"Outstanding work, Doctor. Do you know how long before his death he would have consumed the antifreeze?"

"Not for certain, as we don't know what time he vomited. But it had to have been within a couple hours of vomiting to have any antifreeze still in his stomach. What time did he get home the night before?"

"We can't nail that down. The wife claims she was in bed and didn't hear him come home."

"I also found small traces of ethanol. This tells me Vincent also had an alcoholic beverage sometime prior to vomiting," explained Dr. Ballard. "It is likely he consumed both at the same or about the same time."

"Do you think antifreeze was mixed into his drink?" asked Mitchell.

"Quite possible, but no way to know for sure."

"Thank you, Doctor."

Mitchell had a sense of excitement at the news. *At least now I know he was poisoned the night before his death,* pondered Mitchell.

Now I just must prove who did it. It must either be the wife or whoever he was with before getting home.

With this information, Mitchell decided she needed to confront Kristy Vincent again. This time, however, she wanted it to be at the police station in the interrogation room, where Kristy could be recorded and videotaped. Mitchell called Kristy.

"Hello," answered Kristy.

"Hi, Kristy, this is Detective Mitchell. I've gotten some additional information about your husband's death, and I need to discuss some details with you. Would you mind coming down to the police department this afternoon so that we can talk?"

"Why don't you come here?"

"I have some reports I want to show you that can't leave the office," lied Mitchell. "I also want to make sure I have the timeline of events correct. You can help me with this."

There was a long pause.

"Kristy, I know you were angry at your husband, and you had a right to be. But now he is dead, and you were the last person to see him. I know you loved him at one time. Can't you do this for him? For the good times you had together?"

Finally, Kristy answered. "I suppose so. What time?"

"How about one o'clock? Would that work?"

Again, a pause. "Alright, I'll be there."

"Thank you, Kristy. Do you know where the main building is for the Metro Dade Police Department?"

"Yes."

"Alright, I'll see you at one o'clock. Bye, Kristy."

Baez was still not in the office, so Mitchell called him on his cell phone. "Where are you?"

"I'm at the Lopez dealership with Steve Logan checking Lopez's work computer. Why?"

"I now know for certain Vincent was poisoned just hours before his death, and I've got an interview set up with Kristy here at the PD. I'm sure you'd like to sit in."

"Oh yeah, any chance to talk to that lovely lady I'll jump at," laughed Baez. "I still have at least an hour here, though."

"That's okay. The interview is not until one o'clock."

"Yeah, I can make it. I'll see you then," said Baez.

Baez and Logan continued to scan Lopez's computer in his work office, looking for any references to dating sites, escort services, or the name Mandy. After a couple of hours of searching, Logan could not find any links to dating sites.

"Should we confiscate the computer?" asked Baez.

"That won't be necessary," said Logan. "I've copied all the browsing data, bookmarks, emails, and history on this hard drive. Based on what I've seen, I don't think we will find anything useful. However, I'll go over it again back at the lab."

"Alright, thanks for your help. When will you have a chance to go through his iPad?"

"I'll have something later this week. Between you and Mitchell, it's been busy."

Baez returned to the police department at around 12:30 pm. He found Mitchell at her desk going over notes. "Are you ready for this interview?"

"Yes," said Mitchell. "I'll take the lead, and you can play the hard-ass if that's okay with you."

Baez smiled. "Aren't I always the hard-ass?"

"Yes, you are," said Mitchell, without even looking up. "Once Kristy gets here, I'll bring her into the interrogation room."

"I'll be ready."

Kristy arrived at the front desk at 12:50 pm. The receptionist called Mitchell to let her know Kristy was waiting. Mitchell walked downstairs to the reception area and greeted Kristy.

"Thank you for coming, Kristy."

"My pleasure," said Kristy sarcastically.

Mitchell then led Kristy through the police department to the hall containing four interrogation rooms. She placed Kristy in room number two, which she had already set up for the interview.

Mitchell then joined Baez in the adjoining observation room to watch Kristy for several minutes to gauge her demeanor.

"She looks like she always does, angry," observed Baez. "She also seems nervous."

Kristy was looking down at her hands, picking at her nails. She then looked up and scanned the room, slightly opened her mouth, and took in a deep breath. She then slowly exhaled. Baez and Mitchell then entered the room.

"Kristy, you remember Detective Baez, correct?"

"How could I forget?" answered Kristy.

"Hello, Kristy," said Baez.

Mitchell started. "Kristy, we need to go over the events of the night before Tyler died. Please give us as much detail as you can."

"I've already told you everything. I had worked that day and came home. Tyler had not yet come home. We seldom ate dinner together anymore, and I didn't know when he would be home, so I fixed myself some dinner. I was tired, so I went to bed somewhere around nine o'clock. I didn't see Tyler until the next morning when he was drunk in bed."

"Did you wonder where Tyler was?" asked Mitchell.

"No, he would often stay out late."

"Did you try to call him?"

"Nope!" said Kristy sharply.

"You weren't concerned?"

"Do you even listen to my answers? I told you he would often stay out late."

"What time did Tyler get home the night before?"

Kristy glared at Mitchell and slowly said, "I don't know."

"Do you know when Tyler last ate at your house?"

"What is the point of all this?" asked Kristy.

Now Baez interrupted with a stern voice. "The point, Kristy, is that your husband was poisoned, and you were the last one to be with him. Now, when was the last time he ate?"

"I'm a grieving widow, and you're yelling at me?"

"Grieving widow, my ass. And I haven't even started to yell yet. You have some explaining to do. How did Tyler get poisoned in your home?"

"I don't know!" said Kristy in a loud voice.

"You were the only other person there, Kristy. What did he have to eat or drink that night?"

"I don't know! He didn't get home until after I went to bed."

"Kristy," warned Baez, "he was poisoned with radiator fluid, the same stuff we found in your garage. I believe you were so angry about the affair, you added it to his food or drink over the last several days."

Kristy now appeared less confident. "In my garage? I don't even know what it is."

"Kristy," said Mitchell softly, "now is the time to tell us the truth. It will make things much easier. The affair and how Tyler treated you can be used as mitigating factors."

Baez and Mitchell could see that they were getting to Kristy. She was slumped back in her chair, and her eyes were tearing up.

"I didn't ask for this, you know," sobbed Kristy.

"No one does," said Mitchell. "You can relieve the pressure you are under by telling us the truth."

"How did you give him the poison, Kristy?" asked Baez.

"I didn't give him poison."

"We already know you did. We just don't know how."

Kristy just sat in silence.

"Kristy," Baez continued, "relieve the pressure you are under and tell us the truth."

Still crying, Kristy shouted out, "I didn't kill my husband!"

"Yes, you did, and we are going to prove it," shouted Baez right back.

"You are an asshole," said Kristy as she looked directly at Baez while wiping tears off her cheeks. "I didn't kill my husband, and if you think you can prove it, then arrest me."

Mitchell interrupted, "Tell us who Sugar is."

"Who?"

"The woman your husband called Sugar. The one who sent you the letter."

"I've never heard of Sugar. Who is she?"

"Your husband's lover."

Kristy huffed, "What is she, a hooker?"

"You tell us," said Baez.

"You people are a piece of work."

"Why didn't you call for help for your dying husband?"

"He looked drunk to me. I did not know he was dying."

"By him dying, you are going to make out well, aren't you?" asked Baez.

"I've had enough of your accusations, Detective. I'm done answering questions. I want an attorney now."

"Are you sure you don't want to clear this up and tell us your side of the story?" asked Mitchell.

"My side? I've been telling my side. You just haven't been listening or believing me. Now arrest me or get me my lawyer!" shouted Kristy.

Baez walked out of the room. Mitchell then told Kristy she was free to leave, and they would continue to investigate Tyler's death. She told Kristy she hoped Kristy was telling the truth for her own sake. Mitchell then escorted Kristy back to the lobby.

"We'll keep in touch, Kristy," said Mitchell. Kristy ignored the comment and walked out without saying another word.

Back in the Detective Bureau, Mitchell asked Baez for his impression of Kristy's statements.

"I think she's telling the truth," stated Baez.

"Why do you say that?"

"She seemed confident in her answers and stuck to her story. I also don't believe poisoning fits her. She would most likely lash out in a fit of rage if she wanted to kill someone."

"I have to agree," said Mitchell.

"In both cases, we are missing a critical link, the mysterious lover. We need to find out who this person is," replied Baez.

Later that evening, Baez watched the ten o'clock news while an update on the investigation into Lopez's murder was being aired. In this segment, the reporter talked of a second, similar case, that of Tyler Vincent. Two key points were made. One, that both victim's deaths initially appeared to be suicides, and two, that both wives had received anonymous letters describing an affair. The reporter discussed both cases now being investigated as possible homicides, and the mystery woman was still unknown.

This did not surprise Baez. Many people now knew about the investigation, and it was nearly impossible to keep the information confidential. Reporters are like hound dogs chasing a fox. They will talk to anyone and everybody connected to a case to piece together bits of information. This time, it didn't bother Baez. *Maybe with the publicity, someone will step forward to identify Mandy or Sugar,* hoped Baez.

Chapter 8

It was now 11:00 am Wednesday, a full week after Lopez's death, and Baez was going over the details trying to determine if he was missing anything when Mitchell approached him.

"You're not going to believe this," said Mitchell. "I just got a call from Detective Roger Paxton from Ft. Lauderdale PD. He saw the news about our cases and called to tell me they have a similar case."

"Really?"

"Yeah, suicide by asphyxiation. They found the victim in his car in a small park. A hose was attached from the tailpipe to the window, and the car was running."

Baez's mouth dropped open as he looked at Mitchell.

Mitchell continued. "The victim had been having an affair, and the wife had received an anonymous letter five weeks before the suicide."

"What!?" exclaimed Baez. "Was it the same letter as in our cases?"

"He sent me a copy. Here it is."

Baez looked at the letter.

Mrs. Carter,

This letter is to inform you that your husband, Dylan Carter, has been engaging in an affair with another woman. This is a fact and can be proven should he deny it. This affair has been going on for several months. We will spare you the gritty details. How you handle this situation is totally up to you. However, should Dylan deny this fact, we will publicly expose him. We have photographs and other physical evidence of his infidelity.

Signed,

The Marriage Counselor

Baez shook his head. "Did Carter have money as well?"

"Yes," said Mitchell. "He was an investment banker with a big firm in Ft. Lauderdale. He did very well. Also, he had a life insurance policy for $600,000."

Baez sat back in his chair and thought for a moment. "Are they investigating it as a homicide?"

"No, they ruled it a suicide. Detective Paxton said they could not prove otherwise."

"When did this happen?"

"He said it happened two months ago. It wasn't until he saw the news about our cases that he started having doubts."

"Were the Carter's getting a divorce?"

"Yes. The wife inherited all their assets and the insurance money. The suicide clause had expired. I shared with him what we knew about our cases."

"Are they going to re-open their case?"

"Not yet. He wants to see what we come up with first, but he is concerned."

"As he should be," said Baez. "With this latest information, I may have to rethink my theory."

"I have a meeting with Steve Logan this afternoon to go over the results of Vincent's cell phone records," stated Mitchell. "I'll let you know what I find out."

"Thanks, Leah."

Baez sat at his desk pondering the new information while trying to formulate theories. He kept coming back to the same thought. *We've been looking for a connection between the affairs. Now, I'm wondering if there isn't a connection between the wives. We need to explore that angle.*

Baez picked up the phone and called Detective Roger Paxton with the Ft. Lauderdale Police Department. Baez explained who he was and why he was calling. They talked about the similarities with all three cases and how strange it was that each wife had gotten the same letter.

"Did you ever track down who Carter was having an affair with?" asked Baez.

"We tried," answered Paxton, "but never able to track it down. Maybe we should have tried harder to find her, but all the evidence pointed to a suicide. We believed the motive for the suicide was the letter, and then, of course, the divorce."

"Who wanted the divorce?"

"The wife, Ava Carter."

"Were you able to get anything from Carter's cell phone or computers?"

"We found a series of numbers on the cell phone that were not traceable. On his work computer, we found visits to several dating sites. We assumed that's where he found the woman he was having an affair with."

"You couldn't track it down?"

"No. Of those we could track down, there were no records of Carter ever using the sites. On one, which seemed to target married men, the IP address was hidden on a Virtual Private Network. We could only track it to an area."

"Did you ever suspect the wife had something to do with it?"

"We did thoroughly question her and her friends. We couldn't come up with anything to believe she had anything to do with the suicide."

"Would you mind sending me the cell phone records and the information on the websites you got off his computer?" asked Baez.

"No problem," said Paxton. "I'm eager to see what you guys come up with. The fact that you have similar letters appearing in two of your cases is cause for concern."

"Alright, thank you. I will let you know what we find out," concluded Baez.

Within an hour, Baez had the records from Detective Paxton in his email. He quickly opened it and downloaded the documents. He looked at the cell phone records first, and sure enough, he found an unknown number that appeared multiple times. Unfortunately, the number did not match the unidentified cell phone number from the Lopez case. Next, he looked at the websites provided by Paxton. Baez was interested in the site the Ft. Lauderdale Police could not track down. It was a site called "Secret Affairs."

Baez's phone rang. "Hello."

"We need to meet in the captain's office," advised Mitchell.

"What for?"

"He needs an update. This case is getting more coverage, and he wants to know where we are on it. I'll see you there."

When Baez arrived at the captain's office, Mitchell was already inside giving him some updates. "Come on in, Rick," said Captain Jim Gonzalez.

Once seated, Captain Gonzalez asked for Baez's thoughts.

"I've gone from thinking likely suicide to possible homicide, to the wife did it, to the mistress did it, and now I'm back to leaning toward the wife did it."

"Are you now certain it's not a suicide?" asked the captain.

"No, not certain. But I'm more inclined to believe it is a homicide."

"Leah, what about you?" questioned the captain.

"In my case, I still believe it is a homicide, and the wife is my only suspect. However, like Rick, I'm concerned about the anonymous letters and how they tie in. Now we have this other case from Ft. Lauderdale."

"This is all so strange," said Captain Gonzalez. "If these all turn out to be homicides, do we have a serial killer on our hands?"

"Right now," said Baez, "I think the wives have been involved, and maybe they are connected. One wife gets the idea from the other and vice versa. Make it look like suicide, bypass the entire divorce process, collect all the money, and life is good. A group of women whose husbands have cheated. The so-called anonymous letters may be just to throw us off."

"Interesting theory," said Captain Gonzalez. "As you know, we are getting more publicity now. With this similar case in Ft. Lauderdale, media attention could get out of hand."

"We are aware of that, sir," said Mitchell. "We are working as fast as we can. Part of the delay has been waiting on all the computer forensic stuff."

"Alright," said Captain Gonzalez. "I'll make sure forensics knows this is a priority now. You two keep me informed."

"Yes, sir," said Mitchell.

As they were walking back to their desks, Mitchell asked, "When did you come up with the wife conspiracy theory?"

"About an hour ago," laughed Baez. "After hearing about the Ft. Lauderdale case, I started thinking maybe we were approaching this from the wrong way. Maybe the connection between all the cases is the wives and not the mistresses.

However, we still need to find out who these mistresses are. If they are connected, then who knows what we have."

Mitchell shakes her head. "Just when I think we are getting closer, something else pops up. Do you think there are more cases like this out there?"

"At this point, I wouldn't bet on anything."

An hour later, Mitchell was back at Baez's desk with information on the cell phone records from Vincent's cell phone. The records had one unknown number that showed up numerous times, just like on Lopez's phone, but a different number. The number was also from a burner phone and not traceable.

"Whoever these guys are communicating with, they are good at hiding their tracks," said Baez. "The website Secret Affairs may be where these husbands are meeting the women they have affairs with. According to the location data provided by Detective Paxton, this site originates from the small town of Miami Springs, just north of Miami International Airport."

"You think the women on this dating website are involved?"

"No, but it's possible the wives found out about this website. If we can connect them to this, we may have more reason to suspect the wives in each case."

"That makes sense. What is your next move?" asked Mitchell.

"I'm calling Logan right now to get his ass moving on our computer forensics. I need to know if this website shows up on our victim's computers as well."

Baez called Logan to check on his progress in downloading the data from the iPads and the laptop. Logan assured him he would have the results later in the day. Baez then called Detective Paxton again to ask a favor.

"Roger, would you be willing to contact Ava Carter to see if she knew either Valerie Lopez or Kristy Vincent? We are looking into the possibility these women may have known each other."

"Absolutely," said Paxton, "I'll get on this tomorrow and get back to you."

"Thank you."

Baez had been so intense with the day's work he had not even eaten lunch. Since all he had to do now was wait, he decided to grab a late lunch at his favorite place, Sadie's Sub and Grub, about four blocks from the police department. He grabbed his jacket and walked the four blocks.

When he walked in, he was greeted loudly by Sadie. "Hi there, Detective Rick. It's been a while."

"I've had a busy week, but sure looking forward to a wonderful lunch."

"I know. I've seen the news. Well, if it's good food you want, you've come to the right place. What will it be today?"

"What's the special?"

"Our six-inch meatball pizza sub, a large drink, and a slice of fresh peach pie for ten dollars."

"Sounds great. I'll take it."

Baez sat eating his lunch, careful not to drop pizza sauce on the front of his shirt, and thought more about the three cases. He could not get the coincidences out of his mind. He was hoping the results of their computer searches would come up with the same dating site found by the Ft. Lauderdale Police. That might make things a little easier. Once he had finished his lunch, he left a $4 tip. He thanked Sadie as he was walking out. "Thank you, Sadie. That was one great slice of peach pie. See you next time."

Back at the PD, Mitchell was waiting for Baez. "We finally got some results on the computer searches."

"Yeah? What did Logan find?"

"He found the website you were looking for, Secret Affairs, on both Lopez's iPad and Vincent's laptop."

"Bingo, we finally have a connection. Could he locate the IP address?"

"Somewhat," answered Mitchell. "He said it originates from the Miami Springs area."

"Fantastic. That means whoever is operating that website is in Miami Springs. That helps narrow things down."

"We could probably get a subpoena to get the records from the operators of the Virtual Private Network," said Mitchell.

"We could, but that would probably take weeks. Those companies fight to keep their client's information private. And if a judge doesn't think our evidence is powerful enough, we could lose the fight. I have another idea."

"Yeah?"

"I'm going to find this website and attempt to set up a date. Then I can find out who these people are."

"No one's going to want to date you, Rick," laughed Mitchell.

Baez looked at Mitchell with a frown. "What are you talking about? I'm prime bait, baby."

Mitchell laughed again. "Just joking, Rick. I'm sure you'll get picked up right away."

Chapter 9

First thing Thursday morning, Baez searched the internet looking for the website called Secret Affairs. It did not take him long until it was on his screen. He was surprised at how forward the dating site was about only looking for married men who wanted an affair. The site claimed to have women who were not interested in a serious or long-term relationship. Thus, they were only looking for married men who were still committed to their marriage but wanted some excitement in their lives.

The site promised to be discreet and never to reveal who its clients were. It promised confidentiality. One requirement was proof of marriage. A marriage license and a photo with the wife could be used as evidence of marriage. Men could apply, but there was no guarantee a woman would be interested. The application fee was $300. If a woman was interested and the man agreed to set up a date, an additional fee of $3500 was required before the date. *This certainly limits the clients to men with money,* thought Baez. If accepted by a woman, a picture and short bio would be provided before a man had to decide if she was acceptable. *Almost sounds more like an escort service.* Men also had to provide a home address and current photo. *How am I going to get the captain to agree to pay for this?*

Baez informed Mitchell of what he had found and the requirements of the dating site.

"Do you think the captain will approve of you doing this?" asked Mitchell.

"There's only one way to find out. And by the way, you are going to be my wife."

"What?"

"I have to prove I am married, so you are going to be my wife."

"And how are you going to do that?"

"A marriage photo and fake marriage license."

Mitchell just looked at Baez with a look that said, *I don't believe this.*

"It will work," assured Baez. "Now, let's go see the captain."

Once in the captain's office, Baez explained his plan. Captain Gonzalez was not convinced the plan would work.

"We have to try it," pleaded Baez. "This is the only connection we have to all three cases right now. Let me get inside this group, whoever they are, and find out what is going on."

"You are talking about possibly spending thirty-eight hundred dollars on a scheme that may not provide any evidence of who killed these men if, in fact, they were murdered. They all might be suicides."

"You are right, Captain, but you have to admit, the similarities in each case are reasons to investigate fully. We would be remiss not to follow up every lead."

Captain Gonzalez interlaced his fingers on top of his desk and looked at Baez, then looked at Mitchell. "You are both good detectives, and I trust your instincts, so I am going to support you on this. But I'm only going to authorize an expenditure of thirty-eight hundred. If it doesn't yield the evidence you are looking for, I will not authorize another thirty-eight hundred."

"Thank you," said Baez.

"You can use our undercover account for payment, and I will have Narcotics get you a fake driver's license for ID. Just let me know what name you will be using."

"Don't worry about the money, Captain," said Mitchell. "I doubt anyone will select Rick anyway."

Both Captain Gonzalez and Mitchell laughed at her comment.

"That's twice now, Leah. I may decide not to marry you after all. I also need to have a home address that is real and a cell phone."

"Narcotics have various locations they rent out to use for their operations. I'll have them provide you an address and get you a phone," said Captain Gonzalez.

"Thank you, sir."

After the meeting, Baez got to work on getting a fake marriage license from the county clerk's office. He explained it was to be used only as a prop in a murder investigation. The County Clerk agreed to give him a fake license. Baez then had one of the crime scene photographers meet him and Mitchell the following day at the courthouse for a phony marriage photo.

"You're going to have to get a nice dress for the photo," Baez told Mitchell.

"I was thinking more in line of jeans and a t-shirt," responded Mitchell.

"Why, are you trying to look like Kristy Vincent?"

"Funny," said Mitchell. "I'll be ready. You just make sure you look decent. How long have we been married?"

"I told the clerk to make it seven years. You know, the seven-year itch thing."

"I don't think I could make it seven days with you, let alone seven years," laughed Mitchell.

Baez laughed, "after seven days with me, you'd be converted."

"Ha! Not a chance."

"By the way, you're going to be Julie Martinez on the marriage certificate, and I'm going to be Michael Martinez."

"Julie Martinez. That has a nice ring to it," said Mitchell.

Baez spent the rest of the day setting up his fake account through Narcotics and taking a photo for his phony driver's license.

***

On Friday, the following day, Baez had a new driver's license and marriage license sitting on his desk. *Perfect,* he thought. Later that morning, Baez and Mitchell went to the courthouse to pose for a marriage photo. Baez wore a dark suit with a blue tie, while Mitchell showed up in a long, beige chiffon dress.

"You look very nice for our wedding," said Baez.

"You do too," responded Mitchell.

Late that afternoon, Baez spent an hour filling out an application on the Secret Affairs website. He frequently went back and changed things to make the application as appealing as possible. There were many personal questions he had to answer. Questions included those about employment, level of income, and life insurance policies. Narcotics had quickly set up a fake website for "Michael Martinez" that described him as an attorney. In one section of the application, Baez had to explain why he was looking for an extramarital affair. He wrote that his wife, Julie, no longer had the same passion for sex as when first married. He was looking for some sexual satisfaction, but still loved his wife and did not want a divorce. He also had to agree that any affair started was for fun only and not for permanent relationships. He also had to submit a photocopy of proof of marriage, a photo with his wife, and a recent photo of himself. This was risky, as Baez had been on TV for past homicide investigations. He downloaded an image of the marriage license and a photo they had taken earlier that morning. He just hoped no one associated with the site would recognize him or Mitchell. He then took a selfie with his new cell phone, making sure nothing in the background would give him away, and downloaded it to the site. Next, he had to submit an address and cell phone number. He used the address and cell phone provided by the undercover Narcotics Unit. Finally, he had to provide a username and password for logging into his account. Once the application was completed, he submitted the $300 payment from the undercover account, which allowed him to use his fake name.

Within ten minutes, he received a text message on the cell phone acknowledging receipt of his application. The message advised that his application would be reviewed, and he would get a response within 72 hours. Now, he just had to wait.

"How did it go?" asked Mitchell.

"Fine, I hope. It was a detailed application. I just hope I can remember everything I put in there. I got a message that said it could take up to 72 hours for a response."

"It sounds like whoever is behind this takes it seriously."

"I'll say. It seems well organized," said Baez. "I was surprised they asked about life insurance. What do they care? Only the wives would care about this."

"Maybe because the wives are behind this somehow?" questioned Mitchell.

"I intend to find out. I've asked Paxton to follow up with Ava Carter to see if she knew or had any connection to Kristy or Valerie. I'm also going to re-interview Valerie to see if she will admit to knowing either lady."

"I'll do the same with Kristy," said Mitchell, "although I'm not sure she will speak to me."

"Good luck with that. Let's touch base on Monday to share notes."

"Okay, I'll see you Monday."

***

On Monday morning, twelve days after the death of Lopez, Baez once again responded to the home of Valerie Lopez. He explained he had further information and would like to ask her a few more questions. Valerie agreed and invited him into the living room. Baez explained what he had found about the Secret Affairs website and believed that is where Lopez had found his mistress.

"He found his lover on a website?" asked a surprised Valerie.

"Yes, Valerie, I believe so. We are still investigating it, but we found references to that website on his iPad. It is a website that caters to married men only."

"Why did he do that?"

"I don't know. Some men just find a need for more excitement in their life, I guess. I need to ask you if you've ever heard of Kristy Vincent or Ava Carter?"

"Those names don't ring a bell," answered Valerie.

"It is important, Valerie, as we believe there are now three cases related to this website. The other two wives involved were Kristy Vincent and Ava Carter. Are you sure you have never met them or talked to them? We will find out if you have. It will just make it easier if you tell us."

"I'm sorry, Detective, I don't know anyone by those names."

"Each of those women received a letter just like you did."

Valerie now looked surprised. "A letter about an affair?"

"Yes, and other than the names, they were an exact copy of the one you received."

"I'm trying to think, but I do not remember ever meeting anyone by those two names."

"Alright, Valerie, thank you for your time. I'll keep you informed as we find out more information."

"I guess he was unhappy," sighed Valerie.

Baez did not respond to the last comment. "As I said, I'll let you know if I find out anything more."

"Thank you, Detective."

Meanwhile, Mitchell responded to the home of Kristy Vincent. Kristy answered the door wearing a yellow nightgown and fuzzy pink slippers.

"What the hell do you want?" groaned Kristy.

"Sorry to bother you again, Kristy, but I have to ask a couple more questions."

"I'm not answering anymore of your dumbass questions."

"Kristy, we found the website your husband used to find his mistress. There are a couple of names I need to ask you about that may help us."

"Website? What kind of website?"

"It was a dating website for married men only."

"That figures," grumbled Kristy. "He went on a website to cheat on me?"

"It appears so. May I run some names past you?"

Still standing in the open doorway, Kristy snapped, "What names!"

"Did you know an Ava Carter or Valerie Lopez?"

"Never heard of 'em."

"Are you sure?"

"Detective, what did I just say? I've never heard either of those names. Now, is that all?"

"Yes, Kristy, that is all."

As Mitchell turned to leave, she heard the door slam shut.

Baez was driving back to the department when his undercover burner phone buzzed. He quickly turned into a parking lot to read the message. It was from the Secret Affairs website. He was informed he had been accepted for the "program" and needed to log into his account for more information. Baez then called Mitchell.

"Hey, it's me, Rick."

"Oh, hi Rick. I didn't recognize the number."

"It's my burner phone. I just got accepted by Secret Affairs."

"Did you get set up with someone?"

"No, I need to get back and log into my account. That is probably why we have little information from the cell phones. They do business through an online account that requires a username and password. Meet me at my desk in fifteen minutes."

"Alright, I'll be there."

Back at his desk, Baez sat down at his computer. Mitchell quickly joined him. Baez proceeded to the website and signed in. A page appeared congratulating him on finding a match and directing him to a link for more information. He clicked on the link, and a new page appeared with a full-figure photo of a strikingly beautiful woman with long, flowing blonde hair. She was turned slightly to her left, looking back over her shoulder with her right hand on her hip in a seductive stance. She had a brilliant smile and a well-sculpted hourglass figure. She was wearing a mid-thigh length, strapless black lace dress. Her bio listed her as 5'-7", 125 pounds, 41 years old, with blonde hair and blue eyes. Her background included work as a waitress, secretary, and assistant manager for a full-service restaurant. Her status was listed as divorced. The most intriguing thing about her bio was her name: Mandy.

"Look at that," said Baez. "Probably the same woman that dated Lopez. She certainly matches the description provided by Miguel Rodriguez."

"How lucky can you get?" asked Mitchell.

"As I said before, maybe these women are all one woman."

"I think you are about to find out."

There was a box with the question; Do you accept Mandy as your date? Yes or No. Baez selected yes and hit enter. "We'll see what happens," said Baez.

"I forgot to ask," said Mitchell, "what amount did you put down for life insurance?"

"I made it interesting by putting in seven hundred and fifty thousand."

"If life insurance is a factor that should get their attention."

"Now we wait to see what happens," said Baez. "By the way, did you get anything from Kristy?"

"No, she was her usual friendly, cheerful self. She denied knowing the other two women."

"Yeah, Mrs. Lopez denied it as well."

Chapter 10

It was now Tuesday, and Baez was sitting at his desk looking at the photograph of the woman who called herself Mandy. He couldn't get over how good-looking she was. *Rodriguez was right,* he thought. *Mandy is beautiful and seductive.* Just then, his burner phone rang.

"Hello?"

"Hi, is this Michael?" said a woman in a soothing voice.

"Yes, it is."

"This is Mandy, your secret affair girl. How are you doing today, Michael?"

"I'm doing very well, thank you. And you can call me Mike."

"Okay, Mike, are you ready for an adventure?"

"Yes, that is what I signed up for."

"Great, we just have to go over a few things," she said in a soft tone. "Are you sure this is what you want to do, Mike?"

"Yes, I've thought about it, and this is what I want. I need some excitement in my life."

"I can provide that, I promise. I want to assure you we are discreet and do everything we can to keep your affair confidential. However, your wife may find out, and it could ruin your marriage. Are you willing to take that chance?"

"Yes, I am."

"You also know that this is completely voluntary on your part, and we take no responsibility should this arrangement cause problems in your marriage."

"Yes, I read the warnings on your website."

"Alright then, the next step is to set up a meeting someplace, preferably where no one will likely know you. You pick the place and time, and I will meet you there. After that, you can decide if you want to continue to move forward. I am available tomorrow evening, Friday evening, or Saturday."

"Weekends are not great, as I need to be with family. How about tomorrow night at seven o'clock at the Royal Surf and Turf? They have a friendly bar there. Do you know where that is?"

"Yes, I know right where it is. I'll see you tomorrow. What color do you like?"

"I'm sorry, what?"

"What color would you like me to wear?"

"I'm sure anything would be nice."

"Yes, it would, but I'd like you to pick a color, and that is how you will know it is me."

"Okay, how about red?"

"See you then, Mike."

Once he was off the phone, Baez just sat and thought about the phone call for a few minutes. *She has such a sultry and pleasant voice,* he kept thinking, *and the body to back it up.*

Baez called Mitchell to tell her about the phone call and the planned meetup. He told her he was going to ask another detective to be in the bar to observe.

"Why don't you let me do it?" asked Mitchell.

"You are in the photo we sent in, Leah. You might be recognized."

"Rick, other than my skin being black, I won't look anything like I did in that photo. I'm going to be there."

"Alright," agreed Baez. "But I need you to stay back. I don't want to risk anything going wrong."

"Oh, stop worrying. It now makes sense why we can only find phone numbers on our victim's cell phones. I expected you to get a text message."

"She, or they, seem to know what they are doing to keep things as confidential as possible."

"Did the number she called from match the unknown number on Lopez's or Vincent's phone?" Mitchell asked.

"Let me pull it up on my phone. Let's see, uh, nope, it is a completely different number. Must have changed out her burner phone."

"Alright, I've got more work to do. I just picked up a sex assault, so I'll be working on that the rest of the day. See you tonight."

"Right, bye, Leah."

Baez was eager to meet this woman known as Mandy. He believed she might hold the key that would lead to answers in the death of Lopez and Vincent. At least maybe they could find out who sent those anonymous letters, and why? Was it someone inside the dating service? Or was it someone outside who was angry and trying to ruin their business by exposing them? So many questions and not enough answers.

***

It was now Wednesday evening, a full two weeks after Lopez's death, and no further progress had been made in the investigations. Baez was preparing for his first date with Mandy. He was excited over the possibility of breaking the case open but also nervous. He knew he would have to role-play the entire time he was with Mandy. Could he pull it off? He had to gain her confidence to get her to share information. He wanted to find out details of the operation, where she lived, and where the website was managed. Finally, he wanted to find out how many other people were involved in this website for cheaters.

Baez arrived at the restaurant ten minutes early. He went inside and requested a booth for two. He was shown to his table and sat down. He declined to order any drinks until Mandy showed up. A couple of minutes later, Mitchell walked in and sat across the room. She had her partner, Grace, with her. Mitchell had been right. She did not look like the same person in the fake wedding photo. She was wearing jeans, a western-style button-down shirt, and a cowboy hat. Baez almost didn't recognize her.

At 7:02 pm, Mandy walked into the room wearing a slinky red dress that hugged her hips. The dress had a V neckline, revealing deep cleavage. Her blonde hair hung down past her shoulders in a flowing fashion, with some hanging in front of her shoulders. Baez waved at her. As she approached, Baez stood up to greet her and noticed she had bright blue eyes. Her lips looked the color of strawberries.

"Hi Mandy, I'm Mike. Please have a seat."

"Thank you, Mike. It's good to finally meet you," she said in her sultry voice.

"Same here," said Baez.

The waiter came by, and Mandy ordered a glass of chardonnay. Baez ordered a Corona beer with lime. They then engaged in small talk for a time until Baez started to probe into Mandy's business.

"How long have you been doing this type of thing?" asked Baez.

"Why do you ask that?"

"Just curious. I'd never heard of a service like this before I found your website."

"I wouldn't call it a service, Mike. It's just a dating website like any other, except this one is for married men."

"Your website is incredible and quite functional. How long did it take you to set it up?"

"No time at all because it's not my website. I simply find men on it like you find women."

That's interesting, Baez thought. *That tells me there are more people involved in this operation.* Baez decided not to pry any further. He could tell Mandy was uncomfortable talking about the dating service, and he did not want to scare her off. He needed to build her trust. For the rest of the evening, Baez made small talk and tried to talk about her background. If she was telling the truth, he learned she was originally from Des Moines, Iowa. She had been married once but had now been divorced for 11 years. She had primarily worked in the restaurant service industry and was currently working as an assistant manager at a local restaurant. She also liked to walk on the beach and regularly exercised to keep in shape. Baez could feel a connection building between them.

"Why have you never married again?" asked Baez.

"After my divorce, I decided I didn't want to be married anymore. The divorce ruined me financially. I don't want to go through that again."

"Is that why you only date married men? You don't want a serious or permanent relationship?"

"Why do I feel like I'm being interrogated?"

"Oh my, I'm sorry. I was simply curious, that's all. I'm happy to be with you right now, and if you don't want to talk about your life, I'm okay with that."

"You are right. I don't want to get serious with anyone. That's why this dating program is ideal for me. Are you interested in me?"

"Very much," answered Baez.

"Great, then let's plan to have good times for as long as they last. When either of us is tired of the arrangement, we can leave with no hard feelings."

"When can we get together again?"

"If you want to continue with me, go back online and pay your membership fee. Once that is done, I'll be in touch."

"I do want to continue," said Baez, "but only if you feel the same way."

"Yes, you seem to be a pleasant gentleman, and I've enjoyed your company. I'll get back to you once you've paid your membership fee."

Mandy then got up to leave. Baez stood up. "Can I drive you home?"

"Not tonight," said Mandy. "Maybe next time."

As Mandy walked toward the door, Baez got Mitchell's attention and nodded toward the door, indicating he wanted her to follow Mandy. Mitchell nodded yes. Once Mandy had walked out, Mitchell and Grace went out behind her. Baez then paid the bill and walked out to his car.

Baez got in his car and immediately called Mitchell. "Are you following her?"

"Yes, just got on the Dixie Highway, and we are heading south. She's in a taxi."

"South?" questioned Baez. "Miami Springs would be northwest."

"Yep, but we are headed south."

"Keep me posted," said Baez. He then disconnected.

Baez drove to the Dixie Highway and headed south. He knew Mitchell would call him back as soon as they exited the highway. After about ten minutes, Mitchell called.

"We just got off at Southwest 27th Avenue. It looks like we are turning right onto Orange Avenue."

"Alright, I'm about five minutes behind you."

"They just pulled into a parking lot. It will be the second townhome complex on the right. I'm going to jump out to see if I can tell which unit she goes into."

"Sounds good. I'll be there in a few minutes."

"Grace drove just past the complex and pulled over. You'll find her there."

"Okay."

A couple of minutes later, Baez pulled up behind Grace. Both exited their vehicle and met on the sidewalk.

"Where is she?" asked Baez.

"She followed our subject into the complex," said Grace. "I'm just waiting for her to return."

"Thanks for helping with this, especially on your night off."

"Once Leah said she had to do surveillance, what else was I going to do? It sounded exciting."

Several moments later, Mitchell came walking out from behind some bushes. "She went into unit one thirteen B."

"Good, now we know where she lives," stated Baez. "But this doesn't fit the general location of the website IP address. I was hoping she would go somewhere in Miami Springs."

"Maybe she has nothing to do with the website," said Mitchell.

"Either way, I've got to get into her home to snoop around. I'm not even sure her real name is Mandy."

"I'm surprised she didn't invite you back to her place. It looked like you were getting along well."

"This was just a meet and greet. Now I've got to pay the fee for the privilege of seeing her again."

"Did you learn anything tonight?"

"Not much. She didn't say anything to lead me to think she was a killer. She was cautious about talking about this dating service, so I avoided asking too many questions. I found out she is divorced, and it was not a pleasant experience for her. She said that's the reason she doesn't want another long-term relationship. Thus, she only dates married men."

"Sounds hokey to me," interjected Grace.

"Maybe," responded Baez, "but we won't figure it out tonight. Let's get out of here. I'll see you tomorrow, Leah."

***

The following morning, Baez went onto the Secret Affairs website, logged in, and submitted a $3500 payment to continue his dating of Mandy. Now all he could do was wait to hear back from her.

Baez then called Computer Forensics and talked to Steve Logan about the cell phone data. He asked Logan if he could search the text messages received on Lopez's phone for a text telling Lopez he had been accepted into the program and to log into his account.

"What program?" asked Logan.

"It's this dating service for married men called Secret Affairs."

"A dating service for married men?"

"Yes, and that is probably going to be the only text message received. I received a similar message while posing as a customer. I want to know if it came from the same number as mine. You may have to go back for several months or more to find it. Sorry."

"It won't be much of a problem. Once I know what you are looking for, I have a nifty word search program that works on text from almost any source. I need to finish analyzing a computer I'm working on right now, then I'll run the texts through the search software. Shouldn't take long."

"That would be great. Thank you, Steve."

After hanging up, he noticed he had a message on his phone. It was from Detective Paxton with the Ft. Lauderdale Police Department. Paxton left a message to call him back for an update. Baez immediately called.

"What have you got for me, Roger?" asked Baez.

"We pulled Ava Carter in for another interview, and she denied knowing either of those other women you mentioned. She claimed not to know of her husband's affair until receiving the anonymous letter. She confronted him, and he admitted to it. She said he was shaken up by the letter and didn't want his situation to become public. We believed that was the motive for suicide."

"And now?" asked Baez.

"I don't know," admitted Paxton. "Since the discovery of your two cases, we are taking another look at our case."

"Did she have any information about the mistress?"

"According to Mrs. Carter, she demanded to know who the woman was, but he refused to tell her. The only thing he told her was that she was a Hispanic woman and very attractive."

"That helps," said Baez. "If you come up with any more information, please let me know, and I'll do the same."

"Will do. Talk to you later."

"Oh, one more thing. Did you find any drugs or alcohol in your victim's system?"

"Yes, they found alcohol and barbiturates."

"Same as in my victim," advised Baez.

"This is sounding like more than a coincidence," responded Paxton.

"Yes, it is. Let's keep in touch."

"Alright, Rick, goodbye for now."

"Goodbye."

Mandy was not Hispanic, so Baez now knew for certain there were at least two women associated with the Secret Affairs website. It was likely there were others as well. There was clearly a secretive service being provided to married men who were seeking an affair. Was there a connection to the deaths of at least three husbands? Baez wasn't sure what to believe. As Baez was running plausible scenarios through his head, his phone rang. Baez answered.

"Rick, this is Steve Logan. I found the text you were looking for. It was sent six months before Lopez's death. I've made a copy and will email it over to you."

"Thanks, Steve. Did it come from the same number as the one I received this past Monday?"

"No, different number. And yes, it is from an untraceable burner phone."

"Whoever is running this service is smart," suggested Baez. "They cover their tracks well."

"I agree," said Logan.

***

On Friday mid-morning, Baez received a call from Mandy. "How are you today, Mike?"

"I'm doing well. I had an enjoyable time Wednesday night."

"Yes, me too. Would you like to go out sometime?"

"I would."

"What night can you get away from the wife?"

"My wife works evenings as a nurse during the week. Any weeknight will work."

"How about meeting me at the Beachside Lanes for some bowling Monday evening? Do you know where that is at?"

"Uh, yeah. Bowling?"

"Yes, I love to bowl, and I'm quite good at it. How about six o'clock?"

"Can I pick you up somewhere?"

"Not yet. I'll meet you there."

"Alright, see you Monday at Beachside Lanes for some bowling," said Baez.

Baez then walked over to Mitchell's desk. "You won't believe what my next date is."

"Candlelight dinner for two at her place?" guessed Mitchell.

"No, bowling."

"Bowling?"

"Yes, she said she loves to bowl and wants to meet me at Beachside Lanes Monday evening."

Mitchell laughed. "Sounds like this romance is heating up."

"This dating site and Mandy are not what I was expecting."

"I suppose you want me to go bowling that night?"

"No, Mandy is harmless. I just need to play this out until I can get more information. I'll let you know on Tuesday how it went."

"Good, because I'm not a big bowling fan." Mitchell laughed again.

"What?" asked Baez.

"Nothing, I'm just wondering what the captain would think if he knew you spent all that money just to go bowling."

"Alright, have your fun. But I'm going to solve this case while you sit there and twiddle your thumbs."

Mitchell rolled her eyes. "I got some more information from Dr. Ballard. Based on further analysis of Vincent's internal organs, he concluded Vincent was poisoned over a period of days, probably in the range of ten days. He also believes the last dose was probably the largest, which was the one that finally killed him."

"What do you make of that?" asked Baez.

"I yo-yo back and forth, but Kristy had the best opportunity to lace his food with the antifreeze. They still lived together, and she certainly has the personality."

"Whoever Sugar is, she probably had the opportunity as well," said Baez.

"That's why I go back and forth on this," responded Mitchell. "I need to find out where Vincent was the night before he died. I'm hoping you will find out through this dating service."

"I'll give it my best," assured Baez. As he said it, he wondered if he could actually pull it off. *Will I be able to act naturally and pretend to be someone I'm not?*

Chapter 11

The following Monday evening, Baez arrived at the bowling lanes a few minutes early to reserve a lane and rent his shoes. Before getting out of his car, he removed his gun and holster and placed them in his glove box. It would be hard to hide a firearm while bowling. Baez had never been a great bowler and hadn't bowled in years. He was concerned about embarrassing himself. At six o'clock sharp, Mandy came walking through the door. Baez waved at her. She was dressed in tight-fitting jeans and a white blouse with wide lapels. She was wearing the same strawberry lipstick as before. She had a swagger as she walked. *What is that she's carrying?* Mandy was carrying a bowling bag. She walked over and sat next to Baez.

"Hi, Mike."

"Hi, Mandy. You have your own bowling ball?"

"Of course, don't you?"

"No, I don't."

Mandy looked at the shoes Baez was wearing and laughed. "Where did you get that smelly pair of shoes?"

"Very funny. They are rentals."

Mandy then pulled out her new-looking pink and white bowling shoes. She slipped off her shoes and bent over to tie on her bowling shoes. Baez could not help but notice Mandy's cleavage as she bent over. Before bowling, Baez ordered them both a margarita.

Once they started to bowl, it was obvious Mandy had not been joking about being a good bowler. They bantered back and forth during the game and had an enjoyable time together. Baez did his best to keep up, but Mandy easily beat him, 225 to 146.

"Where did you learn to bowl like that?" asked Baez.

"I played in leagues for many years. My ex-husband was big into bowling."

"Why did the two of you break up?"

"That's not something I choose to talk about, Mike."

"Alright, I'm sorry."

Baez ordered two more drinks, and they began another game. Baez found Mandy to be engaging and fun to talk with. While playing, Baez attempted to get some more information out of Mandy, hoping the alcohol would lower her guard.

"Where do you live, Mandy?"

"I live in the Coral Gables area off the Dixie Highway."

At least Baez knew she was telling the truth about that.

"How long have you been dating from the website?" inquired Baez.

"Why do you want to know about that?"

"Oh, I'm just curious. An outgoing person like you should be able to find plenty of dates."

"Yes, but my dates only want an affair. They are not looking for permanent relationships. Most of them still want to remain married. Given that I don't want a permanent relationship, it works for both of us."

"How did you ever find this dating service?"

"The same way you did, by searching the internet."

By the end of the second game, Mandy had again beaten Baez. However, it was a closer game, as she scored 187 to Baez's 156.

"At least I wasn't soundly beaten this time," pointed out Baez.

"No, I had a terrible game. Well below my average."

"Let's go sit in the bar, and I'll get you another margarita," suggested Baez.

"Sounds good to me."

Baez found them a table, then walked up to the bar to order the drinks. He ordered Mandy a regular margarita with extra tequila and asked for a virgin margarita for himself. After she was most of the way through her third margarita, Baez began with more probing questions.

"How long do your affairs usually last?"

"It depends on the person I'm dating. If they are real jerks, then I cut it off. If they are nice and we are having fun, it will continue until the guy wants it to stop. Don't worry, Mike. I don't think you are a jerk. I like you."

"Thank you, Mandy. I like you too. I'm having a wonderful time."

"That's what this dating service is all about, having fun, with no strings attached."

Baez could tell Mandy was feeling the effects of the alcohol. "What happened to the last guy you were dating?"

Mandy leaned in closer to Baez and whispered, "Sad story. He committed suicide."

"He committed suicide? How?"

"All I know is he asphyxiated himself with his car exhaust."

"Why would he do that?"

"Beats me, but I think his wife found out about the affair."

"Did he tell you that?"

"Yes, and it's been on the news."

"On the news?"

"Yeah, the police are investigating."

"What was his name?"

Mandy sat back up. "I can't tell you that. It's all confidential. You wouldn't want me to go around telling people your name."

"No, I suppose not. May I drive you home?"

"No, I'll call a taxi."

"I'd like to see where you live."

"You said you are free most nights during the week?"

"Yes, my wife works."

Mandy pulled out a pen from her hand purse and wrote her address on a napkin, then handed it to Baez.

"This is where I live. Come by tomorrow at six o'clock, and I will make you a nice dinner."

"I would love that, but can't I drive you home tonight?"

"No, come over tomorrow night. You can walk me outside."

Baez got on his phone and called Mandy a cab. He was told there was a cab in the area, and it would be there in three minutes. Baez then walked Mandy out the main door. Within a minute, a taxi pulled up. As Baez opened the door for Mandy, she turned, grabbed Baez around the back and over his left shoulder, then pulled him in close. She then pressed her strawberry lips on his and gave him a long, sweet kiss.

"Good night, Mike. Thank you for a fun evening. I'll see you tomorrow night."

"Good night, Mandy."

As Mandy rode away in the taxi, Baez stood there for a moment watching her leave and reliving the kiss in his mind. He hadn't had a kiss like that from a woman in a long time. He felt guilty using Mandy like this to get information. *What if she has nothing to do with either case? She's such a sweet lady.*

The following morning, Baez met with Mitchell to give her an update.

"Mandy didn't name him, but she admitted the last guy she dated had committed suicide through asphyxiation. That at least gives us confirmation that she was the one dating Dominic."

"What about the guy in Ft. Lauderdale?" asked Mitchell.

"That woman was described as Hispanic."

"Oh, that's right, I forgot. So, we have at least two women from this club dating men who end up dead. Our Cuban Sugar may be the same woman from Ft. Lauderdale."

"Possibly," agreed Baez.

"Did she talk about any of the other women?"

"No, but I'm going to press her more tonight."

"Tonight? Another date?"

"Dinner at her house. I'll be able to snoop around a little, and if the moment is right, I'll reveal who I am and try to get more information."

"Well, don't forget to ask about Vincent."

"If the time is right, I will ask her a lot of questions. However, I'm not sure she knows a lot."

"Why do you say that?"

"It was the way she told me about her last date committing suicide. If she were afraid of criminal liability, I doubt she would have revealed that to me. She even told me she heard the news that it was being investigated. She didn't seem concerned about that at all."

"Maybe she is cold-blooded," suggested Mitchell.

Baez laughed. "She doesn't seem to be cold-blooded."

"I'm not sure how you can tell after just two dates."

"Good point. I'll have more for you tomorrow," said Baez.

Baez left work at 4:00 pm to go home and get ready for his dinner date with Mandy. A heat wave had hit Miami, and it was a humid ninety-eight degrees, causing anybody who dared to venture outside to sweat profusely. Baez was happy to get out of his detective dress for some more relaxed clothing. He found a nice pair of beige cotton shorts and a blue button-down short-sleeve shirt to wear. *This will look casual enough,* he thought. He put his wallet with a police badge and ID in his left rear pocket. He took his nine-millimeter semi-automatic handgun and, like he did for bowling, placed it in the glove box of his car. He was not concerned about needing it on his dinner date with Mandy. Baez arrived at Mandy's place right on time.

Mandy answered the door wearing hot pink shorts and a white mid-drift top. She was wearing the same strawberry-colored lipstick, and her eyes were crystal blue, almost like sapphires.

"You look lovely tonight," said Baez.

"You don't look so bad yourself," replied Mandy. "Come on in. Would you like a drink before dinner? I have red or white wine or Corona beer."

"I'll take a Corona."

Baez looked around the living room and noticed it was nicely decorated in southern Florida style. The colors were of pastels, with a vase of multiple fresh flowers sitting on the coffee table in the center of the room. The room carried the scent of the floral arrangement.

Mandy retrieved a beer from the refrigerator and poured herself a glass of chardonnay. She handed Baez his Corona and said, "I'm making blackened Red Snapper, rice pilaf, and asparagus. I hope that is okay with you. I never asked if you liked seafood."

"I love Red Snapper. Everything sounds great."

Mandy sat next to Baez on the living-room couch and raised her glass. "Here's to a great evening."

Baez raised his beer and clinked her wine glass, then took a swig of beer. Mandy did the same with her wine. Mandy then leaned over and kissed Baez on the cheek.

"Did you miss me?"

"Yes, I've been looking forward to this evening."

"Me too. I know we have taken things slowly, but I like to get to know my men before committing to a relationship. You have to be careful when dating men through a dating service."

"I understand," said Baez. "I know you explained why you date married men, but doesn't that limit your relationships?"

"I'm not looking for a permanent relationship. I just want to have fun and companionship. Single men usually get too serious."

"What happens if you fall for a married man?"

"Why are you asking me this? Are you worried I might fall for you?"

"I'm just asking. It's an unusual dating situation."

"Have you ever been divorced, Mike?"

Baez started to say yes, then caught himself. "Uh, no, I haven't."

"If you had, you might understand better. It is not fun, especially for the woman. Some men unceremoniously dump their wives and then leave them alone and destitute. I hope you are not one of those types of guys."

"No, I am not interested in leaving my wife. I just wanted some excitement in my life."

"Then this service is for you. Now, can we stop talking about this and just relax and have a good evening?"

Baez figured he had pushed enough for now. "Yes, that would be nice."

Mandy served dinner in her dining room overlooking the courtyard of her townhome complex. It was too hot to sit outside. Baez found the dinner to be fabulous.

Baez complimented Mandy. "You are an excellent cook."

"Thank you, Mike. I'm glad you enjoyed it. Are you ready for another beer?"

Baez wanted to take it easy on the alcohol. After all, he was working and wanted to remain mentally sharp. "I'll just take a water or soda if you have one."

"Is Pepsi okay?"

"Yes, that would be fine, thank you."

"Why don't you relax in the living room while I clean up?" suggested Mandy.

Baez went into the living room and looked around for anything that might provide information on Mandy's real identity. He could not find any mail or magazines that might have a name on them. There were no photographs on the walls or tables.

After about ten minutes, Mandy joined Baez in the living room and again sat next to him.

"I like you, Mike. You are a true gentleman. Most men would have been all over me by now."

"I'm not that type of guy."

"I know, that's what makes me attracted to you," said Mandy, as she moved closer to Baez and placed her hand on his thigh.

Baez wasn't sure how to respond. *Do I tell her who I am and question her? I haven't found anything yet to confront her about. I don't want to move too soon, yet this is getting serious. I need to find a purse or something to find out who she is.*

As Baez contemplated his next move, Mandy turned and moved onto his lap, placing her strawberry lips on his, kissing him slowly and sensually. Baez continued to play along. Part of him wanted to tell her to stop, and another part of him wanted her to keep going. He hadn't been with a woman in a long time. *I need to get her in the bedroom so I can look around.*

Baez pulled away. "Why don't we take this to the bedroom?"

"Mmmm. You're ready for the good stuff, eh?"

"You could say that," said Baez, as he blushed.

Mandy led Baez by the hand to the bedroom. "Why don't you get ready while I go freshen up?"

"Sure," said Baez.

Mandy then went into the bath just off the bedroom and shut the door. Baez quickly got up and looked around the room. He carefully started opening drawers in Mandy's dresser. In the top right drawer, he found a purse. Baez kept listening for Mandy to exit the bathroom as he quickly opened the purse and saw a woman's wallet. Just as he was about to grab it, he heard Mandy grab the doorknob of the bathroom. Baez quickly shut the dresser drawer and stood straight up.

Mandy walked in stark naked. She was surprised to see Baez standing in the room. "You don't look like you are ready."

"I know. I'm just nervous, is all," stammered Baez. Baez could not take his eyes off Mandy. Nor could he contain his excitement over seeing her naked beauty.

Mandy walked over to Baez. "Let me help you, Mike," she said as she unbuttoned his shirt.

This can't happen. I've got to stop her, he said to himself.

Yet, he could not bring himself to say the words. Before he knew it, he was on the bed, naked with Mandy. By then, it was too late, as Baez could not resist the temptation. It had been so long for Baez, and Mandy was so beautiful and sexual. Afterward, he laid on the bed, both exhausted and ashamed. *What have I done?*

"Was that enough excitement for you, Mike?" whispered Mandy.

Baez looked at her. "Yes, it was." As he said it, he became aware of his weakness and indiscretion. *How could I be so stupid?*

"That's just the beginning, Mike."

Baez felt a nauseous pit in his stomach, knowing he had messed up and may have ruined the case.

After a few moments, Baez turned to Mandy, "I probably should get going now."

"Already?"

"Yes, I want to be sure to be home before my wife gets there."

"I understand," said Mandy softly as she got up from the bed and headed toward the bathroom. Once she closed the door, Baez jumped up and went to the dresser drawer again. He quickly pulled out the wallet and looked inside. Right in front was Mandy's Florida driver's license. Baez stared at the name for a moment. Emily Evans. He checked the photograph to be sure. Yes, it was a picture of the person he knew as Mandy. *This doesn't mean she is involved,* he said to himself, hoping he would be proven right. Baez then put the wallet back and quickly got dressed. Several minutes later, Mandy, now known as Emily Evans, exited the bathroom fully dressed.

"I hope we can do this again soon," she said.

"Yeah, me too," agreed Baez half-heartedly, as his mind wandered. He could not stop thinking about what just happened. How could he have been so gullible and stupid? As he was leaving, Mandy gave him one more kiss goodbye. She watched from the doorway as Baez walked toward the parking lot. He then noticed a white Ford Escape in the parking lot in front of Mandy's townhome. This prompted him to remember the witness description of the car seen parked next to Dominic's on the night of his death. Baez stopped, turned back toward Mandy, and asked, "what kind of car do you drive?"

"Why do you ask?" she said.

"Just curious. I like cars and just wondered what a pretty woman like you might be driving."

"It's that white Ford Escape parked out front."

Baez groaned to himself before saying, "those are nice cars, and thank you for a good evening." As he walked past Mandy's white Escape, he wondered, *could this have been the car parked next to Dominic?* The thought of it made him feel ill.

Chapter 12

On Wednesday morning, 21 days after Lopez was found dead in his car, and the morning after his sexual interlude with Emily Evans, Baez walked into work at about 10:00 am. Mitchell immediately corralled him.

"Well, what did you find out?"

"I found out her real name is not Mandy. It is Emily Evans, and she is 41 years old."

"Okay, so now we know these women use aliases."

"At least Evans does," replied Baez. "Here's another thing, she drives a white Ford Escape."

"She has to be a suspect then, don't you think?"

Baez paused before responding. "I think so. She was the one dating Lopez, and she has a white Ford Escape. She is certainly under suspicion. I snapped a photo of the back of her car as I was leaving. I need to show it to Tony Mateo to see if it looks like the one he saw."

"Are you okay, Rick?"

"Yeah, why?"

"You seem down today."

"Probably because I worked late last night."

"Did you get any other information?"

"Only that she dates married men to avoid long-term relationships. I just can't figure out how or why she would want to kill the men she dates. There's a sizeable piece of the puzzle we are still missing."

"Did you press her for information on the other women involved?"

"No, never had the chance."

"Never had the chance? What else did you do?"

Baez ignored the question. "I need to strategize this some more. I'll talk to you later."

Mitchell watched him walk away with a frown. *Something's not right with Rick.*

***

It was around noon when Baez received a call from dispatch. A woman was on the phone who wanted to talk to Detective Baez. Baez accepted the call. The caller identified herself as Cindy Franklin of Pinecrest. She told Baez she had received a letter like the one specified on the news. Her husband, Sean Franklin, admitted to having an affair with a woman from a dating service. Cindy read Baez the letter over the phone. Other than the names, the letter was an exact copy of the other known letters.

"Will you be able to provide me a copy of that letter?" asked Baez.

"Yes, just tell me where to send it," answered Cindy.

"We will pick it up. We are going to want to interview you and your husband in person."

"That will be fine," she said.

"When did you get this letter?"

"Last week. When I read the letter, I was shocked. I had heard about your investigation and the letters on TV. I couldn't believe it when I got one. At first, I thought it was one of my friends playing a practical joke. But when I confronted my husband and let him read the letter, he broke down and admitted he had been seeing someone else."

"Did he give you a name?"

"He said she went by the name of Sugar."

"Do you know what she looks like?"

"Oh yes, he showed me her picture on the dating website Secret Affairs. You have a password to log in, and then you can see who your date is."

"Are you getting divorced?"

"No, my husband has been open and honest about his mistake. He has apologized and agreed to help with your investigation. It was not all his fault. We both have things to work on to strengthen our marriage."

"You sound like a very understanding woman."

"I still love my husband, and I want to make this work."

"Would your husband be available this afternoon for an interview?"

"Yes, I will make sure of it."

Baez chuckled. "Alright, how about three o'clock?"

"We'll see you then, Detective."

After getting off the phone, Baez called Mitchell and gave her the news; they might finally have a significant break in the case. However, before interviewing the Franklins, Baez insisted on Mitchell meeting him for lunch. He had some vital information he wanted to share with her away from the department. She agreed to meet him at Sadie's Sub and Grub.

Baez was already seated in a booth when Mitchell walked in and sat across from him. After ordering some food and drinks, Mitchell looked at Baez. "What's the information you want to give me?"

"Leah, I screwed up."

"What do you mean?"

"With Emily Evans. I probably screwed up our investigation."

"Rick, what did you do?"

Baez could not look Mitchell in the eye. He looked down at the table.

"What is it, Rick?"

When he looked up, his eyes were misty. "I had sex with her."

Mitchell's jaw dropped, and she said nothing for several seconds. "You didn't."

"I'm afraid I did. I never intended it to happen. It just did."

"Damn you, Rick, what do you mean you didn't intend for it to happen? It takes two, you know."

"Yeah, I know. Believe me, I'm as upset as you are."

"How could you let this happen, Rick? You have compromised our entire investigation! You will be crucified if this ever goes to court."

"I know. I'm sorry, Leah. I just lost control. She was so nice and...."

Mitchell cut him off. "I don't even want to hear that crap, Rick. That's like working undercover drugs and shooting up heroin. You don't screw the witness or suspect."

Baez didn't respond. He knew she was right, and he had to take her wrath.

"You do know you will probably be fired for this, right?"

"I very well could," admitted Baez.

"Damn it, I just can't believe this," fumed Mitchell.

Just then, the waitress arrived with their food. She could see Baez and Mitchell were involved in a serious discussion, so she slid the food on the table, saying nothing. Mitchell pushed her food to the side. "I've lost my appetite."

"I'm going to make this right," said Baez.

"Yeah? How do you intend to do that?"

"By solving this case. We have important witnesses to interview this afternoon. Someone who is still alive and willing to talk about his affair."

"I'm not sure I can do this with you, Rick. I can't keep this knowledge from the captain."

"I'm not asking you to. Just give us some time. I think we are close to breaking this case open. Once we do, you won't have to say anything. I will go to the captain myself and tell him everything that happened."

Mitchell put her head in her right hand and started rubbing her forehead as though she were thinking about Baez's proposal.

"I don't know, Rick. If you weren't such a good friend, I'd tell you to go to hell."

Nothing was said for another thirty seconds, which seemed like thirty minutes to Baez. He knew he was asking a lot.

"Alright, but from now on, we do things my way," said Mitchell. "And you will not be with any of these ladies of the night by yourself. If we interview them, it will be as a team. No more undercover dates. When this is done, you immediately go to the captain and tell him everything."

"Agreed," replied Baez.

"I'm pissed at you right now. I still can't believe you allowed your sexual desires to interfere."

"It wasn't like that. It just happened."

"I don't want to hear it, Rick."

"I know, sorry. How do you want to handle the interviews this afternoon?"

"I'm taking the lead. You come in with follow-up questions as needed. Just don't be humping the wife in the back bedroom because she's good-looking."

"Alright, stop. I know you are angry, and I am ashamed. Let's move on, or let's not do this together."

"Okay, that was probably out of line. I won't mention it again. We are going to have to confront Emily Evans as well. Are you up for that?"

"I'll have to be."

Later that afternoon, Mitchell and Baez arrived at the Franklin residence in Pinecrest. The home was in an upscale neighborhood. It was a large two-story home with a large, well-maintained yard. Cindy Franklin answered the door and cheerfully greeted the detectives, welcoming them into their home. She took them into the dining room, where Sean Franklin was already seated. Baez and Mitchell sat across from Sean. After introductions, Mitchell began the interview.

"Sean, tell us what you know about the woman you know as Sugar," said Mitchell.

"I met her through the dating website called Secret Affairs. I only know her as Sugar, but that is not her real name. She goes by that to help maintain confidentiality. At least, that's what she told me. I wasn't looking for a permanent relationship, so I didn't care what her real name was."

"Can you describe her to us?"

"She's a Cuban woman, about five-six, slim, with a nice figure. She has black hair and brown eyes."

"How long is her hair?"

"To the top of her shoulders."

"Anything else distinguishing about her?"

"She has a scar on the top of her left shoulder, about six inches long."

"Did she ever say what that was from?"

"Yes, she told me her ex-husband was abusive, and one day, he tried to hit her in the head with a vase. She moved her head, but the vase hit her shoulder, broke, and sliced open her shoulder."

"Did she ever tell you her ex-husband's name?"

"No."

"How long did you date this woman?"

"About four to five months. It was not a regular thing. Sometimes I would go two weeks without seeing her."

"Can you tell us where she lives?"

"No, but I think it is somewhere near Amelia Earhart Park. She talked one time about liking that park and taking walks around it."

"You never went to her home?"

"No, she never wanted to go there. I always had to arrange a room at a hotel."

Mitchell turned to Cindy. "Mrs. Franklin, when did you receive the anonymous letter?"

"Nine days ago," said Cindy.

"May we have the letter?"

"Yes, I have it right here," said Cindy, as she handed Mitchell the letter.

"When did you confront your husband about the affair?"

"Well, at first, I didn't believe it, but I confronted him that night when he got home from work."

"And he admitted to the affair?"

"Once he read the letter and the threat to expose it publicly, he admitted it right away."

"I wasn't going to lie to my wife," interrupted Sean. "I was already feeling guilty and ashamed before the letter arrived. I'm not even sure why I did it."

"What do you do for a living?"

"I'm a surgeon."

"No surprise. All the men involved so far have had high-profile jobs and healthy incomes. Do you have a life insurance policy?"

"I do," said Sean. "It is a one million dollar policy."

"Neither of you is seeking a divorce?" asked Mitchell.

"No," said Cindy, "we are trying to work it out, and Sean has agreed to go to counseling. We have two children and want to keep the family together."

Mitchell looked at Baez and nodded.

Baez then spoke up. "Sean, do you have any idea who sent the letter?"

"I'm assuming Sugar did."

"Did you ask her?"

"I called her and confronted her about it, but she denied it. She said it would damage her if the information got out, and it would discredit her business."

"Sugar called the dating service her business?"

"Yes."

"One more thing," said Baez. "Do you know what color and type of car Sugar drives?"

"She drives a black Volkswagen Jetta."

"Ever see her in any other car?"

"No."

"Would you be willing to call Sugar to set up one more meet with her? We could be there waiting."

"I'm not sure if she would, as I told her I was done, but I can certainly try."

"That would be helpful," assured Baez. "We'll get back to you on that."

"I have another concern," said Sean. "Am I in any danger?"

"We don't know for sure," answered Mitchell. "Until we find out what is going on, I would not meet with Sugar without us being around to protect you."

"Don't worry, that won't happen," said Sean.

"Thank you, Mr. and Mrs. Franklin," said Mitchell. "You've been a tremendous help."

When they returned to their car, Mitchell turned to Baez. "We are getting closer to identifying who runs this dating service. If he can set up a meeting, that would be great."

"It's got to be Sugar," replied Baez. "You know where Amelia Earhart Park is, don't you?"

"No, I don't."

"It's just outside Miami Springs. That is the general location of the website IP address. Sugar may have an office or maybe runs it out of her home. Even if Franklin cannot set up a meet with Sugar, I think we have enough to get a subpoena to serve on the VPN provider."

"When do you want Franklin to set up a meet with Sugar?"

"Soon, but I'd like to do two things first. I want to show Tony Mateo a photo of Emily's Ford Escape and then confront Emily Evans with what we know."

"Didn't you get her real name illegally?" asked Mitchell.

"What do you mean?"

"You searched her dresser and purse without consent or a warrant. How can you confront her about her name?"

"I don't need to use that," said Baez with a smile. "I ran the plate off her car, which was parked in an open parking lot. You don't need a warrant for that."

Mitchell just looked at Baez and nodded in agreement.

Baez continued. "I'll call Evans tonight and try to set up another date for tomorrow, and then..."

"No more dates," interrupted Mitchell. "I told you that."

"Not an actual date. I will set it up so that you and I can confront her. I don't think she works tomorrow. I will ask if I can pick her up for lunch. If so, we can confront her then."

"Okay," agreed Mitchell.

When they returned to the police department, Baez called Emily Evans. She did not answer, so he had to leave a voice message. *Hi Mandy, this is Mike. If you are not working, I would like to take you to lunch tomorrow. I know a great out-of-the-way place close to where you live. Let me know as soon as you can.*

It wasn't until Baez got home that night when he received a call back from "Mandy."

"Hello, Mandy."

"Hi, Mike. I wasn't sure you would call back."

"Why is that?"

"You seemed kind of shook up when you left yesterday."

"Just nerves. I've never done anything like this before, but I'm okay now. Are you working tomorrow?"

"No, I have Thursday off. I would love to go to lunch with you."

"I will pick you up at one o'clock if that is okay."

"See you then, Mike," responded Mandy in a tender voice. "We can then have dessert at my place."

"Looking forward to it. Goodnight, Mandy."

Chapter 13

The next morning, Thursday, Baez called Tony Mateo to set up another interview. Mateo agreed to meet Baez at 10:00 am. Baez left at 9:30 and headed toward Mateo's apartment building across the street from Stratton Park. Traffic was hectic this day, making the drive longer than expected. Baez arrived at 10:05 am. The apartment building was an older, eight-story white stucco building. There was a private underground parking lot for residents only. Baez parked on the street and walked to the lobby. Baez rode the elevator to the third floor, where Mateo lived in apartment 314.

Baez knocked on the door, and it took several seconds before Mateo opened the door. "Hi, Detective," he said, "I was wondering if you were going to show up."

"Sorry about that," said Baez. "Traffic was a mess."

"No problem. Come on in. What can I do for you?"

"I have a photo of a car I would like you to look at. Tell me if it looks like the car you saw the night of Mr. Lopez's death." Baez pulled a couple of photos from his inside jacket pocket and handed them to Mateo.

Mateo looked intensely at the photos. "This could be the car, but I can't be sure. The taillights look like what I saw that night."

"Take your time," said Baez.

After another twenty seconds of looking at the photos, Mateo spoke. "From the back, it looks like the car, but I didn't get a look at the sides or front. That's the best I can do."

"You think it was a Ford Escape?"

"It could have been, but I'm not positive."

"Is there anything else you remember from that night that you might not have told me?"

"No, I've told you everything I know. It was just strange seeing the only two cars in the lot parked next to each other, and one of them was running. I thought it might have been two lovers meeting in the park."

"Did you see anyone else?"

"No, it was dark, and the windows were tinted."

"Alright, thank you, Mr. Mateo. I appreciate your help."

On his way back to the department, Baez called Mitchell. "Mateo couldn't positively ID the car as a Ford Escape, but said it could be the car he saw. He said the taillights looked the same as he remembered."

"That's better than saying it didn't match," responded Mitchell.

"It's enough that I can use it against Evans today. I may just have to embellish the strength of his identification of the vehicle."

"What are you planning?"

"We need to approach the interview as though we know more than we do. If she is involved, then letting her think we know the car is hers, and we know who Sugar is, maybe we can get her to give up information. We already know she dated Lopez."

"I like that approach. Would you like to take the lead, or would it be uncomfortable?"

"No, I'd like to challenge her."

"Alright, I can go with that," agreed Mitchell. "But if things go off course, I'm stepping in. What time are you supposed to meet her?"

"One o'clock. I'm headed back to the office now."

***

Back in the office, detectives Mitchell and Baez strategized how to go about interviewing Emily Evans, aka Mandy. They agreed to assume she was involved in Lopez's death and possibly others. They would challenge her with what they knew and what they thought was possible. They needed a break in the case before anyone else turned up dead. Mitchell surprised Baez with something else; a warrant to search Evan's cell phones and computers.

"When did you get that?" asked Baez.

"I started working on it last night after our interview with the Franklins. Evans admitted her last affair ended in suicide, and we know she goes by Mandy. After your call this morning, I added the information from Mateo. We now have two possible connections between Evans and Lopez. I figured a judge might agree we had probable cause to search her phones and computers. Judge Francisco agreed and signed the warrant a half hour ago."

"That's fantastic. Excellent work, Leah."

Detectives Baez and Mitchell arrived at Emily Evans' townhouse at 12:55 pm, and Baez knocked on the door. Emily Evans answered the door looking her usual beautiful self. She was wearing a blue mini dress with a low-cut neckline. The collar was lined with rhinestones.

"What's this!?" said Evans. "You brought your wife?"

Baez pulled out his badge from his left front breast pocket and showed it to Evans.

"She is not my wife. I'm Detective Baez, and this is Detective Mitchell. We need to talk to you, Emily."

Evans' eyes got wide after hearing the name Emily.

"My name is Mandy."

"No, it is not," responded Baez. "We are investigating a couple of homicides, and we need to talk to you, Emily."

Evans just stood there, looking back and forth between Baez and Mitchell. She found it hard to believe what Baez was telling her. "Why do you want to talk to me?"

"We have reason to believe your dating service is behind the killings," said Baez. "We need to understand what you know about the service. May we come in?"

"I didn't kill anyone."

"That may be, but we still need to talk to you. You may have valuable information."

"Alright, come on in," said Evans as she stepped back, away from the door.

As they walked in, Mitchell noticed the townhome was nicely decorated, but not overly so. She also noticed and smelled the large vase of fresh flowers on the coffee table.

"Do you mind if we sit at your kitchen table?" asked Mitchell.

"No, that will be fine."

Baez and Mitchell waited for Evans to sit down. Baez then sat directly across from her, and Mitchell sat at the end of the table, ninety degrees off to Evans' right side.

"You are not under arrest, Emily, but we have to ask you some questions. It is important for you to be honest with us," advised Baez.

"I don't know what you are talking about. My name is Mandy."

"Stop right there," warned Baez. "We know your name is Emily Evans. Your car lists to Emily Evans, and we have a witness who knows you."

"What witness?"

Baez noted Evans did not again deny her name, but was interested in who the witness might be.

"That doesn't matter right now. What matters is that you tell the truth and keep yourself out of deeper trouble."

"Why did you lie to me?"

"I was working undercover, Emily. We needed to find out who the people are behind this dating service for married men."

"Is that why you slept with me?"

Mitchell turned and looked at Baez with the look that said, *yeah, Rick, why did you sleep with her?*

"That was a mistake, Emily, and I apologize. Now, we need to get some answers from you about this dating service."

"Did I not please you enough?"

Mitchell looked down at the table and tried not to laugh.

"Emily! Stop it now. I know you were with Lopez in Stratton Park the night he died."

"I don't know what you are talking about."

"Your white Ford Escape was seen parked right next to Lopez's car the night he died. Not only that, a woman matching your description was seen with Lopez, and I know you were dating him." Baez was bluffing, of course, hoping she would believe him.

Baez then pulled out the two photographs of Evans' car and laid them on the table in front of Evans. He then pulled out a photo of Lopez lying in the parking lot, dead.

Evans looked down at the photos but didn't say anything.

"Emily, you need to tell us what happened."

"I don't know what you are talking about. I don't know a Mr. Lopez."

"Emily, I found two long blond hairs on Lopez's bed. I'm sure when we compare them to your hair, they will match."

Emily swallowed but didn't respond.

Now Mitchell spoke up. "Emily, it's best you tell us the truth. We have warrants for all your cell phones and computers. What do you think we will find on them? We will find evidence that you are lying to us right now."

"I didn't kill him," blurted out Evans. "You will also find evidence that Mike, or whoever you are, and I were dating. And if you take my sheets from the hamper, you will find his DNA all over them. Doesn't lying to have sex with me constitute rape?"

"No more than you lying about your name to me," retorted Baez. "Let me make this clear for you. I'm willing to take whatever comes my way. My goal right now is to find the killer of Mr. Lopez, and I believe that killer is you. Once we find what is on those records, you will find yourself in jail on a murder charge."

"I didn't kill anyone!" yelled Evans.

It was time for Baez's best bluff. "Then why were you with Mr. Lopez in Stafford Park the night he died!" yelled Baez.

Evans began to tear up. She sniffled a bit, then said, "I didn't kill him. I was only meeting him there."

Baez exhaled in relief. He had finally broken through. "Tell me, Emily, why were you meeting him in the park?"

"I was dating him as you said."

"Yes, but why meet him that night in the park?"

Evans sniffled some more, and Mitchell pulled out a tissue, handing it to Evans.

"I was told to meet him there."

"Who told you that?" continued Baez.

"I can't say."

Mitchell then reached out and placed her hand on Evans' right forearm. "Emily, now is not the time to protect anyone. You need to tell us everything."

Evans continued to cry and stare at the table in front of her.

Baez interrupted the silence. "Was it Sugar?"

Evans quickly glanced up at Baez. Baez now knew he had struck gold.

"How do you know Sugar?" asked Evans.

"Emily, I told you, I know much more than you think I do. Detective Mitchell is right. Now is not the time to protect anyone. We need to know the truth. Sugar runs the website, doesn't she?"

After a few seconds, Evans said in a soft voice, "yes."

"Why did she want you to meet Mr. Lopez?"

"I was supposed to get him drunk and high on some downers."

"Why was that?"

"I don't know."

"That's not true, Emily. You know why. Why did Sugar want you to get him drunk and drugged?"

"To teach him a lesson, I guess."

"A lesson? What do you mean?"

"He was cheating on his wife and was divorcing her."

Baez and Mitchell looked at each other. Both were a bit puzzled.

"You run a website to entice men to have affairs, and then you punish them for it?" asked Baez.

"No, only if they are getting divorced."

"I don't understand," said Baez.

"If the wife wants them back, we do nothing. We do not want to punish the wives. They are innocent."

"What kind of game are you playing, Emily?"

"It's not a game. We provide what some men are looking for, but if they cheat, there are consequences."

"The consequences are murder?"

"I know nothing about murder. We just publicly embarrass the men to teach them a lesson. I guess Dominic couldn't take it and decided to commit suicide."

"You were with Dominic."

"Only long enough to get him drunk and drugged."

"What was the purpose of that?"

"I was told so that he would be found by police and embarrassed by the publicity."

"And who told you this?"

Evans hesitated.

"Tell us," said Mitchell.

"Sugar."

"Sugar told you to get Dominic drunk and drugged?" asked Baez.

"Yes."

"Did he pass out?"

"Yes."

"Is that when you hooked the hose to the tailpipe?"

"No! I told you I didn't kill him."

"Then how did that happen if he was passed out?"

Evans hesitated. "Maybe it was Sugar."

"Was she there too?"

"Not while I was."

"She came later?"

"I don't know."

"What do you mean you don't know? You just said maybe it was Sugar who hooked up the hose."

"I never saw her there."

"But you know she came later, right?"

"All I know is that she said to call her after he was out. She was going to make sure the police found him so that he would be arrested and embarrassed. That's why I was told to leave the car running, as then he could be arrested for DUI."

"What did Sugar do?"

"I didn't ask anything. We are taught not to talk about anything or ask questions."

"By whom? Sugar?"

"Yes."

"Did you know Tyler Vincent?"

"No."

"Who was dating Vincent?"

"I can't tell you that."

"Why not."

"That is confidential to protect clients and the women who date them."

"Way too late for that, Emily. You need to come clean with everything you know if you want to protect yourself from more serious charges."

Evans looked down at the table again. "It was Sugar."

"Thank you, Emily. What is Sugar's real name?"

Evans looked at Baez, then looked at Mitchell.

"Come on, Emily, we need to know," said Mitchell.

"Her name is Miranda Castaneda."

"She runs the website, correct?" asked Baez.

"Yes."

"She lives in Miami Springs, right?"

Evans looked up at Baez.

"I told you I know more than you think," stated Baez.

"Yes, she lives there."

"What is her address?"

"That I don't know. I've never been there, and she has never told me her address."

"How many other women are involved in this dating service?"

"At least a few."

"What are their names?"

"Are they in trouble?"

"We don't know, Emily, but we need to talk to everyone involved."

"I don't know their names."

"I'm sure you know some of them. We're going to find out who they are."

"The only other one I know is Carla Delgado."

"Who is she dating right now?"

"I don't know. Last I knew, she was meeting with someone from Ft. Lauderdale."

"Was it Dylan Carter?"

"I don't know who it was."

"Tyler Vincent, Dominic Lopez, and Dylan Carter are all dead, Emily. And each of their wives received a letter telling them about the affair they were having. We believe each one of them was murdered."

"I didn't kill anyone. I told you that."

"But somebody did. Your involvement makes you an accessory. It's best that you tell us all you know."

"I have. I know nothing else."

"Do you have anything else, Detective Mitchell?"

"Yes, we are going to take all your cell phones and computers with us, pursuant to the search warrant. We are also going to have officers impound your vehicle, and we will get a warrant to search it as well," advised Mitchell.

"I need my phone and car," protested Evans.

"Too late for that," said Mitchell. "You will get your car back once we are finished with it. You probably won't get your phones or computers until after the case is completed. You can always rent a car and buy another cheap convenience store phone. You seem to like those. We also need your password to your computers and phone."

"I'm not going to give out my password."

"Look," said Mitchell, "our computer experts will crack your password, but it will take some time. You've cooperated thus far, don't stop now."

"We also need your access password for the website Secret Affairs," interjected Baez.

Reluctantly, Evans gave Mitchell the passwords. Evans then slumped in her chair while both detectives searched the home for all phones and computers. They found three cell phones, one of which appeared to be Evans' personal phone. The other two were obviously burner phones. They also collected a laptop computer and an iPad. Mitchell then patted down Evans for any other phones but found none. Finally, Baez took a photo of Evans with his cell phone camera.

"What happens now?" asked Evans.

"We still have lots of investigation to do," advised Mitchell. "Until then, you need to stick around. We may need to talk to you again. And don't tell anyone we were here."

"Am I in trouble?"

"If you are telling the truth, probably some trouble, but not as much as you would be if you hadn't told us what you know."

With that, the detectives left and headed back to the department. They had a lot of information to go over. They also knew the next step would be contacting Miranda Castaneda.

During the drive, Mitchell complimented Baez on his interview with Evans. "I thought you handled that well, especially given the circumstances."

"Thank you. What do you think about what she told us?"

"Not sure I buy the story that she left while Lopez was still alive."

"I know. That was strange. And then they were only going to embarrass him. I suppose they were only going to embarrass Vincent and Carter as well?"

"And yet they all end up dead."

"Exactly," said Baez.

Mitchell then used her cell phone to call the records division. She asked them to search for an address and vehicle information on a Miranda Castaneda with an address in Miami Springs.

"We need to get officers to Castaneda's house to secure it before she finds out we are looking for her," cautioned Mitchell.

"What about having Sean Franklin set up another meeting with her?"

"I don't trust that Evans won't warn her."

"You're probably right," agreed Baez.

When they returned to the department, Baez took the evidence collected from the Evans home and logged it into evidence. He then began the paperwork requesting a forensic analysis of the phones, laptop, and iPad. Meanwhile, Mitchell walked to the Records Division to get the information requested on Castaneda. Records had come up with an address on Wayside Avenue in Miami Springs. Castaneda was the registered owner of a black VW Jetta, license number MAX413. She had a Florida driver's license describing her as a forty-four-year-old Hispanic female, 5'5", with brown hair and brown eyes. Mitchell copied her driver's license photograph and noted that Castaneda was an attractive woman. Having obtained this information, Mitchell called Dispatch and asked them to send patrol officers to the Castaneda residence to secure it, pending a search warrant. Mitchell did not want to risk Castaneda being warned by Evans and destroying evidence. Mitchell then sat down at her desk to type out an affidavit for the search of Castaneda's home and vehicle.

It was approaching three o'clock in the afternoon when Mitchell received a call from Officer John Adonsky. He told Mitchell that officers had secured the home, but Castaneda was not home. While they were sitting watching the house, they observed a woman matching the description of Castaneda drive by in a black VW Jetta. She drove slowly past, saw the police cars, then continued driving on without stopping.

"That's okay," said Mitchell. "We don't have enough to arrest her right now, anyway. Once I have this warrant signed, we'll put out a BOLO for officers to stop her and impound the car for a search."

Mitchell was still working on the affidavit when Baez walked up to her with the look of a kid who had just found a cookie jar. "We are hitting the jackpot," said Baez.

"Yeah? What do you have?"

"Computer Forensics did a quick search of Evans' Secret Affairs account, and it gave us access to the men who have been clients of the dating service. All three of our victims are listed as clients. It also provides the stage names of each woman they were hooked up with. Sugar was dating Vincent at the time of his death."

"This case is certainly getting stronger," replied Mitchell.

"I'm going to go call Detective Paxton over in Ft. Lauderdale to give him the news. I'm sure this will cause them to reopen their case."

"Good, now leave me alone. I need to finish this affidavit."

Chapter 14

It was now five o'clock, and Mitchell had just finished the affidavits for search warrants on the home and vehicle of Miranda Castaneda. She called the county courthouse, hoping to find a judge still in the building. To her surprise, the clerk told her Judge Addazio was still in her office. She put Mitchell on hold to ask the judge if she had time to review the affidavit before leaving. Fortunately, she did. Mitchell quickly left the office and drove to the courthouse. She met with the Judge, who carefully read the affidavit.

"This is an amazing story," said Judge Addazio. "I remember seeing the news about this investigation with the letters and all, but never imagined anything like this."

"We've been surprised a few times as well, Judge."

"I hope you can figure it all out," said Judge Addazio as she signed the warrants. "Good luck, Detective."

"Thank you, Judge."

On the way back to the department, Mitchell called Baez. "I got the search warrants. I'll pick you up out front."

"You need to come into the office first," insisted Baez.

"What's up?"

"I just got a call from Sean Franklin. Sugar called him and wants to meet him somewhere. We need to brainstorm how we want to handle this."

"Okay, I'll be there in ten minutes."

Once in the office, Mitchell found Baez, Detective Sergeant Leon Marquez, and detectives Tom Boyd and Lisa Warren in the captain's office.

Captain Gonzalez invited her in. "Come on in, Leah. We've been waiting for you."

"What's going on?" asked Mitchell.

"Rick was filling me in on what you had going on, and I decided this was getting too big for just the two of you. I'm assigning Tom and Lisa to help you two out."

"Thank you, Captain. We could use the help."

"Yes, especially now that your suspect wants to meet a client and you have searches to conduct. Why don't you and Rick focus on finding....what's her name again?"

"Castaneda," answered Baez.

"Yes, Castaneda. You two find her and her car. I'll have Tom and Lisa search Castaneda's home. I don't want this woman getting away, and I certainly don't want any more murders."

"Thank you, Captain," replied Mitchell.

Mitchell and Baez then took the next thirty minutes briefing detectives Boyd and Warren on the case, making sure they knew what evidence to look for in the search of Castaneda's home.

"There are more details for you in the affidavit," advised Mitchell. "It will provide plenty of direction on what we are looking for in the Castaneda home."

"Don't forget to look for coolant or anti-freeze," reminded Baez.

"We'll be very thorough," assured Warren. "You two just need to focus on finding Castaneda now."

After Warren and Boyd left, Mitchell and Baez conferred on the next steps in finding Castaneda. Baez explained that Sean Franklin told him Castaneda called him and asked if he would meet with her. She told him it was important and that he might be in trouble.

"Do you think she wants to kill Sean?" asked Mitchell.

"Who knows, but she saw the police at her house, so she's probably scared."

"What do you want to do?" asked Mitchell.

"Here's my thought. Let's have Franklin set up a meeting with her in a public place. Then we will be waiting to impound her car and bring her in for questioning."

Just then, Baez's phone rang. It was dispatch advising him Castaneda had been spotted in her black VW Jetta driving north on I-95. Two officers were trying to pull her over, but she wasn't yielding.

Baez quickly turned on the police scanner sitting on his desk. Mitchell and Baez listened to the radio traffic.

551, the suspect is increasing speed. Still headed north on I-95.
Copy 551.
554, I'm right behind 551.
Copy 554. All units, be advised 551 and 554 are in pursuit of the suspect vehicle, a black Volkswagen Jetta, license number MAX413. The suspect is a Hispanic female.
551, suspect is passing on the shoulder!
Copy 551.
Vehicle has now exited onto westbound 395. Speed is eighty-five.
Copy 551, suspect now westbound 395 at 85 miles per hour.
554, I got jammed up in traffic, trying to catch up. Do we have any other units nearby?
554, I've got 558 and 561 headed toward your location.
551, do you have an update?
Still westbound 395, speed between 80 and 85 miles per hour.
All units, suspect still westbound 395.

551, looks like she might try to exit at Northwest 12th avenue.

I've got units headed that way, 551.

554, I'm now behind 551.

Copy that, 554.

We've just had an accident!

551, is that you?

554, can you tell me what happened?

Standby!

Several seconds of silence followed.

554, the suspect sideswiped another car while exiting onto Northwest 12th Avenue! Multi-car accident blocking the exit. We need units on northwest 12th Avenue!

Copy 554, multi-car accident on 395 at Northwest 12th Avenue exit. Are you okay, 554?

Yes, but we are stuck in traffic. Multi-car accident.

Where is 551?

He got hit, but he is okay. Do we have any units in pursuit?

554, I've got units in the area. Do you have an update on the suspect vehicle?

Negative, last seen on the exit headed north onto Northwest 12th Avenue. The vehicle will have damage on the passenger side.

554, do you need medical to respond?

Yes, I've got an injured woman in one of the cars. Head is bleeding, but conscious.

Copy 554, we will send medical immediately.

562.

Go ahead 562.

Myself and 548 are on Northwest 12th Avenue. Suspect vehicle has not been located. We will continue searching the area.

Copy 562.

Baez turned off the scanner. "Damn it!" he shouted. "I can't believe she got away."

"This woman is a fighter," said Mitchell. "At least we can pick her up on charges now. We now have eluding police, reckless driving, and leaving the scene of an accident."

"I'm calling Franklin right now," said Baez. "We need to set the trap. Do you know a place called Miami Moon?"

"The restaurant in West Miami?" asked Mitchell.

"Yes, that's it. It would be a good place to have Franklin meet with Castaneda. There is off-street parking and no major highways nearby. We could wait inside and have officers stationed outside should she try to run."

"Sounds good to me," agreed Mitchell.

Baez called Franklin and gave him the instructions and address for Miami Moon. He also provided instructions on what to do.

"Only agree to meet her there, inside the restaurant," instructed Baez. "Get there early and pick out a booth along the wall. We will be inside watching the whole time. Once she sits down, we will approach and have her trapped. We'll then place her under arrest."

"Got it," said Franklin.

"Tell her to meet you at seven o'clock. After you talk to her, call us immediately."

"Will do," said Franklin.

It was 6:10 pm when Baez's phone rang. It was Franklin.

"She agreed to meet me at Miami Moon, seven o'clock."

"Good job, Sean. You should leave now and get a booth when you get there. We will meet you there to go over everything again. We should be there by six thirty-five."

"Thank you, Detective. See you there."

Mitchell arranged to have uniformed officers stationed near the restaurant but out of sight. Baez and Mitchell then headed to the Miami Moon to meet with Franklin. They arrived at 6:38 pm and found Franklin sitting alone at a booth along the west wall, near the back of the restaurant. *Perfect,* said Mitchell to herself. Both detectives met with Franklin and again assured him they would arrest Sugar once she sat down in the booth. They would sit four tables across from the booth. Franklin was told not to look at the detectives once Sugar walked in. When there were no more questions, Baez and Mitchell took their seats at the table.

Seven o'clock came and went without Castaneda walking into the restaurant. "Do you think she decided not to come?" asked Mitchell.

"Possibly, or she may be nervous and taking her time. After that chase, she is probably being extra cautious," said Baez.

Finally, at 7:08 pm, a woman matching the description of Miranda Castaneda came walking through the front door. She was wearing black slacks, a white blouse, and black flat-soled shoes. She was also carrying a white purse. She stood there for a few seconds, scanning the room. Baez glanced toward Franklin and saw him waving his hand to get her attention. Once Castaneda recognized Franklin, she walked toward the booth. Neither Baez nor Mitchell looked at her, but could see her walk by from the corner of their eye. Baez turned his head toward his left jacket sleeve and spoke into his undercover microphone attached to his shirtsleeve.

"All units, suspect is inside. Take your positions."

Baez waited to hear through his earpiece that officers were positioned at both exits outside. After about two minutes, he got the word. "All units in position." Baez nodded to Mitchell. Both got up and walked to the booth.

Baez walked up quickly and stood at the end of the bench seat, looking down at Castaneda. She looked up and was a bit startled. Baez showed his badge and identified himself as a detective.

"Miranda Castaneda, you are under arrest. I need for you to slide out and stand up, slowly."

Castaneda quickly glanced at Franklin with a scowl, then slowly moved to the edge of the seat. Once she reached the edge, she quickly jumped out of the booth and slammed into Baez, who was surprised and caught off guard. Baez lost his balance and fell backward into an adjoining table where an older couple was having dinner. Baez slammed into the table, knocking dishes and food onto the floor and pushing the table backward. The older woman screamed as Baez rolled off the table and onto her lap. Drinks and food went flying in all directions, and soon others started screaming as well. Ketchup, mustard, ranch dressing, and beer were smeared on the back and sleeves of Baez's jacket.

Mitchell, upon seeing this, first tried to grab Baez to keep him from falling. She could not grab hold of him. In the instant Mitchell was distracted, Castaneda violently pushed Mitchell to the side and ran past her. Once Baez had already fallen, Mitchell turned her attention back on Castaneda, who was now running toward the front door. *Oh, no you don't,* thought Mitchell. Her athletic skills kicked into action, and Mitchell sprinted toward Castaneda, catching up to her just before she reached the door. Mitchell reached up and grabbed a handful of dark-brown hair, then yanked Castaneda's head backward. Castaneda let out a loud scream.

"Let go of me!" yelled Castaneda.

"Shut up!" yelled Mitchell. Mitchell then grabbed Castaneda's left arm and started to bring the arm behind her back when she saw the gun. Castaneda had reached into her purse with her right hand as she was running toward the door and pulled out her snub nose thirty-eight caliber revolver. She was lifting the gun up and toward her left shoulder in an attempt to shoot Mitchell.

By now, Baez had picked himself off the floor and saw Mitchell struggling with Castaneda. He bolted toward Mitchell to assist her. As he ran toward Mitchell, he could see her attempting to pull Castaneda's left arm behind her.

Upon seeing the gun, Mitchell released her grip on Castaneda's left arm and grabbed her right hand, which was holding the gun. Castaneda attempted to turn on Mitchell to shoot her, but Mitchell turned to the side and clamped Castaneda's right hand between her arm and body. As she did this, the gun went off, creating a loud BANG in the restaurant. Patrons started screaming and running for the exits. It quickly became mad chaos.

Mitchell forcefully shoved Castaneda toward the wall, banging her head hard into the wall and then slamming Castaneda's right hand into the wall, causing her to release the gun. Blood started to run down Castaneda's face. Mitchell then swung Castaneda to the right and slammed her to the ground. By now, Castaneda had stopped struggling, and Mitchell was able to get both arms behind her back to handcuff her.

Upon hearing the gunshot, uniformed officers rushed into the restaurant and saw Mitchell on the ground with Castaneda. Two officers went over to assist Mitchell in completing the arrest.

Mitchell was kneeling on the floor, wiping her brow with the back of her right hand, when she heard the words.

"Officer down! We need medical at our location!" shouted one of the uniformed officers.

Mitchell quickly stood up and looked around. "Oh, my god!" She saw that Baez had been shot and was lying on the floor. Two officers were attending to him. Mitchell quickly ran to his side and kneeled next to him.

Baez was conscious but had sustained a gunshot wound to his lower right abdomen. An officer was holding the wound closed to stop the bleeding.

"Rick, I'm so sorry," said Mitchell.

Baez groaned, "for what? It's not your fault."

"Are you going to be okay?"

Baez grimaced from pain. "I'm going to try my best. Not ready to go quite yet."

Mitchell held his hand and waited for medical help to arrive. Once they got there, a compress was put on his wound to help stop the bleeding. He was put on oxygen and then hoisted onto a gurney and taken to the waiting ambulance.

One officer approached Mitchell and told her Castaneda was being taken to the hospital to treat her injuries. "Where would you like us to take her after she is released?" he asked.

"Not to jail," said Mitchell. "Take her to the station and put her in an interrogation room. I need to talk to this bitch before the lawyers get to her."

Mitchell then walked over to talk to Franklin, who had hidden under the table once the fighting started.

"Thank you for your help," said Mitchell.

"Is Detective Baez going to live?"

"He's a tough guy, but he could use our prayers right now."

"I will say a prayer for him," said Franklin. "Do you need anything else from me?"

"We will need a written statement from you, but not tonight. Go home to your family and get some rest."

"Alright, thank you, Detective."

Once the crime scene technicians arrived to process the scene, Mitchell left and drove Baez's detective car to the hospital to check on his status. Upon arrival, she found several other detectives, officers, and Captain Gonzalez already there.

"How is he doing?" asked Mitchell.

"He is in surgery right now," said Captain Gonzalez. "We will know more once he comes out."

"Where is our suspect?"

"She's being treated in the emergency room. Nothing serious, just some stitches to her face and a sprained right wrist."

"Wish it was broken," said Mitchell.

The captain grinned. "Are you planning to interview her tonight?"

"Yes."

"Then you should go back to the station and get cleaned up. I'll keep you informed on Baez's status. I'll also have Lisa Warren sit in with you on the interview. They should be about done with the search."

"Thank you, Captain."

Chapter 15

It had been a long day, but the fight and shooting at Miami Moon had amped up the adrenaline in Mitchell's system. She was itching to interview Castaneda while also worried about Baez. She had received word that Baez made it through surgery and was now in recovery in serious condition.

Detectives Tom Boyd and Lisa Warren had returned from the search of Castaneda's residence with good news. They had located a desktop computer believed to be the primary computer used for the Secret Affairs website. They also found several burner cell phones. In the garage, detectives found several gallons of anti-freeze and a partial roll of plastic hose, similar to that used in the Lopez case. Detective Boyd was busy entering the evidence for analysis while Detective Warren had joined Mitchell to prepare for Castaneda's interview.

"I'll be primary," said Mitchell, "but you can feel free to ask any follow-up question."

"Of course," responded Warren. "Do you think she will talk to you?"

"She is now facing attempted murder of a police officer, assault of a police officer, and multiple other charges from that pursuit. With the information from Evans, I have plenty to pressure her with. So, we will see."

It was 9:30 pm when officers arrived with Castaneda in handcuffs behind her back. She was placed into one of the interrogation rooms. Castaneda was now wearing blue scrub hospital clothing. Officers had taken her clothes as evidence. She had six stitches just above her right eyebrow, and the area was swollen and turning dark-colored. Her right upper lip was also swollen and red. Her hair was no longer neatly brushed.

Mitchell turned on the recording equipment, and then both detectives walked into the room. Mitchell introduced herself and Detective Warren.

"Yeah, I remember you," said Castaneda with a scowl.

Mitchell then walked behind Castaneda and removed the handcuffs. "I'm going to allow you to be comfortable, but if you make any attempt to move out of that chair, I will smash you against that wall harder than I did the first time. Do you understand?"

"Yes."

Mitchell then walked to the other side of the table and sat next to Warren, across from Castaneda.

"You are in some serious trouble, Miranda," said Mitchell.

Castaneda just looked at Mitchell without saying a word.

"We know all about your dating service and the women who work for you," continued Mitchell. "I want to hear your side of the story, but I've got to read you your rights first."

Mitchell then proceeded to read Castaneda her right to remain silent.

"Are you willing to talk to us, Miranda? Or should I call you Sugar?"

"I don't know. I think I probably need an attorney."

"That is your right, Miranda. But we only have one side of the story right now. If Detective Baez dies, you will be facing First Degree Murder of a Police Officer. That's a death penalty case. Any information you can provide about these other murders might help you in asking for some leniency."

After a pause, Castaneda stated, "It was simply a dating service for married men. Nothing more to tell."

"Does that mean you are willing to answer questions, Miranda?"

"Sure."

"Good. Now, I think your dating service was more than that. You used the dating service to lure men into the game you were playing."

"There was no game. It was just a dating service."

"A dating service that murdered its clients," challenged Mitchell.

"I don't know where you got that idea."

"Okay, tell me how it worked."

"I set up a dating service for married men who were looking to have an affair. Most married men are not looking to get divorced and remarried, so it is a way for us to date men with no expectations or commitments."

"Yet, some of them get divorced," added Mitchell.

"Sure, but not because of anything we did. The men are the ones who desired the affair. We just provided the women. We never made the first move to entice a man to cheat."

"It sounds more like a prostitution ring."

"Not at all," objected Castaneda. "Many times, a date did not include sex. Once the registration fee was paid, there was no other payment other than the cost of the date itself, such as meals, drinks, or whatever. Sex was never promised."

"Who sent the letters telling the wives about the affair?"

"I don't know what you are talking about."

"The anonymous letters, Miranda. We have your computer. If those letters were composed on that computer, you don't want to be lying to me about it. We will easily find them."

There was a long pause. "They were to let the wives know what type of man they had for a husband."

"I'm confused," said Mitchell. "I thought you wanted to date married men? Why ruin it by telling the wives?"

"So that the wives could decide on whether they wanted to stay married to a man who cheats!" replied Castaneda.

Mitchell had a puzzled look on her face. "I still don't get it. What was the point?"

"Men who cheat are scum."

"Maybe, but you said you wanted to date them because they were married."

"We provided the opportunity for those who were looking."

Warren interrupted. "Miranda, was this some sort of litmus test for men? A way to identify those who would cheat on their wives?"

"I suppose you could describe it that way," agreed Castaneda.

"Is that why you then sent the letter? To somehow punish these men?"

"No, that was to make the wife aware. Then she could decide if she wanted to stay with him or not. And, sometimes the man decided he wanted a divorce as well."

"I think I understand this better," stated Mitchell. "You didn't set this dating service up for yourselves. It was to trap and punish men who cheated."

"Not a trap," insisted Castaneda. "If a man is looking to cheat, he can find someone. We just made it easier."

Mitchell shook her head. "Is part of the punishment to kill them?"

"We didn't kill anyone. Some of them committed suicide, or I suspect the wives killed some of them."

"How many are we talking about here?"

"I don't know. You're the detective. How many killed themselves?"

"They were only made to look like suicides, Miranda. Men have been murdered."

"I wouldn't know anything about that," insisted Castaneda.

"You know Emily Evans, right? She told us how you wanted her to get Lopez drunk and drugged. You then came by and murdered him by making it look like a suicide."

"She's lying. If anyone killed him, it had to have been Emily. She was the one dating him."

"Yes, but she said you wanted her to get him to pass out. Once he was passed out, she left, and you showed up later."

"Not true."

"Miranda, we found a black plastic hose in your garage. My guess is it will soon be matched to the hose used to kill Dominic."

Castaneda just sat and looked up at the ceiling. The detectives sat in silence. After about fifteen seconds, Castaneda broke the silence.

"You don't understand."

"Then explain it to us, Miranda," urged Mitchell.

After another pause, "We have all been divorced over our husbands having an affair. It was devastating for all of us. Some of us were abused as well. We were left with virtually nothing after the divorce. Some of us got more than others, but it was hard. Having your life torn apart because your husband wants to be with another woman? It's disgusting and painful."

"I understand, Miranda," sympathized Mitchell. "How many women are involved in this?"

"There are seven of us."

"Who are they?"

"I'm not telling you, but you will find it all in the computer."

"How did you poison Tyler Vincent?"

Castaneda had a look of shock. "His wife must have poisoned him."

Mitchell bluffed about how much they knew about the anti-freeze found in Castaneda's garage.

"Miranda, we found the anti-freeze used to poison Tyler in your garage. You live alone, so it had to have been you who poisoned him. How did you do it?"

For the first time, Mitchell could see fear in the eyes of Castaneda.

"I didn't punish all of them," said Castaneda.

"How many are there?"

There was a long pause as Castaneda's eyes watered. "Seven."

"You have killed seven men?" asked a surprised Mitchell.

"No, I told you I didn't punish all of them."

"Who did you kill?"

"You already know about Tyler. Emily and I punished Dominic, and I punished Ed Sanchez."

"Ed Sanchez? Who is Ed Sanchez?"

"Oh, you didn't know about him?" asked Castaneda. "I should have kept my mouth shut."

"Just tell me who he was."

"You'll have to find that out for yourself."

"You keep saying punished," interjected Warren, "but that is the word you are using to describe killing them, correct?"

"They deserved what they got. That's all I'll say," responded Castaneda.

Warren frowned. "They deserved to be murdered?"

"But not for their own actions, they would still be alive. It was their desire that killed them. You might call it a deadly desire."

"That's a twisted way to look at it, Miranda," replied Warren.

"Who killed Dylan Carter?" asked Mitchell.

"You can get everything else you need from the computer," answered Castaneda. "I'm not ratting out anyone."

"Was it Carla Delgado?"

"You'll have to ask her," snapped Castaneda.

"Alright, then tell us how you and Emily killed Dominic. Who hooked the hose up to the tailpipe?"

"I'm done," smirked Castaneda. "My head is hurting, and I've already said enough."

"Okay, Miranda, we will end this interview. But before we go, I want you to unbutton your shirt and show me your left shoulder."

"What for?"

"Just do it, Miranda, or I will do it myself."

Castaneda unbuttoned her shirt and lowered the sleeve. Sure enough, there was a large scar on top of her left shoulder.

"Alright, you can button up now," instructed Mitchell.

Mitchell then leaned over and whispered something into Warren's ear. Warren got up and left the room. Once outside, she shut off the video recording equipment.

Mitchell then got up, walked around the table, and re-handcuffed Castaneda behind her back. Mitchell then grabbed the hair on the back of Castaneda's head and pushed the right side of her head hard onto the table.

"Ahhhh," screamed Castaneda, "You're hurting me! My eye hurts!"

Mitchell held Castaneda's head against the table and leaned down toward her left ear. She then whispered, "I'll do a lot more to you if Detective Baez doesn't make it, bitch. You'll think that little skirmish in the restaurant was a picnic. The only scum in this case is you."

Mitchell then pulled Castaneda's head back up and stood her up. She jerked on the handcuffs, causing Castaneda to yell out again. She then walked Castaneda out into the holding area and handed her over to a uniformed officer.

"Please take this scumbag to the county jail," said Mitchell.

"Gladly," replied the officer.

It was now 10:35 pm, and the adrenalin had worn off. Mitchell could feel the energy draining from her body. She had been at work since 8:00 that morning. She noticed Captain Gonzalez was in his office, so she walked in to get an update on Baez.

"He is still listed as serious. How he responds tonight is critical," said the captain.

"I feel like this is my fault," said Mitchell sadly. "I should have seen the gun earlier."

"Nonsense. You did a great job containing her and disarming her. You probably saved some lives, Leah. There is no reason for you to feel any responsibility. The responsibility falls only on Castaneda."

"Thank you, Captain. I just feel so awful. I'm worried about Rick."

"We all are, but Rick is a fighter. He will pull through this. Now, you go get some sleep, and don't worry about being in early tomorrow. You can continue working on this whenever you get in."

"Thank you, sir."

When Mitchell arrived home, Grace was up waiting for her. "How are you doing, Leah?"

"I'm exhausted, worried about Rick, and getting sore from that wrestling match I had with the bitch who shot Rick. I think I pulled a muscle in my back."

"Would you like me to fix you a drink?"

"No, thank you, Grace. I'm just going to take a hot bath and then go to bed. I'm wiped out tonight."

"I understand," said Grace.

Chapter 16

The following day was Friday, the 23rd day since Lopez's murder. Mitchell slowly opened her eyes at 8:05 am and began to stretch. She usually got up by 6:00. As she stretched, she could feel the tightness in her lower back. Grace walked into the room with a cup of coffee.

"Here you go. How are you feeling today?"

"Sore. What happened to the alarm?"

"I shut it off. I figured you needed some extra sleep after last night."

"Yeah, I suppose. I've got a lot to do today. Have you heard anything about Rick?"

"Yes, Captain Gonzalez called and said Rick was awake this morning, and his vitals looked good. He should be upgraded from serious to stable later today."

Mitchell let out a sigh of relief. "Oh good, I was so worried about him, Grace. I thought he might die." As she said this, Mitchell began to cry. Grace sat down on the bed beside her and wrapped her arm around her.

"I know, Leah. Everything's going to be okay now. Rick will be back to work before you know it."

"I'm not so sure, Grace."

"What do you mean?"

"You can't tell anyone this. Rick said he would tell the captain when this case was finished, and I promised I wouldn't say anything until then."

"Leah, what is it?"

"Rick slept with one of our suspects."

Grace jumped up off the bed. "What!?"

"He was undercover and dating a woman from the website. Things went too far."

Grace sat back down on the bed. "I can't believe it. Why would Rick do that?"

"I asked him that same question. I think he just lost his head for a few minutes."

"What are you going to do?"

"Rick will tell the truth. The woman is sure to bring it up once she is arrested. But anyway, we still have work to do. We found out from our prime suspect that there are probably seven victims. We need to find out who they are and who killed each one."

Mitchell wiped her eyes and downed her coffee, then got dressed for the day. She was back at work by 9:10 am. The captain had not yet returned to work, but detectives Boyd and Warren were already working.

"Per direction from the captain, our analysts have made this case a priority and are already analyzing the computer and phones we took from Castaneda's residence," advised Boyd.

"That is good to hear," said Mitchell.

"What's on the agenda for today?" asked Warren.

"We need to look for any deaths that might match the M.O. in our cases. Men cheating on their wives, anonymous letter, men later found dead. We could have as many as seven victims out there somewhere, most likely in other jurisdictions. We know about the one in Ft. Lauderdale already. Tom, why don't you work on sending out alerts to all surrounding agencies. Lisa and I will check our local files and start more background work on Emily Evans."

"On it," said Boyd.

The detectives then started their work while still waiting for any information computer forensics could provide for them. Mitchell called Steve Logan and updated him on the latest information obtained the previous night. He was already attempting to crack the password to get into Castaneda's computer. Mitchell then called Detective Roger Paxton of the Ft. Lauderdale Police Department and gave him an update.

"I'll have one of our lab techs contact your guys so that we can get the hose in our case compared to the hose you confiscated," said Paxton. "Did she say anything about who killed Carter?"

"She wouldn't say, but when I asked her about Carla Delgado, she said to ask Carla. She also said we could find more information on the computer," said Mitchell.

"We believe we know where Delgado is living. If we find her there, we will bring her in this afternoon for questioning. Let me know if you find anything else."

"Yes, we will," assured Mitchell.

After about an hour, Warren approached Mitchell with additional information on Emily Evans. Evans had gotten divorced five years ago from a man named Edward Evans, who was now living in Alabama. Warren contacted him by phone to confirm he was still alive. Evans admitted they had gotten divorced after he had an affair with another woman. He described the split-up as unpleasant. When asked, he claimed to know nothing about Emily's dating of other men or participation on a dating website. He said he didn't even know she was living in the Miami area.

"At least it confirms part of what Miranda told us," said Mitchell. "We'll probably find that all the women involved are divorced."

It was 11:05 am when Captain Gonzalez walked in and told Mitchell and Warren that Baez was doing well and was upgraded to stable condition. He could now see visitors.

"Do you mind if I go to the hospital right now?" asked Mitchell.

"Not at all. You go visit him. This case will still be here when you get back."

Mitchell quickly grabbed her jacket and headed out the door. It took her fifteen minutes to reach the hospital. When she walked into his room, Baez was awake but still hooked up to IVs. He turned to look at her.

"Well, you finally came to see me," he said weakly.

"It's so good to see you, Rick. I was so worried."

"About me? It takes more than one bullet to keep me down."

"How are you feeling?"

"Good, for being shot. They have me jacked up on painkillers. What irks me is that I ruined my good jacket. It has ketchup, mustard, and who knows what all over it."

Mitchell smiled. "That was your good jacket?"

"Very funny," said Baez.

"I'm sorry for what happened, Rick."

"Not your fault, Leah. I should have ducked."

This made Mitchell laugh. "You must be feeling okay. You still have a sense of humor."

"Did you get Castaneda?"

"Yes, she is in jail on multiple charges. We could have up to seven homicides."

"Seven?" asked a surprised Baez. He grimaced a bit from speaking too loudly. He could feel it in his gut.

"Yes. It appears this was a website set up to lure and punish married men who cheated on their wives."

"This is making more sense," said Baez.

Mitchell could see the strain of talking was somewhat of a struggle for Baez.

"I just wanted to check up on you, Rick. We have a lot of work left to do."

"Yes, of course. You go on now and finish up what we started."

"I will, and I will be back tomorrow to see how you are and give you an update."

"I would like that."

When Mitchell got back to the office, the police department was surrounded by news reporters and satellite trucks. The story had broken nationally, and every major news channel had descended on the Miami-Dade Metro Police Department. Mitchell slipped through a side door to avoid the media crush.

Once inside, she learned the police chief and captain would conduct a live press conference at 2:00 pm. *I hope they are not planning to have me there,* thought Mitchell. When she got to her desk, Warren was waiting for her.

"We got some good news from computer forensics," said Warren.

"Yeah, what is it?"

"They were able to get into Castaneda's files and found a treasure of information. She kept records on all the women involved and who they dated. She even tracked the outcomes. And get this, they found a saved copy of the letter sent to the wives. I've got printouts of all the information right here."

"Wow, this is fantastic!"

Mitchell and Warren sat down to review all the data before them. Seven women were identified as participants on the Secret Affairs website, including addresses. The men they were dating and those who had been "punished" were also listed. Mitchell and Warren could match up the following women to men who had been listed as punished.

Dominic Lopez of Miami matched with Emily Evans, also known as Mandy.

Tyler Vincent of Miami matched with Miranda Castaneda, also known as Sugar.

Ed Sanchez of Pembroke Pines matched with Miranda Castaneda, also known as Sugar.

Dylan Carter of Ft. Lauderdale matched with Carla Delgado, also known as Carmen.

Noah Cruz of Hollywood matched with Sabrina Martin, also known as Serena.

Jason Morgan of Ft. Lauderdale matched with Madison Turner, also known as Marilyn.

Adam Barnes of Plantation matched with Anna Bailey, also known as Sandy.

A seventh woman, Kathy Torrez of Miami, had dated men, but none of them had been listed as punished.

"Do you think all these men will turn up dead?" asked Warren.

"The file indicates they were punished, so I would expect so. These women are going to know Castaneda has been arrested, so we need to locate them before they all split."

Detective Boyd walked in with more news. "Bulletins have been sent to all agencies in Florida, and I've already located two other cases. Ft. Lauderdale has a second case they believe is related. A Jason Morgan was found dead of suspected suicide five months ago. Shot himself in the head."

"Shot himself in the head?" asked Mitchell.

"That's what they told me. They initially thought it was a simple case of suicide after the affair was revealed to his family through an anonymous letter. They now believe it is related to the Dylan Carter case and this website."

"They didn't suspect something was up when Carter's wife received the same letter?"

"A separate division handled the case. They never connected the two."

"What is the second case?" asked Mitchell.

"Ed Sanchez of Pembroke Pines. Sanchez was found dead eight months ago in his apartment after separating from his wife. It was ruled a natural death from kidney disease."

"Probably caused by anti-freeze," responded Mitchell. She then handed Boyd the list obtained from Castaneda's computer. He quickly scanned the names.

"I will call the Hollywood and Plantation departments to see if they have anything on Noah Cruz and Adam Barnes."

"Thank you, Tom. Lisa and I are going to start backgrounds on these victims. I'm going to guess all of them were wealthy."

"I know Sanchez was," said Boyd. "I was told he was a high-priced attorney in the Pembroke Pines area."

"Makes sense," said Mitchell. "Find out what type of gun Jason Morgan allegedly used to kill himself."

"I will," said Boyd as he turned and walked away.

Mitchell looked at Warren. "This case just keeps getting crazier. If you start on the backgrounds, I'll work on an arrest warrant for Emily Evans. We need to get her in custody."

"I agree," said Warren.

Chapter 17

It was now Saturday, 24 days since the death of Dominic Lopez. The weather had turned hot and was expected to be a humid day, with a high of 94 degrees. Mitchell was wearing the lightest jacket she owned, a beige cotton blazer, when she arrived for work at 7:20 am. She was already sweating from the humidity when she walked in. Mitchell had emailed the arrest warrant affidavit for Emily Evans to the DA's Office and Judge Addazio on Friday prior to leaving work. All she had to do now was drive to Judge Addazio's home to retrieve the signed warrant on their way to arrest Evans.

By 8:30, Mitchell and Warren were on their way to pick up Evans. Officers had been sitting outside Evans' apartment during the night to prevent her from fleeing. Upon arrival, Warren and Mitchell approached the front door with a uniformed officer accompanying them. Mitchell knocked on the door but got no answer. She knocked louder.

"Emily, this is Detective Mitchell. We need to talk to you. We know you are in there, and we are not leaving until you open this door to talk to us." Mitchell then pounded on the door once more. Finally, the door opened. Evans was still in a mauve-colored robe. Her hair was a mess, she had no makeup on, and it appeared as though she had been crying. Both detectives and the officer stepped through the open door.

"Emily," said Mitchell, "you are under arrest for the murder of Dominic Lopez."

"No," cried Evans. "I told you I did not kill him."

"We have evidence you helped set him up for murder, Emily."

Mitchell then grabbed Evans' arm and walked her to the bedroom. "Get dressed," she ordered. Mitchell and Warren stood and watched as Evans slowly took off her robe and put on some jeans and a blue t-shirt. Once she was dressed, Warren turned Evans around and placed her in handcuffs. Evans began to sob.

"Save it," said Mitchell. "You can do that later. We need to talk to you back at the station."

They then walked her to the waiting patrol car and placed her in the back seat. The officer drove away and headed toward the police station, where she would be placed in an interrogation room.

Back at the station, Mitchell and Warren entered the interrogation room where Evans was seated. She had already been released from the handcuffs.

"Would you like something to drink?" asked Warren.

"Yes, I'll take a diet soda if you have it," said Evans. Warren left to get her a diet cola from the detective refrigerator.

"Emily, as you know, Miranda has been arrested. We talked to her yesterday and learned all about the dating club and how you punished those getting divorced from their wives. It is important to get your side of the story. Can you read and write?"

"Yes."

Mitchell handed her a form. "These are your rights, Emily. Read them, and if you are willing to tell me your side of the story, I need you to check the waiver box and sign and date it. Even if you waive your rights, you can invoke them at any time during the interview. I just think it is important to hear what you have to say."

Evans took several minutes to read over the form. She then took the pen, checked the waiver box, and signed the document.

"Thank you, Emily."

Warren then walked in and handed Evans a diet cola. "Is she going to talk to us?"

"Yes, she is," replied Mitchell. "She wants to tell her side of the story. Go ahead, Emily, tell us how Lopez was killed."

"It was all Miranda's doing. She told us we needed to punish these men for cheating on their wives and then robbing them of their money."

"How were they robbing them of their money?"

"Mostly from selling the house, and the insurance beneficiary would likely be changed to someone else. The wives would lose a husband and be heartbroken, yet not benefit from it financially. Miranda believed they needed to be punished for this injustice against the wives."

"To punish them, you killed them?"

"No, the anonymous letter was sent as punishment to scare and embarrass them."

"Emily, some of them, including Dominic, ended up being murdered."

Emily began to cry.

"You helped her punish Dominic by killing him," insisted Mitchell. "Why?"

Evans wiped tears from her eyes. "I am divorced myself, and I know what it is like to be cheated on and then lose most of your money. It is tough on women, especially those who aren't working."

"We're talking murder here, Emily."

"Yes, I know," she said softly. "I didn't want that."

"Yet, you participated."

Evans just sat staring at the table, not saying anything.

"Emily," continued Mitchell, "Miranda told us how you hooked up the hose to Dominic's car."

"That's not true," blurted out Evans. "Miranda hooked up the hose. I haven't killed anyone."

"It's true that you met Dominic at the park and had a drink with him, correct?"

"Yeah."

"And you drugged his drink, right?"

"That was just to get him to black out."

"Yes, and then you set it up to look like a suicide. Miranda told us all about it."

"She lies! I did not hook up the hose."

"But you know Miranda did."

"Yes."

"Because you were there."

Evans remained silent.

"You knew Miranda was going to show up and finish the punishment. We have a witness who saw your car there, Emily. Only your car. You have been placed at the scene of a homicide by a witness and by Miranda."

"Miranda came after he was asleep," cried Evans.

"Okay, Emily. Now tell us what happened after she arrived."

Evans hesitated before speaking. "She checked to be sure he was asleep. Then she got the hose out of her car and hooked it up. I didn't do any of that."

"Why didn't you just hook up the hose? Why make Miranda come out there?"

Evans continued to cry. "I couldn't do it. Miranda said she would do it. All I did was give him a drink to put him asleep. He was still alive when Miranda arrived. I swear it."

"I believe you, Emily. Detective Warren now has a few questions."

"Emily," said Warren, "what about the other men? Who killed the other six men?"

"I heard Carla did the same thing with a hose."

"Would that be Carla Delgado?"

"Yes."

"What was the man's name?"

Evans mumbled something unintelligible.

"I'm sorry, Emily, what did you say?"

"Dylan Carter," she sobbed.

"Carla Delgado killed Dylan Carter by hooking a hose up to the tailpipe of his car. Is that correct?"

After a pause, Evans replied softly, "yes."

"How do you know this?"

"She talked about it with me. It was hard for her, but afterward, she said she felt satisfaction. She said it was like getting back at her ex-husband by punishing another cheater, or something like that."

"Is this how you felt after Dominic's death?"

"No, that's why I couldn't kill him. I didn't feel the same way."

"Yet, you took part in this dating website for cheaters."

"Yes, to punish them, but not kill them."

"Do you know of any others who killed men?"

"I heard of things, but never for sure."

"Emily, if you know more than you are saying, now is the time to tell us before someone else does. All the women involved will be interviewed."

"I've told you what I know."

"How many women are in this dating club?"

"Just seven."

Warren handed Evans a list of names. "Look at these names, Emily. Are these the women involved in the Secret Affairs dating website?"

"Yes."

"Is that all of them?"

"That's all I know of."

"Alright, thank you, Emily."

Mitchell then continued. "Emily, did Miranda ever explain why she wanted to kill the men who were getting divorced?"

"She said if the wives were going to be without a husband, the men didn't deserve to go on with a successful life. She described cheating as a dangerous game and would often show us news stories about cheating being the motive for many of the domestic murders that occur. She said men knew cheating could ultimately lead to someone getting murdered. She called it their deadly desires."

"I'm curious," said Mitchell. "If Miranda wanted these deaths to simulate suicide, why no suicide note?"

"She wanted it to look like suicide but also leave some mystery to it. I always thought she looked at it as a game with dangerous consequences."

"Alright, Emily, I think we are done now. Detective Warren, do you have any other questions?"

"No," said Warren.

"Am I free to go now?" asked Evans.

"I'm afraid not, Emily," said Mitchell. "You are going to be charged with murder, as well as other charges.

"What are you talking about!? I told you I didn't kill anyone, and you said you believed me."

"I believe you didn't hook up the hose, but you certainly assisted in the murder of Dominic Lopez. You were instrumental in setting him up and assisting Miranda by getting him to drink a concoction that would make him unconscious, knowing full well what was going to happen. That makes you just as guilty as Miranda."

"NOOOOoooooo!" screamed Evans, as she started crying hysterically. "I did not want to kill anyone!"

"Stop with the hysterics, Emily. You knew full well what this club was all about. If you didn't want to participate, you should have left the club a long time ago."

"I'm going to tell everyone what that detective did to me!" screamed Evans. "He tricked me into having sex with him!"

"Do what you've got to do, Emily. You are still going to jail for murder. Now stand up. I need to put the cuffs back on."

Emily Evans was turned over to a waiting female officer to be taken to the county jail for booking. Mitchell did not want any other male officers to be accused by Evans of anything inappropriate. Afterward, they met with Detective Boyd and Sgt. Marquez to share what they knew. Mitchell shared the information they had gotten from Evans.

Sgt. Marquez then explained that all the other agencies had been contacted and confirmed the deaths of the men identified in the computer data. Each case had been re-opened, and detectives in the other agencies were in the process of locating the other women and bringing them in for questioning.

Detective Boyd reported that Detective Paxton had already brought in Carla Delgado, the woman who had dated Dylan Carter. She had been interrogated and confronted with the evidence retrieved from Castaneda's computer. She was also told other women had already confessed and identified her as the killer of Carter. After an hour and a half of questioning, she finally broke down and admitted to setting Carter up to be "punished." She also claimed that Castaneda assisted her in hooking up the hose to the tailpipe of Carter's car. Delgado told detectives she would not have known how to do this without Castaneda's help. Boyd was still waiting on results from the other jurisdictions.

Marquez added that computer forensics continued to find additional information from the computer and cell phones taken from Castaneda. According to the data, nineteen men had used the Secret Affairs dating site. They would attempt to contact the remaining 13 to confirm they were still alive and well.

Sgt. Marquez then gave an update on the status of Detective Baez. "If his condition continues to improve, he should be able to go home soon."

"Oh, that is good news," said Mitchell. "Sarge, would you mind if I go see him now?"

"Not at all, Leah. We have things under control here."

Mitchell grabbed her jacket and headed out to the hospital. When she entered Baez's room, he was joking with one of the nurses. *He is feeling better,* thought Mitchell.

"Hey, Leah! Good to see you. I hear you almost have this case wrapped up."

"We are getting there, Rick. It was quite the setup. It looks like we have seven homicides made to look like suicides or natural death. But never mind that right now. How are you feeling?"

"Never better."

Mitchell just rolled her eyes.

"I saw you on the news walking into the station," laughed Baez. "You looked tired."

"I was tired! I've only been home to sleep. I need you to come back and help me out."

"Not sure that's going to happen, Leah."

"Have you told the captain yet?"

"No, I don't want to disrupt the investigation. I'll wait until you have all the arrests made."

"Just so you know," advised Mitchell, "Evans was threatening to tell the world you took advantage of her. Be prepared."

"I'm prepared. I messed up, and I'm willing to take whatever comes my way. I'm simply happy we, I should say you, broke this case."

"Nonsense, Rick. Without the work you did on this case, we wouldn't be anywhere close to where we are right now."

"Thank you, Leah. You probably should get back to it. I'm sure you still have a lot to do."

Mitchell walked to the side of the bed, leaned over, and hugged Baez. "I'm happy you are going to be okay, Rick."

Chapter 18

It was now Sunday, but not a day of rest for the detectives working the Secret Affairs case. Information continued to come in from other agencies, and detectives Mitchell, Boyd, and Warren had their hands full. It would take weeks to put together a complete timeline of the events that led to each death perpetrated by members of the Secret Affairs dating site. By late afternoon, all seven women had been located, contacted, and interviewed by detectives in each jurisdiction. All but one woman eventually confessed to actively "punishing" one or more of the seven identified victims. Detectives in Plantation could not get Anna Bailey to admit her involvement. Her date, Adam Barnes, had been asphyxiated in a closed garage. However, detectives still had enough information to charge her with conspiracy to commit murder. They believed her cell phone and laptop computer information would provide enough additional information to charge her with murder.

FOX News and CNN were talking about the case non-stop. Captain Jim Gonzalez was busy answering telephone calls from media all over the country.

Sgt. Marquez, Computer Analyst Steve Logan, and detectives Mitchell, Boyd, and Warren met in the captain's office to review the case. All victims had been accounted for, and all were now considered homicides. Sgt. Marquez had a list of victims and manner of death which he handed out to everyone in the room. The detectives reviewed the list of victims and causes of death.

Dominic Lopez, cause of death: asphyxiation. (Emily Evans and Miranda Castaneda)

Tyler Vincent, cause of death: poisoning. (Miranda Castaneda)

Dylan Carter, cause of death: asphyxiation. (Carla Delgado and Miranda Castaneda)

Jason Morgan, cause of death: gunshot to head. (Madison Turner and Miranda Castaneda)

Noah Cruz, cause of death: hanging. (Sabrina Martin and Miranda Castaneda)

Adam Barnes, cause of death: asphyxiation. (Anna Bailey and possibly Miranda Castaneda)

Ed Sanchez, cause of death: poisoning. (Miranda Castaneda)

"Tell us about Jason Morgan," requested Boyd.

"According to the Ft. Lauderdale detectives," said Sgt. Marquez, "Morgan was shot in his right temple. According to the statement by Madison Turner, she talked Morgan into driving to a remote spot in the forest for some steamy sex. She gave him a couple of drinks laced with barbiturates, which, of course, knocked him out. Castaneda then shows up with a snub-nosed thirty-eight caliber revolver, puts the gun in his right hand, holds it up to his head, and pulls the trigger."

"Sounds like Castaneda was the driving force behind all these killings," added Mitchell.

"Yes, it would seem to be that way," agreed the sergeant.

"Was the gun registered to anyone?"

"No, it was an unregistered gun."

"Castaneda was carrying a thirty-eight snub-nose when she shot Rick. Must be her gun of choice," responded Mitchell.

"And what about the hanging in Hollywood?" asked Warren.

"That was an interesting one," said Sgt. Marquez. "He was found in the parking garage at his place of employment, hanging from a support beam. He was not a big guy, so two women could have hoisted him up. It looked like a suicide. According to the woman dating him, Sabrina Martin, Castaneda and she had to lift him up together. It was not a one-person job. It sounds like six women will face murder charges, with Castaneda being the ringleader."

"What about Kathy Torrez?" asked Mitchell. "Was she not involved in any of them?"

"Not that anyone can prove. She dated a couple of men over time, but neither ended up dead. To avoid conspiracy charges, she has agreed to be a state's witness. She has a lot of information but claims she had nothing to do with any of the murders."

"As of right now," interjected Logan, "we have found no evidence on the computers or cell phones to tie Torrez to any of the murders."

"Did every case involve the anonymous letter to the wives?" asked Boyd.

"Yes, they did," answered the sergeant. "And I find it strange they used the same M.O. in each case. Each time, they used the same letter. As smart as Castaneda was, she wasn't too bright about that one. That's what eventually tied the cases together and raised the suspicion of Baez and Mitchell."

"Do we know yet how two of the victims were poisoned?" asked Warren.

Logan again spoke up. "Yes, we found instructions on Castaneda's computer on how to poison someone slowly over time with anti-freeze. Once the organs have been damaged, one last larger dose will usually kill the victim. The medical examiner suspects Vincent was given a larger amount the night before, which was fatal."

"Are there any more questions?" asked Sgt. Marquez. Hearing none, he continued. "I want to thank each one of you for the work you've done in this case. It was a tough one to crack, but the work of Detective Baez and Mitchell was incredible. And our forensics people were great. Please pass that on to your colleagues, Steve."

"I will, sir."

"And everyone who stepped in to help, it could not have been done without the work you did. Thank you to everyone. Now, I know there is still a lot of work to do to get all the evidence processed, statements transcribed, and such, so I'll let you get back to work. I will give the captain an update once he is finished dealing with the media. Oh, one other announcement. Detective Baez will be released from the hospital later this afternoon."

"Yeah!" shouted everyone.

"That is good news, Sergeant," said Mitchell.

"I told him you would drive him home from the hospital, Leah."

"I'll be glad to, Sergeant. Thank you."

***

Baez was scheduled to be released at 5:30 pm. Mitchell was at the hospital waiting at 5:00. At 5:22, Baez was wheeled down the hall to the lobby where Mitchell was waiting. Her car was parked just outside the door. The nurse rolled Baez to the car and assisted in getting him into the front passenger seat. Mitchell thanked the nurse, and they were on their way home. Mitchell gave Baez the full rundown on the investigation, including who was involved in each murder. Once she was done, and Baez had no further questions, Mitchell had to ask.

"Have you talked to the captain yet?"

"I have."

"Really? When?"

"Early this afternoon. The captain came by to see me. Ms. Evans has told anyone who will listen at the jail that I sexually assaulted her. The captain came by to find out what happened."

"And?"

"I told the truth. I told him everything that happened and that I lost control and was stupid. I apologized and told him I was ready to accept whatever the department wanted to do."

"Do you still have a job?"

"I won't know that for a while. After he reamed me out, he said a final decision would be up to the police chief. He said they would also have to run it by the district attorney. He said he knew I was a good detective, and it was out of character for me, but he wasn't sure how the chief would want to deal with it. He said once it became public, to expect some bad press."

"The captain hadn't said a word to me about it," said Mitchell.

"I told him you had no knowledge of it until afterward and that I had promised you I would tell him myself. He accepted that. Let's forget that for now. We have some celebrating to do."

"Yes, we do, Rick."

Once at Baez's residence, Mitchell helped him out the door and walked him to the house. When he opened the door, he was shocked to see detectives and officers there to greet him.

"Hooray!" they all shouted. "Welcome home, Rick!"

"That's one heck of a way to get a vacation!" shouted Sgt. Marquez.

"Thank you, everyone," laughed Baez. "Great to see you all."

Baez was also surprised at how picked up and clean his home was. "Who did all this?"

"Leah told us how your house might be a little messy, so we came over and cleaned it up before you got home," explained Boyd.

"Well, thank you," said Baez. "This is quite the surprise."

After an hour of laughter and cheer, Mitchell announced it was time to give Rick some peace and quiet. He still needed his rest. Baez sat near the door and thanked everyone as they left.

"Thank you, Leah. That was nice. But you are right, I'm tired."

"Alright, I'll leave you to yourself, but you call me if you need anything."

"Don't worry. I will."

Chapter 19

SIX WEEKS LATER

During the weeks following the arrests of all the suspects, information gathered from the Miami-Dade Police Department and other jurisdictions was freely shared in collaboration to build the strongest cases against the six women charged with murder. By now, the case was well known by people across the country as the case of the Secret Affairs Murders. The district attorneys of Broward County and Miami-Dade County had agreed to have Miranda Castaneda, the mastermind behind the killings, tried in Miami-Dade County. She was charged with six counts of first-degree murder and six counts of conspiracy to commit murder. Emily Evans was to be tried in Miami-Dade on one charge of first-degree murder and conspiracy to commit murder.

The other four women, Carla Delgado, Sabrina Martin, Madison Turner, and Anna Bailey, were all charged in Broward County for first-degree murder and conspiracy to commit murder.

Detective Baez had been on injury leave for the past six weeks, but was now back at the police department to meet with the police chief and Captain Gonzalez to learn what punishment he faced for his misconduct. He knew this could very well be his last time in the building as a police officer. Given the sensitivity of the case and possible implications on the criminal cases, the internal affairs investigation had been handled by an outside investigator. The investigator's report was then reviewed by both the district attorney and police chief.

"Come on in, Detective Baez," commanded the chief. "Have a seat."

"Good morning, sir," said Baez.

"As you can imagine, Detective, I was disappointed to hear about your conduct in this case."

"Yes, sir. I understand."

"However, after a thorough investigation and review by the district attorney's office, they found no basis for any criminal charge. It was agreed that Evans only knew you as a client, not as a police officer. Thus, her consent was not coerced. You will not be facing any criminal charges."

Baez let out a sigh of relief. "Thank you, sir. I'm sorry to have put the department in this position."

"Now, we just have the matter of what the appropriate discipline will be for your indiscretion."

"Like I told the captain, I'm ready to accept whatever you believe is appropriate."

The chief looked at Baez for several seconds without expression. "The captain here tells me you are a fine detective, and if it wasn't for your work on this case, it might not have been solved."

"Thank you, Chief, and thank you, Captain. I would like to think my work was critical in the case."

"I've reviewed your record," continued the chief, "and it is quite good."

Baez nodded.

"The troublesome part for me is the embarrassment you've brought to the department. But you know what? It's not the first time the department has been embarrassed by something, and it won't be the last. We'll survive. In taking all things into consideration, I accept that this was a one-time lapse in judgment.

I can't overlook all the good you have done. I'm not going to fire a good detective over one mistake."

"Thank you, sir. I appreciate it. It will never happen again."

"Alright, here's what I'm going to do. I'm going to suspend you for four weeks without pay. Get away from here, do something fun, and clear your mind. When you get back, you'll be all healed up, refreshed, and ready to go. And most of this will be forgotten by then."

Baez stood up to shake the chief's hand. "Thank you, sir. I'll make sure you never regret your decision."

"I know you will, Detective Baez. Now that we have that dirty business taken care of, I want to thank you for the job you did on that case. Without the work you and Mitchell did, those ladies would probably still be out there trolling for victims."

"Thank you, sir," said Baez once more. He then left and walked to the Detective Bureau in search of Mitchell. He found her in the detective lounge, drinking a coffee and eating a cinnamon roll.

"Hey, Rick! Good to see you back," said Mitchell.

"I'm not back yet. I just wanted to say hi to you."

"Do you still have a job?"

"Yes. I've been suspended for four weeks without pay, which is more than fair."

"I'm happy to hear that, Rick. What are you going to be doing?"

"I'm going to take some time off and do some traveling to clear my head and refresh myself. I want to see my parents in New Jersey and maybe get to see my brother in Indiana. I'm also thinking of buying a new fishing boat."

"Good for you, Rick. I think you are on the right track. I look forward to working with you again when you return."

"Yeah, me too."

Mitchell stood up and gave Baez a hug. "Take care of yourself, and I'll see you when you get back."

"You can count on it," said Baez as he turned and walked out the door with a renewed sense of purpose. A burden had been lifted off his shoulders. He had faced death and the potential loss of his job and was given a second chance. It was time to start fresh, and he knew he would have to approach the job differently when he returned. The job could no longer be the only thing in his life. He was determined to get out and enjoy what life had to offer.

Amarillo

Billy

Chapter 1

It was a scorching hot day in Amarillo, Texas, and the humidity level was higher than usual for a summer day in July. At around 4:00 pm, the female clerk at the Circle K in northern Amarillo was behind the counter when she saw a large male come through the front door. It caught her attention because of the size of the individual. He was well over six feet tall and looked very muscular, similar to how a bodybuilder might look. He was dressed in casual khaki pants and a medium-blue polo shirt. His brown hair was cut short in a military-style. His shirt was wet under his arms from the sweltering heat, and beads of sweat were on his forehead. He looked to be in his early twenties. The male looked around the store and appeared to be confused. After several minutes, the clerk responded.

"Is there something I can help you with?"

The male looked at her and said in a deep bass voice, "is there somewhere to sit down to eat?"

"This is a convenience store," said the clerk. "If you want to sit down to eat, go to a restaurant."

"And where would I find a restaurant?"

"There is a Denny's just down the street. They have lots of choices, and the food is good," said the clerk as she pointed south.

"Alright, thank you," said the man as he turned and walked out the door.

That was strange, thought the clerk. *Who doesn't know Circle K is not a sit-down restaurant?*

At approximately 5:30 pm, Officer Stella Turner, a three-year officer with the Amarillo Police Department, was on patrol when she received a radio call of a theft at the Denny's restaurant in her beat. A manager had called reporting a male customer had eaten two meals and then left without paying. Police officers sometimes refer to this as a dine and dash. Not the most exciting call, thought Turner, but it had to be handled. She arrived at 5:38 pm and contacted the manager.

According to the manager, a large white male, about 22 to 24 years old, came into the restaurant and ordered chicken fried steak with all the fixings. After consuming this meal, he asked for a second meal of a deluxe hamburger and fries. He also drank three glasses of milk. Afterward, he started to leave the restaurant without paying. The manager stopped him and told him he had to pay for his meal. The male looked at him and asked how to pay for the meal. The manager explained he could pay with cash or a credit card. The male said he had neither. The manager did not detain him, as he was much too big and muscular.

"This guy asked you how to pay?" asked Officer Turner.

"Yes, as though he didn't understand. He said something about this being a cafeteria where people bring you food to eat. I explained this was a restaurant where you must pay for the food you eat."

"Do you think he is mentally challenged?"

"I did not get that impression," the manager responded. "He seemed intelligent enough, but it was like he didn't know the concept of working to get paid and using money to buy stuff. He seemed a little immature to me."

"Did he threaten you?"

"No. He asked how to get money, and I said to get a job and work to get paid. He then asked what work he could do for me to be paid. I told him it didn't work that way. He got frustrated and just walked out."

"Can you describe him to me?"

"Sure, he was massive. He was probably at least six foot six and two hundred and fifty pounds of all muscle. He had short brown hair."

"What was he wearing?" asked Officer Turner.

"He was wearing beige pants and a blue collared shirt with buttons at the top."

"Like a polo shirt?"

"Yes, like a polo shirt."

"Anything else about him?"

"Not that I noticed, other than him being very large."

"Alright, thank you for your help," said Officer Turner before leaving the restaurant. She wasn't sure what to make of the report but thought the whole thing was strange.

Officer Stella Turner was a 27-year-old white female who had been with the department for only three years. Stella was an attractive woman who stood at 5'9" and 136 pounds. When working, she pulled her mid-length blond hair back and tied it up in a short ponytail. When not working, she let it hang down to just above her shoulders, slightly curled toward her neck. Turner grew up in the Dallas area and was a star tennis player at her high school, taking fourth place in the state tournament her senior season. She was considered the best player in the Dallas-Fort Worth district. After high school, she attended Texas Christian College and majored in criminal justice. Her father had been a police officer, and she was always fascinated with the work. She still played tennis through a local tennis club and occasionally played in tournaments. Officer Turner worked the afternoon shift four days a week from 3:00 pm to 1:00 am.

Back in her patrol car, Turner cranked up the air conditioning. Wearing a police uniform with a bulletproof vest and twenty pounds of equipment made days like this highly uncomfortable. She then used her in-car computer to enter the suspect information into the online watch log to alert any officers who might respond to a similar incident or observe someone matching the suspect description. Turner then patrolled the area looking for the suspect until she was dispatched to assist with traffic control at a warehouse fire.

***

The following morning, forty-two-year-old Detective Jack Webster was having breakfast with his wife, Eileen. His two children, 13-year-old Sierra and 11-year-old Matthew, were still sleeping. Both children were out of school for the summer and enjoyed the extra time sleeping. Webster rarely saw his children on summer mornings before he had to leave for work. However, he enjoyed the additional alone time with his wife.

Webster had light brown hair cut close on the sides, with a tassel of hair that hung slightly over the top of his forehead. He was rather tall at 6'2" and a stocky 230 pounds. He had well-tanned skin and hazel eyes. His defining trait was the light brown cowboy hat he wore every day. A sweat stain showed along the base of the hat. Webster was known in the department as a tough, experienced cop with 21 years of service in the Amarillo Police Department. He did not have a college education, but he knew more about policing through advanced investigative training and experience than most.

"What do you have going on today?" asked Eileen.

"More follow-up on the homicide from last week. I need to meet with the lab folks to see where we are on the forensics," replied Webster.

"Do you still suspect the boyfriend?"

"I do. He has an alibi, but I don't buy it. He had ample time to kill her before leaving. Some of his statements didn't ring true, and I think the forensics will support my suspicion."

"What does Alec think?"

Webster laughed. "He's still taking it all in. Given his lack of experience, he hasn't developed that sixth sense yet. He likes to wait until all the evidence is in before developing any theories. I'm going to have him review all the statements today and then see if he has any suspicions."

After breakfast, Webster kissed his wife goodbye and headed to work. He arrived a little past eight o'clock. His partner, Alec Velez, was already at his desk. Alec Velez was young and inexperienced as a detective. He was only 29 years old and had only been in the department for five years. After four years in patrol, Velez had been selected as a detective and assigned to work with Webster. Velez was a graduate of West Texas A&M with a degree in psychology. He was born and raised in Amarillo and had wanted to be an Amarillo police officer ever since having an officer visit his sixth-grade class.

Detectives Webster and Velez were assigned to the Violent Crimes Unit, which investigated homicides, serious assaults, and some robberies. Occasionally, they would be given other complex cases that Detective Commander Martina Lopez believed required the experience of Detective Webster.

"Good morning, Alec," said Webster as he walked past Velez, sitting at his desk. "Anything new assigned to us?"

"Good morning, Jack," replied Velez. "Nothing new that I've seen."

"Good, that will give you some time to go over the statements from last week's homicide," said Webster. "I have my theory, but would like to know what you think. In the meantime, I will visit our evidence techs to see if they've come up with anything we can use. We can touch base later this morning."

"Sounds good," replied Velez.

Later that morning, around 10:00, Detective Commander Martina Lopez approached Velez at his desk. "Where is Webster?"

"I believe he is at the lab talking to the evidence techs," answered Velez.

"All of our property detectives are busy, and we've just had a theft or robbery at the Clothes Mart on the north end of town. It sounds like someone may have gotten hurt. I'd like you and Webster to go there and find out what happened."

"Alright, I'll get in touch with Jack, and we'll head out there."

"Thank you, Alec."

Velez called Webster to give him the news. Webster said he would meet Velez in the back parking lot in twenty minutes. Velez was outside waiting for Webster when he pulled up eighteen minutes later. Velez jumped into the passenger seat, and Webster drove out of the parking lot and headed toward the Clothes Mart in the north part of Amarillo.

"Do we know what we have yet?" asked Webster.

"Yes," replied Velez. "I talked to a patrol officer on the scene, and he told me someone came in and took a bunch of clothes. One of the male employees attempted to stop him, and the suspect assaulted him. According to the officer, the suspect gave the employee a forearm to the chest and knocked him back so hard, he fell and cracked his head on a table."

"Is he okay?"

"The officer thought he would be, but he was taken to the hospital to be treated. He had a gash on the back of his head."

"This is more important than our homicide?" growled Webster.

"The commander didn't have anyone else available and asked us to respond. The suspect matches the description of an incident in a restaurant from yesterday," explained Velez.

"What was the incident from yesterday?"

"A dine and dash."

"What? Now we're investigating someone who doesn't pay a food tab?"

"I don't know what to tell you, Jack, just doing what the commander wants. It caused quite the commotion."

Webster just shook his head and kept quiet. Upon arrival at the Clothes Mart, the detectives met with the manager, Mia Harper. She told them how the suspect entered the store and started grabbing clothing. When he attempted to leave without paying, one of her male employees, Lucas, tried to stop him. The suspect gave Lucas a hard push with his right forearm in a punching fashion, knocking Lucas backward and into a display table, causing a severe gash to the back of his head.

"Did this person say anything?" asked Velez.

"There was some shouting before he pushed Lucas. I thought I heard the suspect say he had no money. Other than that, no, I could not tell what was being said."

"Please describe him to me."

"He was very noticeable. Very big and muscular."

"How tall was he?" continued Velez.

"I'm not good on height, but he was a huge, scary-looking guy."

"Could you tell what race he was?"

"Yes, he was white."

"Hair?"

"Very short. I think it was brown."

"Clothing description?"

"He had on a blue polo shirt and tan colored pants."

"Had you ever seen this person before?"

"No, never."

"Did he have a car?"

"None that I saw. He just ran off toward the road."

"How much did he steal?"

"It is hard to say, but from what I saw in his arms, probably at least four hundred dollars in merchandise. It was all shirts and pants."

"Okay, Mia, thank you for your help. Here is my card. Please call us if you remember anything else."

Back in the car, Webster asked Velez what his thoughts were. "I don't know," said Velez. "Maybe a homeless guy with no money? How many of them wear polo shirts?"

"I don't know," said Webster, "but hopefully, we can just turn this over to one of the property guys."

"Do we need to go interview the victim?"

"No, I talked with the patrol sergeant, and he said it was all handled. The victim is going to be kept overnight but should be fine," explained Webster. "Now, let's go work on our homicide."

Chapter 2

Amarillo is the largest city in the panhandle of Texas, with a population of approximately 200,000. In Spanish, amarillo is the word for yellow. It is believed the Spanish named Amarillo after the many yellow wildflowers that grow in the surrounding dense prairie land. Residents of Amarillo are sometimes referred to as Amarilloans. The city rests in the Western High Plains region near the Canadian River that runs north of town.

Amarillo is known for ranching, the meatpacking industry, wheat and cotton fields, and the nearby nuclear weapons plant. It is also big enough to have its share of civic attractions, such as museums, a nature center, a zoo, and an amusement park. Located twenty-five miles south of the city is Palo Duro Canyon State Park. The Palo Duro Canyon is the second largest canyon in the United States. Another attraction on the west side of Amarillo is called Cadillac Ranch. It is an art attraction comprising ten Cadillacs buried nose-first into the ground. Visitors are welcome to spray paint the cars while visiting.

The Amarillo Police Department is a full-service police department headed by Police Chief Anson Boone. Chief Boone has been with the department for 24 years. He started his career in Lubbock, Texas, when he was 27 years old. After six years of policing in Lubbock, Boone took a job with the Amarillo Police Department. He liked the smaller town atmosphere, and his wife was originally from Amarillo. Boone worked his way up the chain until becoming the Police Chief four years ago. He was well known in Amarillo for having solved a serial killer case as a detective 19 years ago.

Anson Boone was 58 years old and stood 5'7", with a belly that hung over his belt. He was mostly bald, with gray hair on the sides of his head. Boone was a no-nonsense, old-school cop. He was honest but tough. He could tell jokes with the best of them, but he wasn't one to put up with a lot of nonsense when it came to police work. While not required as Police Chief, Boone still wore his uniform every day of the week. He believed it was essential to be highly visible to both department members and the public.

One of Chief Boone's habits was to have a packet of Copenhagen wintergreen snuff tucked into one of his cheeks. He quit smoking at the age of fifty, but still needed the nicotine the snuff provided. He knew he should quit, but some habits are just hard to break. If Chief Boone ever got in your face to chew you out, you could smell the wintergreen and tobacco on his breath.

Boone has been married to Daisy for 33 years. Together, they have three children, a son, and two daughters. They also have five grandkids. When he can get away from work, they enjoy taking road trips through the western states, often camping in their travel trailer.

The day after the incident at the Clothes Mart, Chief Boone was reviewing the watch logs in his office when his administrative assistant, Laura Ramirez, knocked on his door.

"Chief," says Laura, "there are two federal agents here who would like to speak to you. They say it is important."

Slightly irritated they did not make an appointment, Boone responded, "did they say what it was about?"

"No, Chief, just that it was important they talk to you."

"Alright, bring them in," Boone said.

As the two agents entered his office, Boone stood up to greet them. He noted they were both sharply dressed and appeared to be in their mid-thirties. The male agent was in a tailored suit and tie, and the female agent had a conservatively styled dark business skirt, white blouse, and dark jacket. He shook hands and introduced himself.

The male agent introduced himself as FBI agent Levi Rucker. The female agent introduced herself as Clara Chen, an investigator with Homeland Security.

"This must be important to have an FBI agent and someone from Homeland Security here to see me," said a surprised Boone. "What can I do for you?"

"We have some information to pass along and ask for your assistance," said Rucker. Two nights ago, we believe a dangerous escapee entered Amarillo. We will take him into custody when found. We would like your officers to be on the lookout for him."

"We'll be happy to help," said Boone. "Who is this character?"

"We can't share much, but he goes by the name of Billy. He is a large white male, about six foot six, and is very muscular."

The chief thought for a moment, then said, "You know, we had a couple incidents of theft I read about in our watch logs. The person you describe sounds like the suspect in our cases."

"It very well could be," agreed Rucker. "We will have agents in the field ready to respond if your officers find him."

"What crimes has he committed in the past?"

"He hasn't done anything yet," said Rucker, "but we believe he has the potential to be dangerous."

The chief was now puzzled. "If he hasn't committed any crimes up to now, why was he in custody?"

"We can't tell you that," said Chen. "However, he could present a threat to our national security."

"Do you think he is a terrorist?"

"No, not that. But he could present us with some problems if his existence is discovered," explained Chen.

"How dangerous is he?"

"We don't know," answered Chen. "He could be dangerous, but we aren't sure to what extent."

"Tell me, Ms. Chen, how is this person a threat to national security?"

Chen and Rucker looked at each other. "I can't tell you that, Chief," answered Chen. "It is classified information."

"What do you mean you can't tell me that? You just asked for our help. If this person is a potential danger to my community, I need to know everything. Give me this person's full name and date of birth, and we can start looking for him."

"Chief, this is a national security matter," said Chen. "If we could tell you more, we would. I know this is hard. We just wanted to let you know we will be in town looking for him and could use your help. If your officers see him, call us, and we will do the rest."

Chief Boone sat back in his chair and crossed his arms as he looked at both agents. "What is this guy going to do, blow up the city?"

"No, nothing like that, but he could be dangerous to other people," said Rucker.

"Then tell me his damn name!" shouted Chief Boone.

"We just call him Billy," said Rucker.

Chief Boone laughed. "If this guy is dangerous, why not give me the information we need to help you?"

"Let's call him Billy Jones," responded Rucker.

"Call him Billy Jones?" said an incredulous chief. "This is ridiculous. Investigator Chen, how many criminals have you arrested?"

Chen just looked at the chief, saying nothing.

"Yeah, just what I thought. We arrest people every day here. If you want our help, you need to work with us. I'm not endangering our officers by not providing them what they need to know."

"Chief," said Rucker, "we understand how strange this is. I can assure you this is a national security concern. His name doesn't matter. He was in federal custody and escaped. We simply need to get him back in custody. We are calling him Billy Jones, and here is his description." Rucker handed the chief a flyer. "Help us find him, and we will get out of your town."

"No picture?" asked Boone.

"No, we don't have a picture."

"I thought you said he escaped from custody?"

"He did, but it was a special circumstance. No picture."

"Alright, just get out. I've listened to enough. You feds come here wanting our help and are not even willing to give us all the information. If we see this guy, we're going to arrest him, and then you can come pick him up."

"I hope you will call us first, Chief," said Chen. "It is important."

"Well, not important enough to tell me what is going on. You can leave now."

"I understand, Chief," said Rucker. "Tell your officers to be careful. This individual is very strong."

"My officers will be careful," Boone assured them.

After the agents left, Chief Boone called his assistant Laura into his office.

"What do you need, sir?"

"Please get Commander Lopez up to my office. I need to talk to her about something."

"Okay, I'll call her right away."

Fifteen minutes later, Commander Martina Lopez appeared in Chief Boone's office. "You wanted to see me, sir?"

"Yes, Martina, come on in."

Commander Lopez was the highest ranking Hispanic in the department. She was 45 years old, with short dark hair, brown eyes, and stylish wire-rimmed glasses. Lopez had been with the department for 22 years, working her way up the ranks. For the last three years, she has overseen the Criminal Investigations Division. She was well respected in the department and was a graduate of the FBI National Academy, a ten-week professional development program for law enforcement leaders.

"I received a visit from two federal agents this morning who told me there was a person who escaped from federal custody, and they believed he was in our city," explained the chief. "They also said he could be dangerous."

"Do we know who this person is?" asked Lopez.

"Not exactly. The feds called him Billy Jones, but I suspect that is just a name they called him. They wouldn't tell me anything more. Here is a flyer with his description on it."

"Did they give you a picture of him?"

"Nope, said they didn't have one."

Lopez looked at the chief with a frown on her face as if to say, whaaaat?

"Yeah, I know," responded Boone. "It is crazy. They wouldn't tell me much other than he could be a threat to national security. They want us to help track him down and then call them to pick him up."

"Who were these agents?" asked Lopez.

"An FBI agent by the name of Levi Rucker and an investigator from the Department of Homeland Security by the name of Clara Chen."

"Homeland Security?"

"Yep. I tried to find out why this person was a danger and why Homeland Security was interested in him, but they wouldn't say. There's some secret they don't want to share."

"You said he escaped. Do you know from where?"

"No, but the only federal high-security prison in Texas is in Beaumont, about one hundred miles east of Houston."

"If he escaped from Beaumont, that's over six hundred miles away," said Lopez. "How did he get to Amarillo?"

"Good question," said Boone. "This guy matches the description of those two thefts I read about, the one in the restaurant and then the clothing store yesterday. Have patrol be on the alert and put a couple of detectives on the case. Have one of them contact the Beaumont prison to get more information on this guy. I don't know why they think he is dangerous, but the sooner we have him out of here, the better I will feel."

"I'll get this information out immediately to all patrol officers and list him as highly dangerous. Once we have more information from Beaumont, I'll let you know, Chief."

"Thank you, Martina."

After yesterday's incident at the Clothes Mart, the male suspect, referred to as Billy, had tried to keep a low profile. He was scared and confused. Not knowing how to provide for himself, he had to improvise to survive. He was learning to get things he needed without others seeing him. He preferred to avoid confrontation, if possible. During the night, he needed to get more food. Rather than going into an open store or restaurant, Billy found a small café that was closed. He broke through the rear door and gathered enough food to last for a few days. He carried the food in a makeshift backpack he had made from a pair of pants he had stolen from the Clothes Mart. He tied the legs shut, and with the use of a belt, he flung it over his shoulder.

Billy spent some of his time wandering around in the north end of Amarillo, observing the sights and sounds unfamiliar to him. He wanted to learn how other people lived their lives. He found it fascinating to see all the activity.

Having not slept the night before, Billy found a place to sleep in Cottonwood Park, a wooded park in one of the northern neighborhoods of Amarillo. There was a small lake in the park that was kept filled by a small creek. The cottonwood trees along the banks of the creek were numerous, providing shade and concealment. Billy found a culvert to hide his belongings and used stolen clothing as bedding along the creek bank. Billy was so tired, even the heat of the night couldn't keep him awake.

In the morning, Billy's muscular body prevented him from wearing most of his stolen clothing. None of the pants he took would fit over his thick thighs. He still had to wear the khaki pants he wore the first day in Amarillo. He found an XXXL size polo shirt he could wear among the shirts he had grabbed. It was a yellow Nautica shirt with the Nautica emblem on the left breast. His face was now covered in stubble from not being able to shave the last couple of days.

Billy used the creek water to wash himself with one of the shirts he had stolen. He then pulled some muffins from a pant leg of his makeshift backpack. They were a little smashed but still delicious. He drank one carton of milk he had taken. It was warm from the heat but not yet spoiled. Billy knew he would have to find another source of food.

One thing that intrigued Billy was all the girls in town. He knew several women from the place he came from, but in Amarillo, they were everywhere. Billy wondered what it would be like to be with a woman. It had been prohibited where he lived before. Maybe, Billy thought, *I can find one to have sex with me.* He only knew what he had read and what others had told him. Billy did not know why, but his desire to have sex was powerful. Billy spent the next several hours walking in the surrounding area, learning everything he could about life in Amarillo.

Patrol officers had been alerted to be on the lookout for a male escapee who was a suspect in two thefts and an assault. The suspect was known as Billy Jones. He was described as a white male, six foot six, two hundred and ninety pounds of solid muscle, with brown curly hair, and noticeable hair on his chest. Officers were told he was intelligent and possibly dangerous.

Detectives Webster and Velez were poring over the evidence in their homicide case when Commander Lopez called them into her office.

"I'm not sure what we are dealing with here," advised Lopez. "But we have an escapee believed to be in Amarillo, and the feds are looking for him. He has been described as a national security risk and possibly dangerous. I need you two to do some background on this guy. The feds are not telling us much about him."

"Commander," protested Webster, "we are in the middle of a homicide investigation. Can't someone else be assigned to this?"

"Normally, yes. But we believe he is the same person involved in the dine and dash and the theft and assault at the Clothes Mart. You two covered that case, and we don't know for sure what we have here. Homeland Security wants this suspect, so you know this involves something big. I need my best team on this."

"Alright," said Webster, "where do we start?"

"All we know is that his name might be Billy Jones. The feds called him an escapee, so we think he came from the prison in Beaumont. Here is his description," said Lopez as she handed Webster the bulletin. "See what you can find out."

"Okay, we'll let you know," assured Webster.

Chapter 3

Later that afternoon, Billy was back in Cottonwood Park watching people walk by. He noticed three young women enter the park and sit down at a picnic table. They each had a backpack and appeared to be talking and laughing. There was no one else near the picnic table, so Billy thought it would be an excellent opportunity to ask some questions. He did not realize the three young women were teenagers walking home from a summer arts and crafts program at the middle school. One of the teenagers happened to be 13-year-old Sierra Webster, the daughter of Detective Jack Webster.

Billy approached the girls and asked if he could ask a few questions. Julie, one of Sierra's friends, said yes.

"Have any of you young ladies ever had sex?" he asked.

The girls looked at each other and giggled. "No," said Sierra, "we are only thirteen."

"How old do you have to be?"

"I don't know," said Julie. "I don't know anyone who has had sex."

"Why are you asking us these questions?" said Sierra.

"I'm looking for someone to have sex with," said Billy. "I have a strong desire to have sex, and you are all nice looking young ladies."

The girls all looked at each other, and Sierra began to get worried. "You should not talk to us about this. Talk to someone your own age," she said. "You need to leave us alone."

"Don't you want to have sex?"

"Let's go," said Sierra to her two friends. "We need to get out of here."

The three girls quickly grabbed their packs and began to walk away quickly. Billy started to follow them.

"Wait, I have a few more questions."

"Run," barked Sierra.

All three girls ran through the park toward the sidewalk that would lead them home. After a few seconds, Sierra looked back and saw that the man was not coming after them. She slowed down, and the other two girls followed her lead.

"That was weird," said the third girl, Debbie.

"That was scary," said Sierra. "There is something wrong with that man."

"Did you see how big that guy was?" asked Julie.

"Yes, very big," agreed Sierra. "I need to tell my dad about this."

Detective Webster had made a phone call to the Beaumont Prison and was waiting for a return call. His phone rang, but it was not the prison. It was his wife, Eileen, calling.

"Hi, honey, what's up?"

"Sierra came home today frightened. Some man approached her, Julie, and Debbie in the park on the way home from school today."

"What did he do?" asked a concerned Webster.

"He was asking the girls about sex and wanted to have sex with one of them."

"What!?"

"Yes, he said he wanted to have sex."

"Does she know who this man is?"

"No, never saw him before,"

"Can she describe him?"

"She said he was an enormous man. He was tall and had big muscles."

Webster paused.

"Jack, are you there?"

"Yes, I'm here. Is he a white male?"

"Yes."

"We are looking for someone like that right now. It sounds like this guy might be the same person. You're talking about Cottonwood Park, right?"

"Yes."

"Alright, I'm going to send patrol officers out there right now. I'm going to head out there myself, and then I will come home. Keep Sierra home for now."

"Yes, I will," replied Eileen.

Webster called dispatch to give them the information. Officers were immediately sent to Cottonwood Park to look for the suspect. Billy had retreated to his camp along the creek bank when he heard sirens getting close to the park. He looked over the creek bank and saw a couple of police cars pulling into the parking lot on the far side of the park. Billy grabbed his belongings and shoved them into the culvert. Billy then climbed into the culvert so as not to be seen.

Five officers arrived and walked through the park. A couple was stopped and asked if they had seen a large man anywhere in the park. They said no. Officers continued to search the park. Billy could hear two of them talking as they walked along the creek bank. Billy hid in the middle of the culvert to avoid being seen. None of the officers walked down the bank to look in the culvert. After ten minutes, the officers concluded Billy was no longer there.

Billy was unsure what he had done wrong, but he knew he did not want to be contacted by the police. He was afraid they might want to take him back and wondered if the girls had called the police. *I was only asking questions,* he thought. *Maybe I need to look for older women.*

Detective Webster met some of the patrol officers as they were getting ready to leave the park. "Did you find anything?"

"No," said one officer. "We walked the whole park and even spoke with a couple who said they hadn't seen anyone matching the description."

"I'd like a couple of you to keep patrolling the area. We believe this person is on foot, so he couldn't have gone too far."

Just then, a black SUV came screeching into the parking lot. FBI agent Levi Rucker and Homeland Security investigator Clara Chen got out of the car. This time, they were wearing bulletproof flak jackets.

Rucker flashed his FBI badge. "Were you able to find him?"

"No," said Webster. "How did you know to come here?"

"We are monitoring the police radio traffic," said Rucker.

"So you are the two agents looking for this Billy Jones, eh?"

"Yes, Detective."

"What is he wanted for?"

"As we told your chief, we can't tell you the details. We just need to take him back to where he came from."

"And where is that?" asked Webster.

"Can't tell you."

"Look, this guy approached my daughter and her friends this afternoon and asked them for sex!" stated Webster. "Now, it would be nice to know what we are dealing with here. Is this guy a sexual predator running loose in our city?"

"No, he's never committed a sex crime," said Rucker. "Once we find him, we will take him out of here, and you'll never see him again."

"But you can't give us any more information?" asked Webster.

"Only what you already know. It's just a matter of time before we get him back in custody."

Webster just shook his head as he walked away. "Thanks, guys," he said to the officers as he got back into his car. Webster then drove away and headed home. He needed to talk to his daughter.

Billy had been watching the gathering of police and agents from his culvert hiding spot. Once everyone left, he ate his last remaining unspoiled food. Billy quickly learned that trying to keep food fresh in 95-degree heat did not work so well. He would have to go looking for more food after it got dark.

Once Detective Velez heard about what happened to Webster's daughter, he called Webster. "Jack, is everything okay?"

"Yes, I'm driving home now to talk to my daughter. She is fine. All this creep did was talk about having sex. He didn't touch anyone."

"Do you need me to do anything?"

"No, Alec, but thank you. We'll talk more tomorrow. I'm hoping patrol will find this guy tonight."

"Alright, see you tomorrow," said Velez.

It was almost 5:30 pm and time for Velez to get off work. He called Officer Stella Turner to see if she could meet him for dinner at 6:00. Officer Turner was working the afternoon shift from 3:00 pm to 1:00 am. Velez started dating Turner five months ago. They met each other when Velez was still in patrol, but they did not begin dating until he became a detective. He had always been attracted to her, but he thought it would be awkward to date while they were both working patrol. Four months ago, Turner was the first responding officer on a sexual assault, and Velez was the detective assigned to the case. Working with her on the investigation renewed his interest in her, and the following week, he asked her out. They have been dating ever since.

Turner found the mixed-race Velez to be quite handsome. He stood at six feet and had a slim, muscular body. His skin always looked tanned, and he had dark wavy hair. He was very polite to everyone. She liked that. He also had a smooth baritone voice with which he could sing very well. She found this out when he took her to a karaoke bar on one of their dates. It was one of her best dates ever.

Velez tried to meet Turner for dinner during her shift at least once a week. Given their different hours, it was the only time they could get together, other than on her days off.

"Yes," said Turner, "I am not on any call right now. Where would you like to meet?"

Velez knew Turner worked on the northern end of Amarillo, so he always picked a place within her patrol area.

"How about Chili's tonight?" he said.

"Yes, I like that place. I'll meet you there at six."

When Velez arrived at Chili's, Turner was already seated at a table. He joined her, and they both asked for diet cokes. Turner then ordered the grilled chicken salad, and Velez ordered the queso burger and fries.

"How has your day been so far?" asked Velez.

"Nothing to speak of. I handled a traffic accident earlier. How about yours?"

"We have been asked to check into this Billy Jones character. We believe he escaped from a federal prison."

"Oh yes, I think he was the guy from the restaurant theft the other day."

"Did you hear about the call to Cottonwood Park?" asked Velez.

"Yes, I was handling a traffic accident when it happened. Do you think it was the same guy?"

"He fit the description," said Velez. "And one of the girls he approached was Webster's daughter."

"Oh, my gosh," said a surprised Turner. "Is she okay?"

"Yes, he did nothing other than talk about sex with them."

"That's disgusting," said Turner. "I'll be sure to look for this guy tonight."

"Just be careful. The federal agents have emphasized he could be dangerous, and we know little about him. They are not sharing a lot of information. One agent is from Homeland Security."

"Since when does Homeland Security concern itself with two-bit criminals?"

"That's a question we all have," said Velez.

After eating, they said their goodbyes, and Turner returned to patrol the streets looking for Billy Jones. Velez headed to his parent's house. He hadn't seen them in about ten days and thought paying them a brief visit would be nice.

Meanwhile, Detective Webster was home talking with his daughter, Sierra. He was relieved to know she was okay and that the suspect had only spoken to the girls.

"Did he say he wanted to have sex with you?" Webster asked Sierra.

"Yes, he asked if I wanted to have sex."

"Alright, sweetie, we have officers looking for this guy, and we will find him. You handled things well by running away."

"Eileen, when is the next arts and crafts day?"

"Thursday."

"Will you be able to drive the girls back and forth until we find this guy?"

"Yes, of course."

Detective Velez arrived at his parent's house at 7:10 pm and walked through the front door. "Hi, Mom, how are you doing?"

"Alec, so nice to see you. Thanks for coming by."

Upon hearing voices, Velez's father walked into the living room smiling. "Hello, Alec. About time you came to see us."

"It hasn't been that long, Dad,"

Alec was born and raised in Amarillo, and his parents still lived in the same house. His father, Diego, was Hispanic, and his mother, Katherine (Kat), was white. Both parents were very proud of their son for being an Amarillo police officer. A large photograph of him in uniform was displayed proudly on the living room wall.

"How is that nice girl you are dating?" asked Diego.

"You ask me that every time, Dad. She is doing very well."

"What are your plans with her?"

"Dad, we've only been dating for four months."

"Well, it doesn't take long to know when you've found the right one. Your mother and I knew we were meant for each other after our third date. I took her to...."

"Dad," interrupted Velez, "I've heard that story way too many times."

"Alright, I'm just saying."

"Oh, leave him alone," said Kat. "He'll tell us when he knows."

***

Meanwhile, Officer Turner patrolled her district in northern Amarillo, looking for the suspect known as Billy Jones. She was patrolling in the vicinity of Cottonwood Park, thinking he was probably still in the area. At about 7:30 pm, Turner and another officer were dispatched to a suspicious person walking in the 1800 block of Oaklawn Lane and matching the description of suspect

Billy Jones. Turner immediately drove toward the location. She was first to arrive two minutes later.

Turner observed the person she believed to be the suspect walking southbound on the sidewalk past some small storefronts. She monitored the suspect until her backup arrived. Turner then pulled her patrol car up in front of the suspect and stopped. The second officer stopped just behind the suspect, and both officers exited their vehicles.

"Stop, we need to talk to you," said Turner as she approached the suspect. The second officer walked up behind him, carefully observing his hands.

"What do you want?" asked Billy.

"Are you Billy Jones?"

"No," said Billy, with a confused look on his face.

"You look like Billy Jones. What is your last name?"

"My name is just Billy."

"You have to have a last name," said Turner, while the second officer got closer to Billy from behind.

Billy just looked at her. "What do you want?"

"We need to take you into the police department to clear up who you are. I'm going to handcuff you for our protection. Please turn around and put your hands on top of your head." As Turner was saying this, she was amazed at how muscular he looked. *I sure hope he doesn't want to fight with us,* thought Turner.

"I'm not going anywhere with you," said Billy. "I don't want to go back."

"Please cooperate, Billy. It will make things much easier."

The second officer moved in closer.

"Now put your hands on top of your head and turn around," ordered Turner.

"No."

The second officer then stepped forward, grabbed Billy's right wrist, and attempted to pull it behind his back. Turner moved toward Billy's left wrist. Billy tensed up, and the second officer could not move his arm. As Turner grabbed his left wrist, she immediately knew she could not control him. His muscles were tense and felt like steel. Billy then pulled his arms close to his chest, pulling the officers along with them, and then forcefully flung his arms outward, sending both officers flying in opposite directions. Officer Turner flew backward, slamming against the back fender of her patrol car. She could feel an immediate sharp pain across her lower back. The second officer fell hard on his back on the concrete sidewalk, groaning as he hit the pavement. Billy then took off running down the sidewalk.

Turner fell to her knees and reached for her radio. She immediately called out a code 10, which meant officers needed immediate help. She could hear the sirens wailing as other officers closed in. Two black SUVs pulled up with screeching tires, and then patrol cars began arriving one by one. Soon, there were thirteen officers and four federal agents on the scene.

Patrol Sergeant Anderson advised dispatch that no other units needed to respond. The other officer was already on his feet and appeared to be okay. Sergeant Anderson went to Turner, who was being attended to by two other officers. She was still on her knees when he approached.

"Are you okay, Stella?"

"Yes, I'll be fine. Just some pain where I hit the fender."

"We should get you checked out."

"No, I think I'll be okay."

"Nonsense, we are going to be sure you aren't injured."

Sergeant Anderson then told one of the other officers to transport Turner to the hospital to be checked out. Turner was able to walk on her own to the patrol car and was then taken away. Other officers started searching for the suspect block by block but were unable to locate him.

At the hospital, Turner was waiting to be examined by the doctor. She pulled out her cell phone and called Velez.

"Hi, Stella, what's up?"

"Well, I located your guy Billy."

"You did? Where?"

"In the 1800 block of Oaklawn."

"Congratulations!"

"No," said Turner. "I found him but did not arrest him."

"What happened?"

"We tried to arrest him, but he was so strong, he just violently pushed us away. He threw me against my car, and I hurt my back."

"Oh, no. Are you okay?"

"Yes, but they have me at the hospital getting checked out."

"I'll be right there."

"Nonsense, I'm going to be fine."

"I don't care. I'm coming. Then I'll take you home."

Turner was happy to hear that. "Thank you, Alec."

Velez turned to his parents and told them what happened.

"Do you want us to come with you?" asked Kat.

"No, Mom. She is not seriously hurt. I'm going to take her home from the hospital."

"Tell her to be more careful out there," advised Diego.

"Yes, Dad," said Velez as he walked out the door.

Sergeant Anderson called Chief Boone at home to tell him what happened. "Yes, Officer Turner will be okay. She was able to walk on her own to the car. We're having her checked out to be sure."

"Thank you, Sergeant."

"However," said Anderson, "these federal agents are driving us nuts. They want us to do a building-by-building search for this guy over a five-block area. We don't have the staffing for that."

"How many agents are out there?"

"There are four of them wearing flak jackets."

"Is anyone named Rucker?" asked the chief.

"Yes."

"Put him on the phone."

Anderson looks around and finds Rucker. He motions to him. "The chief would like to speak to you."

Rucker takes the phone. "Hi, Chief."

"What the hell do you have my officers doing out there? We will not disrupt every business in a five-block area simply because your guy might be there. He could be long gone for all you know."

"Chief, we need to find this guy."

"Yeah, I know. He injured one of my officers. We will continue to look for him, but if you want to do a building to building search, do it yourselves. You could easily set up surveillance and watch a large area to see if he reveals himself. And who the hell is this guy?"

"An escapee. That's all I can say."

"Yeah, right. You are in our city, and Sergeant Anderson is the person in charge out there. You work with him or go it alone. Are we clear?"

"Yes, Chief."

"Now, put the sergeant back on the phone."

"Hello, Chief," answered Anderson.

"Sergeant, you are in charge. If the agents don't follow your instructions, let them go it alone. You know how to set up surveillance. I don't want us creating panic in our business district up there."

"Got it, thank you, Chief."

Sergeant Anderson set up a surveillance detail for the next three hours. Unfortunately, no one ever spotted Billy.

Chapter 4

The following morning, Velez walked into the detective room and found Webster already at work. "You're here early."

"Yep, I'm motivated to find this asshole now. How's Stella doing?"

"She is fine, just some bruising. The doctor told her to take some Ibuprofen and rest it for a day. Have you heard from the Beaumont prison?"

"Yes."

"And?"

"They never heard of a Billy Jones and have had no one matching his description in custody. Furthermore, no one has escaped in over twenty years."

Velez looked at Webster. "The feds are lying to us."

"Yeah, and I don't like it," said Webster. "We don't know who we are dealing with or why. I've asked the chief for a meeting with him, the commander, you, and me. We need to be in his office at nine."

Webster and Velez walked into the chief's office at 9:00, and Commander Lopez was already there. Once everyone was seated, the chief started asking questions.

"What do we know about Billy Jones?"

"We know he didn't escape from Beaumont," answered Webster. "They never heard of the guy and have had no one escape in the last twenty years."

Velez then spoke up. "I haven't been able to find anything on a Billy Jones in the criminal database or through motor vehicles or driver's license. There are multiple William Jones' that turn up, but none fit his description or estimated age of twenty-two to twenty-five. There are three William Jones' with criminal records in Texas, but none even close in age."

Chief Boone reached into the breast pocket of his uniform shirt and took out a round tin can of Copenhagen, opened the can, and grabbed a small packet. He then placed the packet in his lower right cheek and leaned back in his chair. "I am not surprised. The feds are not telling us the truth, at least not the whole truth."

"Chief," said Commander Lopez, "what would you think about going public with this information? If we have everyone looking for this guy, we will find him much sooner and get him out of Amarillo before someone gets seriously hurt."

"I like that idea. If you write up a press release, I'll get it sent to the media. This will bring a lot of attention to our city, but as you said, we need help from the community. Someone may know who this person is. Who knows what this character will do next."

"I'll get on that as soon as we are done here," assured Lopez.

"Webster, is your daughter okay?" asked Boone.

"Yes, sir, thank you for asking. He didn't touch her or anything. He just asked them questions about having sex."

"We could be dealing with a mentally ill person," suggested Boone.

"From the reports we've had on each incident, he has acted strangely," said Velez. "Even Stella said there was something different in his mannerisms."

"Is Stella feeling better?"

"Yes," replied Velez, "she is resting at home for the next two days and will then be back to work."

"Alright, thank you, everyone," said Boone. "Now go find this guy."

Commander Lopez quickly spoke up. "Chief, you need to know we had several burglaries on the outskirts of town last night. One occurred at the Big T's food warehouse and another at the same Clothes Mart from the other day. We don't have any witnesses, but the items taken from Big T's were boxes of food, and the only items taken from Clothes Mart were clothing. No other valuables or money were taken. We think it might be Billy, as he went after food and clothing before."

"Damn," Boone said in a raised voice. "This is turning into a crime spree. I don't care who this guy is to the feds; we need to stop him and put him in jail."

"We'll do our best, sir," said the commander as they left the chief's office.

Billy had learned it was easier to get the things he needed when no one else was around. He found the security at most places was easy to defeat. Once he was in the Big T warehouse, he had time to pick and choose the items he wanted. Packaged food was more practical, as it did not spoil like fresh food. He was also more selective in the clothing he took, checking the sizes before taking them. However, he did not have as much time to shop at the Clothes Mart. An alarm went off when he broke the back door. He ran in and quickly grabbed a few pairs of pants and some more XXXL shirts, then left just before the police arrived.

Billy figured he had enough food in the culvert to last him a few days. He was not familiar with a lot of processed food, but he did like it, especially the two bags of Oreo cookies he scarfed down. He washed them down with several cans of soda. He could also change into clean pants. He found the warm-up type pants an athlete might wear with the elastic waistbands to be the most comfortable. He even picked up a beige ventilated wide-brimmed hat to keep the sun off his head and out of his eyes.

Billy still had the desire to have sex with a woman. It was something he'd never done before. He learned about it in his training and first desired to have sex a couple of years ago. However, the few women he had been around were off-limits. He had been promised he would one day be allowed to have sex with someone, but that day never came. Now that he was free to roam wherever he wanted, he could find himself a woman. He was amazed at all the different women he saw on the streets of Amarillo. Some were dressed in nice business suits, while others wore hardly anything at all. He had more interest in tall blond women. With food and clothing taken care of, Billy figured he could spend the next couple of days seeking a mate.

By 11:00 am, the police department had issued a press release describing Billy and listing his suspected crimes. It warned people the suspect was strong and dangerous. Anyone seeing this person was to leave him alone and call the police. The FBI had recently relented and provided the Amarillo Police Department a photograph of Billy. This photo was included with the press release. By noon, all the local TV and radio stations were leading their news programs with this story. The department's public information officer immediately started getting phone calls from the press.

The police chief also got a phone call. This one was from Homeland Security agent Clara Chen. "Chief Boone, why did you release that information? We told you this was a national security matter."

"Yes, but that is about all you told me," responded Boone. "This Billy of yours is starting to wreak havoc on our city, and you were right; he is dangerous. We had to notify the community. We also need their help in finding him to get him off our streets."

"I wish you hadn't done that, Chief. Washington will not be happy about this."

"Washington? What's Washington got to do with this?"

"Do you understand what the Department of Homeland Security does? We protect this country by monitoring other countries and keeping our national security secrets from those countries. We also work with the Department of Defense."

"Alright then, tell me what Billy has or knows that is so important," said Boone.

"Chief, I would like to tell you, but you don't have the clearance needed to know. I understand you need to protect your community, but your community includes the United States."

"I just did what I thought was right, Ms. Chen. I don't know any secrets, so I can't give anything away. All we want is to get Billy whoever, and then you can have him. Just get him out of our city."

"That's what we are trying to do, Chief."

A half-hour later, Laura interrupted the chief to let him know he had another phone call. This time it was the United States Secretary of Defense, Alvin Carter, calling.

"Are you serious?" asked Boone.

"Sorry, Chief, I'm afraid so."

Chief Boone took the phone call. "Hello, Mr. Carter. What can I do for you?"

"Chief Boone," said Carter, "I am calling to impress upon you how important it is that you cooperate with our federal agents in capturing our escapee with as little public acknowledgment as possible."

"With all due respect, Mr. Carter, we've been trying to do that. We are not getting any information about this Billy person, yet we are supposed to protect our community. He is a real pain in our asses out here. I've already had two officers get assaulted, and he's committed several crimes."

"I understand, Chief, but we have interests that go beyond the concerns you have in your city. We will try to get him out of your city as soon as we can. I need your assurance you will downplay this with the press before it gets too much out of hand."

Boone took a deep breath and exhaled. "Look, I'll do what I can not to let it get out of control, but this can't go on for much longer."

"Chief Boone, I appreciate your cooperation. Please follow the guidance of our agents out there. They are only trying to help."

"Can you at least tell me where he came from?"

"No, I can only tell you he escaped from one of our facilities, and he is important to our national security. I will also tell you that once this is over, we never had this discussion."

"Never had this discussion?"

"That's correct," said Carter sharply.

"Alright, Mr. Carter. Thank you for calling."

"You have a good day, Chief."

The chief sat back in his chair and sucked some juice from the snuff packet in his cheek. He kept going over the phone call from the Secretary of Defense. *This thing is more significant than I thought it was. What could be so important about Billy Jones?* Then it came to him. Why hadn't he thought of it earlier? The Department of Energy's Pantex Nuclear Facility was located only twenty miles northeast of Amarillo. It was the only facility of its kind in the United States and was used to assemble and disassemble nuclear weapons. He believed Billy had to be a worker or scientist from the facility who had lost his mind or turned against the United States. The government was probably working on some new nuclear weapon, and Billy threatened to tell the world about it. This had to be why the Department of Defense and Homeland Security were so concerned.

The chief then called his public information officer, Alyssa Reed. "Alyssa, I need you to downplay the Billy story for me."

"Why would we do that?" asked Reed.

"This is important to the feds, and we need to keep everyone calm. Let the public know to stay away from him, but say nothing about the federal government being involved."

"Alright, Chief, I can do that."

"Thank you, Alyssa."

Chief Boone then called Commander Lopez. "Martina, Defense Secretary Alvin Carter called me concerned over too much information getting out about Billy. It all makes sense now. Billy had to have come from the Pantex Nuclear Facility. He probably knows secrets that can't get out."

"That makes some sense," agreed Lopez. "Should I send Webster and Velez out there to get more information?"

"No, I don't think the Department of Defense would appreciate that. However, make sure they know what we are dealing with and make it a priority to find Billy."

"Will do, Chief."

***

It was another hot day in Amarillo, and Billy was tired from being up most of the night. He cleaned himself off in the creek and settled into his makeshift bed in the culvert to rest. Billy would go out later in the day after the temperatures dropped. For now, he needed some rest.

Detectives Webster and Velez continued to work on finding information on a Billy Jones that matched the Billy Jones they were looking for. They were not having much luck. Patrol officers kept their eyes open for anyone matching the description. Once the news story broke, officers had to respond to every call of reported sightings of the suspect. In each case, the person they checked out was not Billy. By 6:00 in the evening, officers had responded to thirty-six reported sightings. It seemed like people were calling on any tall white male who looked strong. Officers occasionally ran into federal agents driving around in their black SUVs. The agents were monitoring police radio traffic and responded to many of the same calls.

Once the sun started to set, Billy thought it was time to go out to find a nice woman who would have sex with him. He knew the police were looking for him, so he had to be careful. He left his culvert dressed in dark blue warm-up pants and a black polo shirt. He thought this would help him hide in the shadows. He also wore his new hat and pulled it low over his forehead. Part of Billy's training included learning how to drive. He figured if he could find a vehicle to use, it would be easier to move around without being recognized.

Billy walked among the trees until he got to the cross street bordering Cottonwood Park. He looked for an opportunity to get a vehicle he could drive, preferably one like those he had been trained on. He was looking for a large SUV.

During his observations of life in the city, Billy had noticed sometimes people would pull up to a store and run in to get something, leaving the car running with someone sitting in the car waiting for the person in the store to return. He believed this presented the best opportunity to get a vehicle. Billy found a place to sit outside a Walgreens to observe the parking lot. He then waited for his chance.

Over the next hour, he saw several people leave their cars running with someone waiting, sometimes even children. Unfortunately for him, none of them had been in a large SUV. Billy remained patient and continued to watch. Finally, a man and woman pulled up and parked a silver Ford Expedition. The driver got out of the Expedition and left it running while the woman waited in the passenger seat. This was his chance. Once the man was inside the store, Billy approached from the passenger side.

Billy flung the passenger door open, startling the middle-aged women inside. "What are you doing!" she exclaimed.

"Get out now," said Billy in a calm voice.

"No, get away from here," said the woman.

Without saying another word, Billy reached into the car, grabbed the woman by her upper right arm, yanked her out of the car, and tossed her to the ground. She immediately screamed.

Billy calmly walked over to the driver's side, got into the vehicle, backed it up, and drove away. Another man who heard the woman screaming ran to her aid.

"Are you alright, ma'am?"

"Yes, but that man just stole our car!"

Billy continued to drive away from the store, knowing the police would come that way. He drove slowly, as he was unfamiliar with driving in cities. Billy had never driven in traffic like this before. It made him nervous, so he looked for streets with less traffic. He wasn't sure where he had gone, but the area was not as pleasant as where he had been staying. It was more run down, and more people were hanging out on the sidewalks, some in dirty clothes sleeping in alleys or against a building. Several bars and nightclubs lined the street. What he did like was that there were a lot of pretty women walking around. Some of them were scantily dressed.

Billy found a side street and parked his SUV. Before getting out, he noticed a purse on the floor of the passenger side. He opened the purse and rummaged through it. To his surprise, he found a pouch inside that contained money. He pulled it out. There were nine bills of cash. Three of them were twenty-dollar bills, two were fives, and four were ones. Billy put these in his pocket. He then got out and walked back toward the street with all the activity.

Once he got there, he was amazed to see the bars and activity. Most of the bars he passed had music playing. A few of the people sitting on the sidewalk asked him for money. He ignored them. He came upon a bar that was playing music that sounded familiar to him. He went inside to see if he could find a suitable woman.

Once inside, he found it loud and difficult to hear with the music and all the talking. He walked up to the bar.

"Yes, sir, what can I get for you?" asked the bartender.

"I'm looking for a woman," said Billy.

"What does she look like?" asked the bartender.

"Tall with blond hair."

"Is she white?"

"Ummm, yeah, white," answered Billy.

"There are a lot of those here. You need to be more specific."

"I want to have sex with her."

The bartender laughed. "Don't we all. What's her name?"

"I don't know; I haven't met her yet."

The bartender was now confused. He thought for a moment. "Are you looking for a hooker?"

"What's that?" Billy asked.

"That's a woman you have sex with."

"Yes, that's what I want," agreed Billy.

"Well, you're in the wrong place," advised the bartender. "You need to go two blocks south of here. There's a place called the Red Rider Pony. Go there, and they can get you what you want."

"Thank you," said Billy. He then left and walked south, looking for a place called the Red Rider Pony. He finally found it on a much darker street with fewer bars. The neon light in the window said Red Rider Pony. He could hear music inside, but the windows were darkened. Billy walked through the door.

The room was dimly lit, and there was a long bar on one side with two topless women dancing on it. Men were sitting on stools along the bar watching the women dance. The rest of the room had small round tables with two chairs at each table. They were about half full of men and a few women. Familiar country music was playing over the sound system. Billy liked it, as it was usually the choice of music at the facility where he had lived.

Billy walked up to the bar and asked the bartender where to find a blond woman for sex. The bartender picked up a two-way radio and said something Billy could not hear over the music. Thirty seconds later, a blond woman in a red bikini top and red mini skirt approached Billy from the hallway that led to the back of the building.

"My, you a big hunk of a man. And so young. Are you that big everywhere?" she asked.

Billy looked at her and just shrugged his shoulders.

"I understand you are here for some fun. Is that right?"

"I'm here because I have a strong desire to have sex," said Billy.

The woman laughed. "You get right to the point, don't you? Follow me."

Billy followed the woman down the hall to a small room with a double bed covered in a red bedspread. There was a small table in the corner with a dimly lit table lamp on it. There were no windows.

"What can I do for you?" asked the woman.

"I told you, I would like to have sex with you."

"That will cost you two hundred dollars cash up front."

"What?"

"I said two hundred dollars cash, sweetie."

"Sex is a natural act between two people. You don't have to pay for sex."

The woman laughed. "Well, you have to pay for THIS sex."

"I'm not paying you," said Billy as he began to take off his pants.

"Whoa, cowboy. I'm not sure what you think this is, but we are not doing this. You need to leave now."

This angered Billy. He had gone to this trouble to find a woman to have sex with him. This woman agreed, and now she was demanding money. He grabbed the woman by the arms. She tried to pull away, but it was no use. "You're hurting me," she shouted.

"I'm not going to hurt you," Billy said as he pushed her onto the bed. He then reached down and ripped off her red skirt. The woman started screaming.

"Get off me! Help me, help me! Larry!" she screamed as loud as she could.

The door quickly opened, and another woman stepped in. "What is going on here? Get off her!"

Billy was feeling rage build up within him. Billy released his grip on the woman in bed and swung his left arm backward with a balled fist, smacking the second woman square in the face, sending her back into the wall. Just then, another relatively large man burst into the room and grabbed Billy around the chest from behind and pulled him off the bed. He attempted to push Billy out the door. This further enraged Billy.

Billy bent forward and down, then reached over his left shoulder with both hands and grabbed the shoulder and elbow of the man on his back. In one quick move, he flipped the man over his shoulder, causing the man to land on his back. The man quickly jumped up and punched Billy in the face, snapping his head backward and causing a slight cut to the inside of his mouth. Blood ran down his chin.

Billy then cocked his right arm, and with one swift blow to the other man's nose, he knocked him back through the door, causing the man to fall backward and hit his head on the opposite wall in the hallway. Billy then walked into the hall, grabbed the man by the shirt collar, and lifted him slightly off the ground. He then reared his right arm back as far as he could before delivering a second blow to the man's face. Blood gushed from the mouth and nose of the now unconscious man. Both women stood in the room screaming at the sight.

Billy knew he had to get out of there. He wiped the blood off his chin and spat the blood in his mouth onto the floor. He then ran down the hall and out the door. Billy did not stop running until he found his Ford Expedition. He got in it and drove off, trying to find his way back to Cottonwood Park.

At the bar, the two women attempted to revive Larry. They could not wake him up. The bartender called for the police and medical help. Upon the arrival of the ambulance EMTs, they recognized the seriousness of Larry's injuries. They immediately put him on a gurney and rushed him to the hospital.

Detective Webster was at home getting ready to go to bed and read a book when he got the call. He quickly got dressed, kissed Eileen goodbye, and headed toward the Red Rider Pony. Detective Velez was visiting Stella Turner when he got the call. He kissed Stella goodbye, then also headed toward The Red Rider Pony.

The crime scene was a mess. There was a lot of blood and multiple witnesses. It would take both detectives several hours to get all the witness statements. Crime scene technicians were called out to process the forensic evidence. They collected blood, saliva, hair samples, and fingerprints.

While finishing up at the scene, Webster received a call from Sergeant Anderson, who had responded to the hospital.

"Alright, thank you for calling," said Webster.

Webster turned to Velez. "We now have a homicide. Our assault victim passed away from severe head trauma. His name was Larry Gamble, a forty-two-year-old white male."

"Sad," replied Velez. "Do you have any doubt our suspect is Billy?"

"No. He matches the description to a T."

Chapter 5

It took a while, but Billy eventually found his way back to his culvert in Cottonwood Park. He took off his bloodstained clothing and disposed of them in a trash can. He then cleaned himself off in the creek. Billy realized he needed to find a better place to live. He would need to find an abandoned home or building for better concealment and protection from the elements. He now believed people on the outside were not very friendly. He had to be ready for anything.

The next morning, Velez and Webster were in early to see if any further information came in overnight. Other than a few false reports of suspect sightings, there was nothing. News of the latest homicide and all the details committed by the suspect, known as Billy, was the top news story of the day. The description of the stolen Expedition had been released to the media as the suspect vehicle. Officers on the street were constantly being asked questions about this mysterious sexual predator and strongman killer.

"The chief believes the only explanation is that our suspect is an ex-employee of the nuclear plant," said Webster. "Why else would the government be so concerned? I believe he may have accidentally been exposed to radiation, and it scrambled his mind."

"You may be right, but how would we find out?" asked Velez.

"We go talk to someone at the facility," suggested Webster.

"I don't think the chief will approve of that," said Velez.

"That's why we won't tell him."

Velez gave Webster a questioning look.

"I know, it's risky," agreed Webster. "If we don't find out anything, no one will have to know. But, if we get information that helps us nab this guy, the chief will overlook it."

Being a new detective, Velez was skeptical. He didn't need to lose his job over this case.

"If something goes wrong, I'll take the blame. I'll tell the chief I coerced you into going."

Reluctantly, Velez agreed. Several minutes later, Webster was driving Velez to the nuclear plant. They were at the front security gate within thirty minutes, asking to speak with the facility director.

"We are detectives with the Amarillo Police Department, and we need to speak to the director about a violent criminal we believe worked at this facility," Webster explained to the armed guard. The guard made a phone call.

"I'm sorry, Detectives, you will have to make an appointment."

"Tell the director this is a matter of public safety, and if he doesn't speak with us, we will be forced to seek a warrant to search the facility."

The guard returned to the security booth and made another phone call. He then came back out. "The director doesn't believe you can get a judge to sign a warrant to search this place."

"Look," said Webster, "we are not trying to create any trouble. We just have a couple of questions about an employee of his. Please tell him that."

The guard made a third phone call. Velez looked at Webster and said, "That bluff certainly didn't work."

"Did you have a better idea?" snapped Webster.

After several minutes, the guard came back. "He says he will see you for only a few minutes. He will meet you in the main lobby."

"Thank you, sir."

The guard opened the gate, and Webster drove to the main entrance. Webster and Velez entered the lobby and were met by a second armed guard sitting at a desk. "The director will meet you here," advised the guard.

Webster and Velez sat down and waited. Ten minutes later, a man dressed in a long white sleeve shirt, red-patterned tie, and black dress pants approached them from the elevator. He had the haircut and walk of someone who looked like they were in the military. He reached out and shook each detective's hand while introducing himself as Robert Krug, the director of Pantex. He then walked them into a small office just off the lobby.

"What can I answer for you today, Detectives?"

"Mr. Krug," started Webster, "we believe a man terrorizing our city was an employee of yours. He is behaving like a madman, and last night he beat someone to death. Federal agents are in our city looking for him and being very secretive. We are trying to get more information so that we can understand what we are dealing with and what his habits might be."

"Why do you think he was one of our employees?"

"Because the FBI, Homeland Security, and the Department of Defense are all concerned about him. We know you assemble weapons here. It makes sense that he either knows something or was exposed to something the government wants to keep secret."

"What is his name?"

"We don't know whether it is his real name, but the feds call him Billy Jones."

"That name doesn't ring a bell to me, and to my knowledge, all our employees are accounted for," said Krug. "Let me make a phone call to personnel."

Krug pulled out his cell phone and dialed. The detectives listened as Krug asked about an employee named Billy Jones. He also asked someone to check under the name William Jones as well. Webster was impressed by Krug's cooperation and willingness to help. Webster overheard Krug also ask if any employees were unaccounted for. After the call, Krug turned his attention back to the detectives.

"I'm sorry, Detectives. I'm afraid we can't help you. No one by that name has ever worked here, and all our employees are accounted for. If one of our employees was out creating problems, I'm sure the government would have contacted us directly, and we haven't heard a word about this."

Webster apologized. "Mr. Krug, I thank you for your time, and sorry to disrupt your day,"

"That's fine, Detective. But next time, please call first."

"Yes, of course," agreed Webster.

On the drive back, Webster couldn't believe Billy Jones was not somehow connected to the nuclear facility. "What other explanation could there be for the government to be after this guy? We know he is not an escapee from Beaumont, and now we know he is not an employee of the nuclear plant."

"Unless they are all lying," suggested Velez.

"That's always possible," said Webster, "but I've been a detective for a long time, and I did not detect any deception from Mr. Krug."

Neither detective said much the rest of the way back. They were both going over the events of the last week in their heads. As Webster turned into the police parking lot, Velez asked, "Do you think Krug will call the chief and tell him we were there?"

"No, but I'm going to tell him."

"Why would you do that?"

"Because I no longer believe the nuclear plant is involved in this, and the chief needs to know that. He still thinks Billy is from that facility."

After they returned to their desks, Webster told Velez he was going up to tell the commander and then tell the chief what they had found out.

"Good luck," said Velez.

"If I still have a job when I get back, how about we go grab some lunch?"

"I'll be here," answered Velez.

Once Webster left, Velez called Stella Turner. "How are you feeling today?"

"Oh, I'm fine," said Turner. "I'll be going to work today for my regular shift. I'm very motivated to find this Billy guy."

"I understand. Just please be careful. I don't want anything to happen to you."

"Don't worry, I'll be cautious with him. I'm looking forward to our night out tomorrow."

"Yes, me too. I'll talk to you sometime tonight. Love you, Stella."

"Love you too. Goodbye now."

After Webster explained to the commander what he had done at the Pantex Nuclear Facility, they both went to explain it to the chief. Webster explained why he had gone and what Director Krug had told him. The chief was upset but understood why Webster wanted to check it out.

"If the feds find out, they won't be happy," said the chief. "But at this point, I don't care. I still think Billy was employed at that plant. I can't think of any other explanation."

"I disagree, Chief," said Webster. "If they were going to lie to me about Billy, it sure as hell wouldn't have been the director who came to talk to me. Do you think he wants to put himself in a position to be accused of lying to law enforcement authorities? No, he would have sent some lowly bottom-tier employee out to talk to us and deny Billy ever worked for them. Then, if it ever became public, he could truthfully say he didn't even talk to us and had no idea the employee talked to us. That's how high-level employees and government officials protect themselves."

"I hadn't thought of it that way," admitted the chief.

"That is why I don't think Billy ever worked there," continued Webster. "It wouldn't make sense for the director to talk to me if he had anything to hide."

"Maybe you're right," admitted Boone. "But what could be so important or dangerous about this man that has the entire government up in arms?"

Webster shrugged his shoulders. "I don't know, Chief."

"Martina," said Boone, "are we doing a press conference today?"

"Yes, sir, at one o'clock today."

Boone leaned over his wastebasket next to his desk and spat out his pouch of snuff. "I'd like you to be the primary speaker today. Say nothing about the federal government's involvement. If they ask, just say they are assisting our investigation, nothing more. But, I want you to stress to the community the potential danger of this individual and ask anyone with information to call us, even if anonymously. Someone out there knows something, and we need to motivate them to come forward."

"I can certainly do that, Chief," responded Lopez.

Webster returned to his desk and looked at Velez. "Are you ready to grab some lunch?"

Velez flashed his big smile. "I guess that means everything went well, and you are still employed here."

"Never in doubt. Is Chuck's Grill fine with you? He has a big TV and will allow us to watch the press conference at one."

"Yeah, I love Chuck's. The burritos are great."

"Then let's go," commanded Webster as he grabbed his signature cowboy hat off his desk.

***

Billy knew he had to find a more secure and safe place to stay. Someone would eventually find him in the culvert, and he wasn't very comfortable living there. During one of his walks exploring the neighborhood, he saw a small storefront several blocks east of Cottonwood Park. There was a sign in the window that said for sale or lease. It appeared the building was vacant. The windows were darkened, which would be perfect for Billy. He figured there would also be a bathroom inside. He planned to break into the back and live there for as long as possible. He first wanted to get a different car, as he knew the police were looking for him. He packed his belongings in preparation for his move.

At 1:00 pm, Webster and Velez were finishing their lunch when the police news conference came up on the TV in Chuck's Grill. They watched as Commander Lopez did an excellent job of describing the concern for the community and stressed how important it was for anyone with any information to come forward. She received some questions about FBI involvement but did a great job of deflecting the questions. As with any major case, she said that the police department appreciated any help the FBI was willing to provide.

Patrol officers were not sure what area of town to focus their efforts. They knew he had been seen in Cottonwood Park several days ago, but no one knew for sure where he might turn up after the assault at the Red Rider Pony, six miles away. However, Officer Turner still believed he was somewhere in the northern neighborhoods of Amarillo. She thought he would return to the area he was most familiar with.

It was now 4:30 pm, and Turner was carefully patrolling her area when she came across the stolen silver Ford Expedition. It was parked on a side street three blocks west of Cottonwood Park.

Just as I thought, he returned to the area. I'm sure he's staying somewhere close by.

Turner called for a tow truck to take the stolen vehicle back to the police department, where crime scene technicians could process it for fingerprints and other evidence. Several other officers responded to help her further search the area. The other officers patrolled in their vehicles while Turner got out on foot and started looking for Billy door to door.

Billy was amazed at what one could find simply by checking out trash barrels and dumpsters. He no longer had to use a makeshift pair of pants as a backpack. He had found a very nice used backpack in someone's trash put out on the street. It was a little dirty but otherwise very functional. He even found an old suitcase in a dumpster that was scratched up but still usable. He now kept his clothes in the suitcase.

He also found several baseball-type hats and a cowboy hat he could use to help alter his appearance. Behind a bakery, he discovered thrown-out pastries that were several days old but still tasty. When he was lucky, he could find fresh produce (at least fresh to him) that had been discarded behind some grocery stores.

Billy still hadn't been able to find shaving cream or razors. His face was now covered with a short stubble beard from not shaving for at least a week. He didn't like the feel but hoped it might help hide his identity. The most significant problem for Billy in remaining unrecognized was his size. It was hard not to be noticed at six foot six and very muscular.

Billy had been watching from his hiding spot and noticed more police cars than usual in the area. He decided to wait until the evening when it would be more difficult to recognize him, and fewer people would be out and about. He would then find another car and move his hideout to the vacant storefront. Besides, it would be cooler at night. Billy was already sweating through his clothing from another scorcher of a day.

Officer Turner continued to search for Billy by walking the streets and talking to people she met. No one had seen him. After a couple of hours, she got a call of a domestic disturbance in her beat. She hustled back to her car to respond. She was happy to get the call. Her feet were tired, her undershirt was soaked with sweat, and her lower back was aching from the weight of her equipment belt resting against the bruise on her back. She was surprised she lasted as long as she did.

Once it was dark, Billy left his culvert to look for another vehicle. He hoped he could take one this time without being seen. The night air was still hot, but at least the sun was not beating down on him. On this night, he wore a baseball cap pulled down low over his eyes.

It didn't take as long this time for Billy to find a vehicle. He was walking down a nearby residential street when he observed a man load his pickup truck with a couple of boxes, then start the truck. The man put the truck into reverse, then stopped and put it back into park. He got out and ran back into the house, leaving the engine running. Billy ran to the truck, jumped into the driver's seat, and backed out of the driveway. By the time the man came back out, the driveway was vacant. "What the hell...." said the owner out loud to no one.

Billy was happy with his new vehicle. It was a white GMC truck. It had plenty of room for his large-framed body. Billy quickly drove to the park. He gathered the belongings he wanted to take and dumped everything else into the creek. He put his stuff into the truck's back seat and then drove toward the vacant shop on Bishop Street.

Officer Turner had just finished a small dinner and was on the phone with Detective Velez. "Nothing much is going on tonight," she told him. "No sign of Billy. My only significant call has been a domestic between a drunk couple arguing over something the woman's teenage son had done."

"Did you arrest anyone?" asked Velez.

"No, it hadn't gotten to that point yet, but it would have if we hadn't gotten there. A neighbor heard screaming and called us. Where are you taking me to dinner this weekend?"

"I was thinking about the famous Big Texan Steak Ranch. You ever been there?"

"Only on a couple of calls. Never to eat there."

"You're kidding me? Oh, you must try it. The place has fantastic steaks."

"I've heard it's good; I just rarely eat that much."

"The food is good, and it's a fun place to be."

"Oops, I've got to go," interjected Turner. "Just got a call about a stolen truck. I'll talk to you tomorrow."

"Okay, goodnight, Stella."

Turner responded to the call and met with the owner. The owner told her he had been loading some tools to take to a friend's house when he realized he had forgotten his wallet. He put the truck into park and briefly ran back into his house. He found his wallet in his bedroom, then came right back out. When he came out, the truck was gone. He didn't see anyone.

It wasn't much to go on, but Turner suspected the thief was Billy Jones. She put the information on the truck, a white GMC pickup with Texas plates, out over the police radio. There was not much else for her to do but look for the truck.

Billy had no trouble defeating the padlock on the back of the vacant store. Once inside, he was pleasantly surprised to see it had been cleaned out and there were two bathrooms. They both still had running water. Even the lights worked. Billy had hit the jackpot. He unloaded his belongings and set them in a back corner of the store. He then put on a light blue polo shirt and dark blue warm-up pants. It was now time to have some fun.

After the fight with the bouncer at the Red Rider Pony, Billy's urge to fight and desire for sex had waned, as though his inbred instincts had been satisfied. However, it had been a couple of days since the incident, and he was starting to feel antsy again. His desire for sex or physical combat was growing. He set out into the night to see what he could find.

Chapter 6

Billy drove for a while, looking for anything he might find interesting. He eventually came across some type of street festival. It looked like several blocks had been barricaded, and the street was full of people. Many were walking, some were standing in groups, and others were dancing. He could hear a band playing country music from somewhere in the crowd.

Billy had to drive several blocks before he found a parking lot with a few spaces still open. He walked the three blocks back to the festival and walked past the barricades. A few people glanced his way, and he could tell they were impressed with his size. But no one seemed to care. After walking a block through the crowd, Billy could see the stage where the band was playing. It was a six-person country band with both a female and male singer. Billy listened for a short time, then moved on.

He came across a tent from which beer was being served. Billy had never tried alcohol, but he was curious. He walked up to the temporary bar and asked for a beer.

"What kind?" shouted the barkeep above the noise of the crowd.

"Just beer," shouted Billy back.

"I know, but what kind? We have light beer, full beers, an amber, a dark, and even an apricot."

"I don't care. Just give me a beer."

"Okay." The barkeep poured Billy a regular full beer and handed it to him. "That will be six dollars."

Billy just looked at him. "What?"

The barkeep shouted louder, "That will be six dollars."

Billy remembered he had some money he had found. He reached into his pocket and handed the barkeep a twenty-dollar bill. He then turned to walk away.

"Hold on there, let me get your change."

Billy stopped and waited until the barkeep handed Billy a ten-dollar bill and four ones. Billy stuffed the money in his pocket and walked away.

He walked a short distance away and stopped to try his new drink. He took a large swallow. It didn't taste terrific, but everyone else seemed to enjoy it, so he continued to drink. As he did so, it began to taste better. When finished, he decided to get another and approached the same barkeep.

"Give me another one," shouted Billy.

"Same thing?" asked the barkeep.

"Yeah."

"Here you go. That will be another six dollars."

"I have to pay again?"

The barkeep laughed. "Well, yeah, it's not all you can drink for six dollars."

Billy did not like the barkeep laughing at him. "Why do you have to pay for everything in this town?" he shouted. "You even have to pay for sex!"

"Hey, man, just give me the six bucks, okay?"

Billy could feel anger building up inside of him, but he controlled a desire to punch the barkeep, and instead, he reached into his pocket, pulled out some more money, and laid it on the bar. The barkeep counted out six dollars and pushed the rest of the money back to Billy.

This time, Billy chugged the beer down. He went back to the bar and asked the barkeep for another beer.

"Hey man, you are drinking way too fast," shouted the barkeep. "Why don't you wait twenty minutes, and then I will get you another one."

"Give me another beer," said Billy as he glared at the barkeep.

The barkeep could see Billy was getting angry and, from the size of him, the barkeep did not want to upset him.

"Here you go. It's on the house. But that is your last one for a while."

Billy didn't know what the barkeep meant by on the house, so he reached into his pocket, took out another twenty, and laid it on the bar. The barkeep took the money and gave Billy fourteen dollars back.

Billy quickly downed his third beer in five minutes and walked away to look for something more interesting. He found some dancers in the middle of the street dancing to the band's country music. They were dancing in circles and twirling each other around. Billy studied the dancing for about fifteen minutes trying to figure out the steps. He thought he would like to try it.

As he was standing there, he felt a strange sensation in his head, which made him somewhat dizzy. *I've never felt like this before*, he thought. He shook his head. It seemed to help some. He then saw a beautiful tall blond woman in a blue cowgirl outfit and a white cowboy hat standing to the side, watching. He had seen her dancing earlier.

I want to try dancing with her, he thought to himself. He approached the woman and said, "come dance with me."

The woman looked at Billy and was impressed with his size. She found him not exactly dressed for the occasion, but she was there to have fun, so why not. She took his hand and walked into the street with Billy.

Billy tried to imitate the dancing he had observed, but it was hard to remember all the steps. To the woman, it was obvious he did not know what he was doing. She tried to lead him. He began twirling her around, sometimes lifting her off her feet.

"Slow down, cowboy," protested the woman.

"Just hang on," Billy said. "I'm going to give you the dance of your life."

He grabbed her around the waist, lifted her, and spun her rapidly in the air. She tried to get out of his grasp, but he was too strong. People watching were laughing, surprised, or horrified.

"Please stop!" the woman cried out. "You're hurting me!"

Someone in the crowd then shouted out, "Hey! That's the guy the police are looking for! Grab him!"

Some women started to scream. Someone else yelled, "Stop him!"

Several men stepped forward from the crowd to rescue the woman being twirled like a ragdoll. Three men grabbed onto Billy, causing him to release his grip on the woman. She fell to the ground, then quickly got up and ran away.

The three men attempted to take Billy to the ground. Someone yelled, "call the police!"

Panic spread through the crowd as more people started screaming and running, knocking some people to the ground. Billy became enraged that these men were attacking him. He began to swing his arms violently and started kicking at the men. One by one, Billy was throwing them off his body. One came back at Billy and ran right into a left-handed haymaker punch from Billy, knocking him unconscious. The other two men then backed off. Another man came running at Billy with a two-by-four piece of lumber and swung it, giving Billy a body blow to his left side. Billy flinched, but it did not stop him. He grabbed the board out of the poor man's hands and swung it overhead, crashing it down on top of the man's right shoulder so hard the bones in the shoulder were crushed. The man collapsed in the street, screaming in pain. Most people now began to run, creating a stampede through the festival.

Police had been called. Several were at the festival, and they were trying to make their way through the crowd. However, it was like a fish trying to swim upriver. People were running away from Billy while the officers were trying to run in the opposite direction. Sirens of more officers coming could be heard in the background. One of those officers was Stella Turner.

Billy stood and looked around at the fleeing crowd of people. He knew the police would be there soon. Billy left the two injured men lying in the street and started to run in the direction where he believed his truck was parked. Once he got through the crowd, it was easier to maneuver. He thought he was getting close to his truck when two police cruisers pulled up in front of him with bright lights blinding him. Within seconds, a third cruiser pulled up, this one being driven by Officer Turner. She was determined not to let him get away this time.

"Freeze! Put your hands on top of your head!" yelled one of the male officers. The officers had their handguns pointed at the suspect. However, they could see he was not armed with a weapon. Turner quickly ran scenarios through her head. I don't want to shoot an unarmed man, she thought. She holstered her duty weapon and pulled out her taser.

"I have a taser!" she shouted to her fellow officers.

"Put your hands up!" the male officer continued to shout.

Billy stared at the bright lights, not knowing how to respond. He did not want to go to jail, nor did he want to go back to the place he had lived his whole life.

"Just let me go, officers, and I will leave," shouted Billy.

"We can't do that, Billy," said one officer.

"He's not armed," said Turner. "Keep me covered, and I will walk up closer and tase him."

"Alright, but be careful, Stella."

The two male officers kept their guns sighted on Billy. Turner slowly approached, telling Billy to put his hands up or be tased. Billy was not sure what that meant. Billy turned and started to walk away.

"Don't let him get away!" shouted one of the officers. "Tase him!"

Turner ran a few steps closer and let loose with her taser, hitting Billy squarely in the back. Billy tensed up as the voltage coursed through his back muscles. Billy was temporarily paralyzed and shaking at the same time. He dropped to his knees, unable to overcome the electrical current. The two male officers ran up to Billy, ready to handcuff him once the electrical current stopped.

When the current stopped, the release of muscle tension caused him to fall forward. Both male officers jumped on the back of Billy to hold his arms as Turner rushed up with her handcuffs. The officers tugged on Billy's arms to put them behind his back. They were so muscular, it was hard to get them back far enough to put the cuffs on. Turner wasn't even sure they would fit around his wrists.

The officers kept tugging. While they were doing this, Billy was recovering from the electrical shock. Once he realized he was about to be handcuffed, he yelled in a deep, canyon-like voice, pulled his arms in, and pushed himself up off the ground with both officers on his back. The officers let go and again reached for their guns. Turner fumbled for her taser to give him another dose of electricity. At the same time, federal agents were trying to make their way through the crowds to find Billy and the officers.

Billy screamed again in his low, guttural voice. "Just leave me alone!" The officers took a few steps back, hoping Turner could get another shot. As she raised the taser, Billy charged at them.

One officer fired two rapid rounds toward the torso of Billy. He didn't even slow down. He knocked the officer who shot at him onto his back and then picked up the second officer and threw him onto the hood of his police car. Turner dropped her taser and reached for her handgun. By the time she leveled it at Billy, there were too many other people around. She was afraid of harming an innocent bystander. Billy continued to run into the darkness.

Turner rushed to the officer who had been thrown onto his car to see if he was injured. "I'll be okay," he said. "I'm sure I'll be sore tomorrow." She then checked on the second officer, and he was fine as well.

More patrol cars pulled up, and two federal agents Turner had not seen before approached them, huffing and puffing. "Did you get him?" one asked.

"Almost," said Turner. "We almost had him handcuffed, but he recovered before we could get his arms behind his back."

"We heard gunshots."

"Yes, I think I shot him," said the officer who shot his gun. "I could swear I had my gun pointed right into his chest. But if I did, it didn't stop him from running away."

An all-points bulletin was issued for Billy with the information that he may be suffering from gunshot injuries.

Billy ran as fast as he could to escape the police. He stayed in the shadows close to buildings. As Billy got further away, he found himself in a neighborhood of single homes and apartment complexes. He was tired and bleeding. Billy found a large hedge in front of a two-story brick home. He crawled behind the hedge, lying down along the front of the house. He rested there while waiting for the police to stop looking for him. He observed several patrol cars cruise by with spotlights shining between the homes. One beam of light swept the front of the hedge. The thickness of the hedge protected Billy from being seen, and he soon fell asleep.

While other officers were searching for Billy, Officer Turner and the two officers involved in the shooting had been taken to police headquarters to write up their reports and then be interviewed by members of the Police Shooting Investigative Team. This was a multi-agency team of investigators organized to investigate all officer-involved shootings. The team included investigators from the Potter County Sheriff's Department, the Randall County Sheriff's Department, the Amarillo Police Department, and both the Potter County and Randall County District Attorney Offices. Some team members responded to the sight of the shooting to process the scene and interview witnesses. Other members responded to the Amarillo Police Department to interview those officers involved. It was going to be a long night for Officer Turner.

Almost two hours after the shooting, Billy woke up startled from a dream. In his dream, he had been strapped down on a bed with doctors sticking needles in his arms. He had beads of sweat on his forehead, and the front of his shirt was soaked in blood. He knew he had been shot and probably needed some medical attention.

He wasn't sure how long he slept, but it was still dark out. The evening air was no longer filled with noise from the festival. Billy reasoned it was safe to go home now. He crawled out of the hedge and started looking for his truck. It took him some time, but he eventually found it where he had parked it. He got into the truck and drove toward his hideout in the abandoned store. Along the way, Billy came upon an all-night urgent care medical facility.

Billy parked outside the facility and watched for a few minutes. It didn't look like anyone was inside, other than a nurse at the front desk. Maybe he could get someone to mend his wounds.

Billy walked inside and approached the front desk. The nurse looked up. "Oh, my goodness, what happened to you?"

"I'm hurt," is all Billy said.

"Come on back, and let's take a look at you."

The nurse took Billy to an examining room. "Wait here, and I will get the doctor."

"How many people are here tonight," asked Billy.

"Just me and Doctor Bakshi."

The nurse left the room and soon came back with Dr. Bakshi. "Hello, I'm Doctor Bakshi. What happened tonight?"

"I think I was shot."

"Shot? How were you shot?"

"Some people on the street attacked me."

"Let me take a look," said Dr. Bakshi as he lifted Billy's shirt. "Wow, it looks like you have two gunshot wounds to your abdomen and chest. We need to get you to the hospital."

"NO," said Billy in a loud voice. "Fix me up here."

The doctor looked at Billy. "We can't do surgery here. This is an urgent care facility for minor injuries. You have to go to the hospital."

The nurse started to leave the room to call an ambulance.

"Stay here!" shouted Billy. "No one leaves this room."

"I'm going to call an ambulance for you," said the nurse.

"No, if you leave this room, I will kill the doctor, and then I will kill you. Fix me up here and do it quickly."

The doctor and nurse stood still and stared in disbelief at what Billy had just said. "You can't be serious," said Dr. Bakshi.

"I've never been more serious. I'm hurt, I'm tired, and I'm angry at the people in this town." Billy stood up and grabbed the doctor's left hand, bending it back toward his forearm. The pain caused the doctor to buckle his knees.

"You're hurting me," grimaced the doctor.

"Then you fix me, or I break your wrist right now."

"Okay, okay, whatever you want," pleaded Dr. Bakshi.

The nurse just stood silent in fear. "Get over here and help the doctor," ordered Billy.

The nurse stepped closer.

"Get me some gauze, a scalpel, large tweezers, lidocaine, and anti-septic," ordered Dr. Bakshi.

The nurse gathered the supplies from a cabinet and placed them on a metal tray.

Dr. Bakshi inspected the entry wounds. One entry wound was on the lower right chest. A second entry wound was in the softer abdomen area, centered approximately two inches below the ribcage. Dr. Bakshi tried to give Billy a shot of lidocaine, but the needle bent.

"You have some of the toughest muscle mass I've ever seen," said Dr. Bakshi. "Linda, will you get me a thicker needle, please? I'm guessing you work out all the time."

Billy ignored the comment.

Dr. Bakshi tried a second time to administer the lidocaine. It was still hard to insert the needle, but he could get it in far enough to administer the drug. Dr. Bakshi then used a probe to feel inside the entry wounds. To his surprise, the bullets were just below the surface of the skin. The bullet in the chest was resting against a rib. The bullet in the abdomen was slightly deeper, but still not deep enough to completely penetrate the muscle tissue or damage any organs.

"What is your name?" asked Dr. Bakshi.

"Billy."

"Billy what?"

"Just Billy."

"Well, Billy, you are fortunate. Your extreme muscle mass helped stop the bullets and protect your organs. Hitting your rib also helped. Linda, I'm going to need a thicker needle to stitch him up."

Dr. Bakshi used his large tweezers to reach into each wound and pull out the bullets. He then stitched the wounds and applied antiseptic. "That should do it, Billy. We've done what you asked us to do. What now?"

"You wait in this room until I am gone."

"We can do that," Dr. Bakshi assured him.

With that, Billy put his bloody shirt back on and walked out the door. He got in his truck and drove himself home.

Once they were sure he was gone, Dr. Bakshi called the police to report the incident.

Chapter 7

After Officer Turner had been interviewed by investigators and completed her reports, her shift was over. She called Velez and woke him up.

"Hey, what's the matter?" asked Velez.

"Sorry to wake you, but we found Billy tonight at the Summer Music Festival."

"You did? Is he in custody?"

"No, but we shot him."

"Is he dead?"

"No. I got him with a taser, and we almost had him arrested, but he recovered before we could get handcuffs on him. He then charged at us, and Miller shot him two times."

"That didn't stop him?"

"He kept running right past us."

"Maybe Miller missed him."

"Nope. Officers received a call later from an urgent care facility where Billy had stopped for treatment. He told the doctor and nurse he would kill them if they didn't treat him."

"Wow. Are you okay, Stella?"

"I'm okay, just shaken up some. Would you mind if I came to your place? I could use a hug."

"Yes, yes, of course. Come right over."

"Thank you. I'll be there in twenty minutes."

Turner spent the rest of the night with Velez. In the morning, Velez allowed Turner to keep sleeping while he fixed some breakfast. He thought it was important to spend the day with Turner, so he called Commander Lopez to ask for the day off.

"I'm sorry, Alec, we need you to come in," advised Lopez. "As you can imagine, it is crazy busy here this morning. We have almost everyone doing something on this case now, and the press won't leave us alone. Webster is already here, and I gave him a tip we received from crime stoppers after the shooting last night. An unknown caller said we needed to talk to Doctor Darren Bradford, who works at G.E.H.R. and Technology Institute. I was hoping you could help Webster run that down."

"Alright, can you give me an hour? I want to be sure Stella is up and feeling well before I leave. I can be in by nine-thirty."

"That will be fine. Webster is doing some research on Doctor Bradford now."

"Thank you, Commander."

Velez finished cooking breakfast, then went in to check on Turner. She was lying in bed, awake.

"How are you feeling?" asked Velez.

"Much better."

"I was going to take the day off to be with you, but the commander needs me to go in. Things are hectic right now."

"Don't worry about me. I'll be fine. I still plan on going to work this afternoon."

"Well, get up then. I've got hot coffee and breakfast ready for you."

"Really? What did you fix?"

"A sausage egg scramble with onions and green pepper, and pancakes."

"Sounds delicious. Thank you, Alec."

After breakfast, Velez got dressed and left Turner in his apartment while he went to work. He arrived at 9:35 am.

"Where have you been?" asked Webster.

"I wanted to spend some time with Stella."

"Yeah, I know. The commander told me. I was just giving you a hard time. She told you about this crime stopper's tip, right?"

"Yes, do you think it is important?"

"It might be. I did some research on Doctor Darren Bradford. He works at the G.E.H.R. and Technology Institute. It's not clear what he does for them, but his background is in genetics. Bradford is a fifty-one-year-old white male and a graduate of Massachusetts Institute of Technology, otherwise known as M.I.T. He has a doctorate degree and was one of the researchers who worked on the Genome Project."

"Didn't that have something to do with human genetics?"

"Yes. It was an international research effort to determine the DNA sequencing of the entire human genome. They identified and mapped all the known human genes."

"That was quite a while ago, wasn't it?"

"The project concluded in two-thousand-three."

"Isn't the institute the gated facility north of here?"

"Yep, that's the place. It's about fifteen miles northwest of here. It's a large white facility surrounded by chain-link fencing and barbed wire. They do research of some type. I've already called them and asked for an appointment to see Doctor Bradford. I'm still waiting for a response."

"If this has anything to do with Billy, I doubt he will talk to us," said Velez.

"However, if it has nothing to do with Billy, he should be willing to talk to us just like Robert Krug at the nuclear plant."

It was ten o'clock when Billy awoke in his abandoned store. Other than being shot, the previous night's activities had been a good release of his built-up desire for heavy physical activity or sex. He realized the release of this energy was good for him, as it allowed him to feel normal for a short time. Other than the soreness from the gunshot wounds, Billy was feeling well. He ate the last of his food supply, knowing he would have to go out that night to find some more.

Commander Lopez called Webster and Velez into her office. "The chief wants to know where you are on Doctor Bradford."

"Still waiting to hear if he will meet with us," said Webster.

The commander started rubbing the temple on the right side of her head.

"Are you okay, Commander?" asked Velez.

"Yes, just trying to figure out how to juggle all the work we have to do today. We have about sixty witnesses who have come forward from the festival. They all saw the assault on the men who tried to intervene with his dancing. This town is going crazy with fear right now."

"How are those two men doing?" asked Webster.

"One had a busted-up shoulder and needed surgery. He has been admitted. The other suffered some fractures in his facial bones. He was released this morning but will need some follow-up work. Oh, I almost forgot, we got some results back on the DNA testing of the blood and saliva collected from the floor at the Red Rider Pony. Here is the report." She handed the report to Webster.

Webster took a few minutes scanning the report. "This doesn't match anyone in the database?"

"I'm afraid not," answered the commander. "We can't seem to catch a break."

"This is strange," said Webster. "It says here that one of the DNA markers is not consistent with known human DNA. What does that mean?"

"I assume it means there is a mixture with some type of animal DNA."

"I'll call the analyst to see if he has any further information," said Webster. "And we'll let you know when and if we talk to Doctor Bradford."

"Thank you, Jack."

Back at their desks, Velez asked to see the DNA report. Webster handed it to him.

After reading it over, Velez stated, "normally they can say if animal DNA is mixed with human DNA. This report doesn't say that."

"That's why I'm calling Seagram right now," declared Webster.

"Hello, this is Nate Seagram. How may I help you?"

"Nate, Detective Webster here."

"Hello, Detective."

"I have a question for you. Your report indicates there is a DNA marker not consistent with human DNA. Does this mean there is animal DNA in the mix?"

"No, otherwise, I would have put that in the report. This DNA has the characteristic of being human, but it doesn't fit what we've ever seen previously in human DNA. In layman's terms, it looks like an alteration or mutation."

"You've never seen that before?"

"Not like this. There have been natural mutations discovered that have given humans special characteristics. For example, there are a few people without fingerprints. This is caused by a defective or mutated gene."

"So, this is a naturally occurring process?"

"It can be."

"You said can be. Does that mean it might not be natural?"

"The markers of this person's genome are so unique, I question whether it occurred naturally."

"Are you saying someone could have altered a human's genetic code?"

"Well, it's already been done in some experiments. We know the Chinese have been working on DNA alteration for years. Do you remember reading about the birth in 2018 of the twin girls in China that were created from edited genes?"

"Yes, I vaguely remember hearing about that."

"Many scientists believe gene-altering will eventually be available to produce humans with certain desired characteristics. Right now, however, it is not ethically acceptable to do so."

"Alright, thank you, Nate."

"What did he say?" asked Velez.

"He said there had been some alteration or mutation of this person's DNA."

"Alteration? Is that even possible?"

"According to Nate, scientists are already experimenting with it."

Just then, Webster's phone rang. "Detective Webster."

"Yes, thank you, Doctor, for calling me back. That's correct. We would appreciate that. We can be there in thirty minutes."

"That was Doctor Bradford. He will talk to us at the research facility."

"Which means he doesn't know Billy," stated Velez.

"Yeah, he will probably have no idea what we are talking about."

The detectives arrived at the G.E.H.R. and Technology Institute thirty minutes later. The institute sat on a plateau overlooking the Canadian River Valley. It was approximately fifteen miles north of Amarillo and three miles west of Highway 87. The road from Highway 87 to the facility was a two-lane asphalt road that led to an eight-foot chain-link gate with barbed wire strung across the top. A guard booth was just outside the gate. Webster stopped and rolled down his window.

"May I help you, sir?" asked the guard.

Webster showed the guard his identification. "Yes, we have an appointment to see Dr. Bradford."

"I've been expecting you. Drive forward a quarter-mile, and you will see a sign that says visitor parking. Park there and then go through the double glass doors covered by the extended roof. The receptionist will help you out."

"Thank you," said Webster.

Once they entered the building, the receptionist greeted them in a friendly manner and then escorted them down a long hallway and into Dr. Bradford's office suite. A secretary sat in the reception area and offered the detectives a drink. Both politely declined.

After only a few minutes, Dr. Bradford stepped out and invited them into his office. The office was lavishly decorated, and there appeared to be several diplomas hanging on the walls, along with various awards. Dr. Bradford directed the detectives to sit in two oversized brown leather chairs facing his desk.

Dr. Bradford's brown hair was thinning, and much of it was already gray. He wore light beige plastic-framed glasses and a white lab jacket over a soft blue button-down shirt. In addition to his name, the name tag on the lab jacket listed his title as Director of Genetic Research.

Detective Webster briefly explained the situation with Billy Jones, the danger he presented to the community, and the tip they received from crime stoppers. Webster explained he hoped the doctor had some information on Billy to help them get him into custody.

"I'm sorry, Detective, but I don't know a Billy Jones."

Webster then handed Dr. Bradford the photograph provided by the FBI. "Does this person look familiar?"

"No."

"What about anyone who worked here who matches his description?"

"No, I've never seen anyone like that here."

"Dr. Bradford, our lab technician believes Billy has some genetically altered DNA. You do DNA research here. One might think Billy came from this facility."

"There are various ways a person might have a mutated gene. Mutated genes are what cause some of the deformities and diseases humans are born with."

"Yes, but this person seems to have superhuman strength."

"Have you looked into the possibility of steroid use?"

"We haven't, but he seems to be beyond that. It's something we will investigate if we ever catch him. I was hoping you could help us. He has already killed a man and injured others."

"I wish I could, Detective."

"Exactly what type of research do you do here?"

"We look for the genetic causes of disease."

"Doctor, an anonymous caller told us you would know something about Billy. He is going to hurt more people if we do not get a handle on this. Even if you tell us confidentially, just give us something to proceed with."

"I know nothing, Detective. But if I think of something, I will call you."

"Doctor," said Velez, "what does G.E.H.R. stand for?"

"Genetic Experimental Human Research."

"That sounds like altering DNA to me," said Webster.

Bradford laughed. "We only do research on preventing disease. Creating a human superman is fantasy. It would also be illegal."

"What about the Chinese? They are not guided by the same ethical standards we are."

"I've heard of ongoing experimentation in China. They won't admit it because of worldwide ethical concerns. There are lots of things the Chinese are doing in science that we would not do here."

"Do you think the Chinese might have created Billy?"

"I suppose it's possible."

"One more question. How is your research funded?"

"Private donations. And before you ask, we do not divulge that information."

"Thank you for seeing us today. Here is my card. Call if you can think of anything else."

"I will, and you are more than welcome."

As they were driving back, Webster asked Velez what his thoughts were.

"He answered every question. You said if he were involved, he wouldn't even meet with us."

"Yeah, that's what I said."

"Have you changed your mind?"

"I'm not sure yet. But something doesn't feel right."

***

As expected, Officer Turner showed up for her scheduled shift at 3:00 pm. She believed Billy had gotten comfortable in his surroundings in north Amarillo and was hopeful she could once again find him. Her first stop was the location of the Summer Music Festival. The festival had been scheduled to go another night. After the assaults and shooting, the remainder of the festival was canceled. City crews had most of the clean-up completed. Turner then drove to the spot where Billy had been shot. By now, all the crime scene tape had been removed. Turner got out of her patrol car and stood looking at the spot where she tased Billy. She re-lived the events in her head, wondering if they could have done something differently.

At 4:30 pm, Webster received a call from an unknown number on his cell phone. He answered the call.

"This is Darren Bradford. If you follow my instructions, I will talk to you."

"Uh, sure, what are your instructions?"

"Do you know where Cadillac Ranch is?"

"Yes."

"Go there tonight at ten o'clock. It will be dark, and no one will be there. Wear only shorts and a t-shirt. I will check for a wire. If you come wired, I will say nothing. I will be wearing a Texas Rangers baseball hat."

"Can I bring Detective Velez?"

"No. Only you. This is your only chance. Meet me at the end of the row, behind the last Cadillac."

"Why....." before Webster could say anything more, Bradford hung up.

"Velez," said Webster, "that was Doctor Bradford. He wants to meet me tonight at Cadillac Ranch to talk."

Velez had a look of shock on his face.

"I told you I had a feeling," boasted Webster. "Oh, I can only wear shorts and a t-shirt. And he emphasized no wire."

"What the hell?" responded Velez. "I'm going with you."

"No, you can't. Bradford emphasized he would only meet with me."

"Jack, this could be a setup. You need me there as backup."

Webster thought for a moment. "Okay, we will arrive early, and you can hide in the cotton field watching with binoculars. You only come out if I'm physically attacked."

"I can do that."

After the sunset, Billy decided to go out to find food and more action. His urge for excitement was building. Finding a car tonight was easy. He came across a blue Chevy truck parked at a convenience store with the motor running. He jumped in the driver's seat, and off he went. His first stop was the dumpster behind his favorite bakery shop. Sure enough, he found more disposed pastries. He filled a box and put it in the truck. Billy then drove until he saw a small, independent grocery store that had closed for the night. He smashed out the glass in the door and walked in. He found a box and started filling it with food items. He hurried, knowing the police would be there soon.

Billy returned to his truck with a box of new food items as he heard sirens getting closer. He calmly drove off seconds before the police arrived. The police no longer worried him, but he would rather not have to deal with them given a choice. Now it was time to have some fun. He was in the mood for some more fighting.

Webster and Velez arrived at Cadillac Ranch at 9:30 pm. Webster was dressed in shorts and a Texas Rangers t-shirt to match Bradford's baseball cap. He was also wearing his signature light brown cowboy hat. They scouted the area and picked a location in the adjacent cotton field where Velez could hide and still view the meeting area. Velez was in place by 9:40. Webster stood at the last buried Cadillac, waiting for Bradford.

Cadillac Ranch is a tourist attraction west of the city off Interstate 40. It comprises 10 Cadillacs buried nose-first in the ground in an open field. They were buried in 1974 by a small group of artists who called themselves the Ant Farm. One attraction is that tourists are allowed to spray paint graffiti on the cars. The cars have been painted thousands of times.

It wasn't long before Webster saw a car pull into the parking area. Someone got out of the car and started walking toward the buried Cadillacs. As he got closer, Webster could see he was wearing a baseball cap. Once he was sure who it was, Webster called out, "Good evening, Doctor Bradford." There was no response. Webster slid his hand to his back waistband and placed his hand on his gun.

Bradford walked up to Webster and reached for something in his pocket. Webster started to pull out his gun. *Here we go,* he thought.

"Hold it right there," said Webster. "What do you have in your pocket?"

Bradford did not answer, but held his hand up to his ear with his pinky finger and thumb extended, the hand symbol for a telephone.

"Slowly," said Webster.

Bradford slowly pulled his cell phone from his pocket. He then typed a message on his phone and held it up for the detective to read. It read, *"Lift your t-shirt so I can check for a wire."*

Webster frowned, then reluctantly lifted his t-shirt, exposing his bare chest underneath. Bradford then typed another message. It read, *"Now drop your shorts."*

"There's no way I'm dropping my shorts!" objected Webster.

Bradford shrugged and turned to walk away.

"Hold on here," said Webster. "I came all the way out here to talk. Now talk to me."

Bradford shook his head and pointed to Webster's shorts.

"Damn it," growled Webster as he unbuckled his belt and dropped his shorts. He had to hold his gun to keep it from falling. Bradford walked around the detective, checking for wires.

Velez, who was observing this through his binoculars, wondered *what in the hell is going on? Is Webster in trouble?* He decided to wait.

Bradford nodded, indicating Webster could pull his shorts up. He typed another message. *"Now, take your hat off."*

Webster took off his hat and showed Bradford the inside.

"Now shut off your phone," he typed.

Webster took his cell phone from his back pocket and turned it off.

Bradford finally spoke. "Thank you, Detective. Sorry about that. I had to be sure you weren't trying to record what I have to say."

"It better be good," Webster grunted.

"I've been following what has been happening in town with Billy. It's gotten to where I can no longer be silent. He has to be stopped."

"So, you know Billy?" said an impatient Webster.

"This is top secret stuff I'm about to tell you. You can never use my name. If you do, I will deny even meeting with you, and the feds will discredit you. I also recorded our conversation in my office, which I would release to discredit your story. Even with all that, if the feds suspected I gave information, I would be in serious trouble, maybe even imprisoned. Therefore, I need to protect myself. I trust you will tell no one."

Webster studied Bradford for a few seconds. "I won't tell anyone," assured Webster.

"We call the person you are looking for, Billy. He has no official last name. He was born and raised in our facility, and until recently, he never left the facility. He is a genetically altered human being. He is officially called Billy X23P."

"What the hell are you guys doing up there?" said an incredulous Webster.

"The federal government has tasked us to conduct genetic engineering experiments to create stronger, more resilient humans for national security reasons."

"What would the national security interests be in a modified human?" asked Webster.

"The Chinese have been working on genetic engineering for years. We believe they are ahead of us in this area. They are attempting to create stronger, faster, more intelligent humans for military service. The United States Military and our government are concerned. The American public is not ready to accept genetic engineering on ethical principles. However, if we stand by and wait, the Chinese will be so far advanced, we may never catch up. Thus, we have this top-secret research sanctioned by the highest levels of government."

Webster was shocked by what he was hearing.

"Billy is the result of our research and experimentation. We believe he is stronger and faster than any other human on the planet. However, we are not sure what the Chinese have developed."

"Has Billy been educated and received training?"

"Yes, he has been educated and militarily trained from the day he was born."

"Doctor," said Webster, "he seems to be very violent. Was he raised to be violent?"

"No, that is a side effect of the DNA alteration that we have not perfected. In the facility, Billy was receiving hormone treatments to control his violent tendencies. If not regulated, he also has a strong sexual desire."

"Yes, we've noticed that. He's already tried to rape a woman and has killed a man."

"I'm aware of that," said Bradford. "That is the reason I have come to you. The longer he is off his treatment, he may become increasingly violent."

"More violent?"

"That's a possibility. We really don't know."

"How did he leave the facility?"

"We found the door to the loading dock broken. We believe Billy got out by hiding in a delivery truck."

"What does the C23P stand for in his name?"

"There are twenty-three chromosomes in the human body, each containing genetic code. In males, they have the X and Y chromosome. We have altered the DNA on the Y chromosome and renamed it the P chromosome in Billy."

"Who is the mother of Billy?" asked Webster.

"Even I don't know that. It was a woman used as a surrogate. The embryo was implanted in her womb."

"How old is Billy?"

Bradford paused for several seconds. "Billy is only twelve years old."

"No way!" exclaimed Webster.

"I'm telling you the truth. The genetic version of Billy grows twice as fast as a normal human being. Our genetic engineering was designed to create much stronger humans. A side effect has been an increased growth rate. Two problems we've faced are the increased tendency for violence, and the brain does not develop as fast as the body. You have a twelve-year-old in the body of a superhuman with strong violent and sexual urges. This can be a deadly combination, as you've already seen."

"Doctor, no one will believe all this.," said Webster.

"I know. But you need to know this."

"Doctor, he got shot in the torso twice, and it hardly fazed him."

"Because of his muscle mass. Part of the genetic code created more robust and denser muscle mass. Some of what we learned came from studying the genetic code of gorillas."

"Are there other Billy's at your facility?"

"I can't go into that. Please understand."

Webster looked at Bradford with raised eyebrows.

"Alright," said Webster. "I'm probably never going to understand the science. Just tell us how we stop Billy."

"You will have to put him down."

"Put him down? You mean kill him?"

"I mean kill him."

"We can't just kill someone like that unless our own life is in danger."

"Detective, our entire country is in danger if the public finds out about this. China wants to dominate the world. We can't allow that."

"No, we'll find a way to detain him and put him in jail," said Webster.

"You don't get it, Detective. The government will not allow you to detain and jail Billy. He must be eliminated. They will make up some story about him being a mentally deranged criminal and say they've locked him up in a secure facility. No one will ever question it or ask about him again."

"And you'll just keep experimenting with genetically altered humans?"

"If not me, then someone else. Again, we need to keep up with our enemies. Someday we will perfect this process, and the entire human race will be better for it. We might someday eliminate all diseases. Wouldn't that be wonderful? Humans have naturally evolved over thousands of years. We are simply trying to speed up the process."

"Were you the one who called in the crime stoppers tip?"

"No, but I think I know who did. I won't give you his name, as he would be in trouble if it ever came out. We had a scientist leave the facility six years ago because he disagreed with what we were doing. We've made mistakes, as you can imagine. He tired of the losses and left when Billy was six years old."

"What losses?" questioned Webster.

"As with all research, there is trial and error. Our experiments sometimes don't work. Use your imagination, Detective."

Webster had a sick feeling in his stomach. "I don't think I want to."

After an uncomfortable pause in the conversation, Webster said, "How will the feds be able to keep this quiet?"

Bradford chuckled. "Did you know about it?"

"No."

"And yet, our facility has done this research since the Genome Project in two-thousand-three, fifteen miles from your city. The government does an excellent job of keeping secrets."

"What would keep us from getting a warrant to search your facility and blow this thing out of the water?"

"Good luck," laughed Bradford. "The government bought that piece of property twenty-five years ago and made it federal land. The building on it is a federal building with national security interests. A state judge has no jurisdiction. Try finding a federal judge willing to issue a warrant. That place is warrant proof."

Webster knew Bradford was right. "Is there anything else you can tell us that might help?"

"Yes, tell your officers to either shoot him in the head or use a rifle. His muscle mass won't stop a rifle round."

Neither said a word for several seconds.

"Well, thank you, Doctor Bradford, for telling me this. I have a lot to process. It still sounds like science fiction to me."

"In some ways, it may be," agreed Bradford. "But the future is upon us."

On the way back to the department, Webster explained everything Bradford had told him as best he could. Velez was shocked by what Webster described.

"I still can't believe this," said a disturbed Webster. "A genetically altered human?"

"In college," said Velez, "I took an advanced genetics class, and we talked about the possibility of some of the stuff he told you. I learned of our ability to grow human ears on the backs of mice and things like that. I've even read where scientists are trying to grow edible meat in laboratories to end the need for killing animals. If we are close to doing those things, then why not this? It's not that far-fetched, Jack."

"I'm sure you're right, Alec. It's still shocking. What are we going to tell the chief?"

Velez shook his head. "You're the one with the information. By the way, why the hell did you moon the doctor?"

"Shut the hell up! He was checking for wires. If you ever mention that to anyone, so help me god...."

Velez started laughing. "I'm glad you wore clean underwear. Did you learn that in the academy?"

"One more word, Alec, and you'll be walking back."

Velez wasn't going to push it to find out. It was too far to walk.

After several minutes of silence, Webster spoke up again. "Can you believe he told me we would have to shoot Billy?"

"Yeah, that shocks me. What do we tell the officers?"

"Well, I will not tell them to shoot him on sight, that's for sure. There has to be another way."

Chapter 8

Billy cruised the streets in his newest truck looking for something exciting to do. There didn't seem to be much action on the streets. Billy remembered the sense of relief after he visited the Red Rider Pony. He decided to try another bar. In the next block, he saw a restaurant/bar on the corner of the intersection. It looked like an excellent place to try.

Once he walked in, Billy saw people playing a game on green tables with hard balls and long sticks. Loud music he did not recognize was blaring throughout the bar. Billy found it annoying. He walked to the bar and asked for some water. The bartender looked at him with a questioning look before giving him a glass of ice water.

Billy took his water and started checking people out as he walked around. *Is there a woman in here who will have sex with me?* Billy saw a long-haired older blond woman sitting with another man. He walked over to talk to her.

"Hello, what's your name?"

The woman looked up at Billy. "Who are you?"

"I'm Billy."

"She's with me," said the man sitting at the table.

Billy looked at the man, then walked toward one of the green tables to watch the game. He was interested in how they hit one ball to hit another ball in a hole. After a few minutes, Billy picked up a ball to feel it. He was impressed with how hard it was.

"Hey!" shouted one of the players. "What are you doing?"

"I just wanted to see what it was made of."

"You can't do that. We are in the middle of a game."

Billy could feel anger building up inside of him. Who did this person think he was to challenge Billy like that?

"Hey, buddy," said a voice from behind Billy. Billy turned around and looked. A shaggy-haired man wearing a purple tank top was looking at Billy. "Would you like to play?"

"Yes," said Billy.

"Great, you can break. I'm Charles."

"Break?" asked Billy.

"Haven't you ever played?"

"No."

"Alright, here is how you do it." Charles then hit the white ball into the aligned group of balls, sending them in all directions on the table. "That's how you break. Now it's your turn. Pick either solids or stripes."

Billy lined up a ball with his stick.

"No, you have to hit the white ball with the cue. Use the white ball to knock other balls into the pockets."

Billy thought that was stupid. It certainly made it more challenging to hit a colored ball into a hole. Billy did the best he could to line up a shot. He pushed the cue stick hard, missing the center of the white ball. The white ball sliced off the table onto the floor. Several men watching laughed.

"Stop laughing," said Billy.

"Come on, big guy, you should be able to handle a cue stick," said one of the men.

"Here, Billy, try again," said Charles.

Billy tried it again. This time, his stick went under the ball, bouncing it into several other balls.

Some men started laughing again.

"You suck at this," said one man.

Billy could feel his rage rising. He stepped toward the man and pushed him back. "I told you to stop laughing."

"Cool it, man. We're just having fun here."

Billy could see many were now looking at him. He looked back and scanned the room.

"You all think I'm a freak, don't you?" he shouted.

Charles stepped forward to calm Billy. "No, they don't. They meant nothing by it. We just want to have fun here. Calm down."

Billy was trying to contain his emotions. He remembered having fun and laughing at the facility, but this seemed different.

"Come on and sit down over here," said Charles. Billy followed him to a table and sat down.

The bartender, who had observed the confrontation, believed Billy fit the description of the man police were looking for. He had called the police to report it.

"What is your name?" asked Charles.

"They call me Billy."

"Alright, Billy, where are you from?"

Billy did not know how to answer the question. Should he tell Charles he had come from the compound north of the city?

"I'm from north of here," answered Billy. Billy then heard some commotion at the front door. He looked and saw three police officers talking to people and looking around. One patron turned and pointed directly at Billy. Officers started making their way toward Billy.

This is getting annoying, thought Billy. He got up and ran toward the back of the restaurant and through a swinging door into the kitchen area. He ran straight into a server carrying a tray of food, sending her and all the food flying. The server hit her head on a metal preparation table as she fell. In a split second, three officers came running right behind Billy, shouting for him to stop. Billy had no intention of stopping.

Billy ran toward a door with an emergency bar on it. He hit the bar and flung open the door. He observed a black SUV come screeching into the parking lot. Billy was running at an incredible speed. Homeland Security Investigator Clara Chen opened the passenger door to jump out. Just as her feet hit the ground, Billy slammed into the open car door, shoving it back into Chen, crushing her against the doorjamb. She let out a scream and fell to the ground. FBI Agent Levi Rucker aimed his Smith and Wesson semi-auto toward Billy. He fired off two rounds. From what Rucker could tell, his shots missed their target. He then ran to the aid of Chen.

The three officers, still in pursuit, ran past the fallen agent. Once he was out of the parking lot, Billy turned north and started running as fast as he could down the sidewalk. The officers were losing ground with every step Billy took. Even with his size, he ran like a gold medal track star. After two blocks, the officers gave up.

Billy continued to run without stopping until he was sure the officers were no longer chasing him. He stopped at a busy intersection. Cars were lined up at the traffic light, and the first car in line closest to him was a red Chevy Tahoe. Perfect for his size. He ran to the driver's side, opened the car door, and told the male driver to get out.

"What the hell? Shut the door!"

"Get out now!" shouted Billy. The driver tried pushing Billy away from the door. Billy tried pulling the driver out of the car, then realized the driver was wearing a seat belt. The driver punched Billy in the face with his elbow. Billy didn't even flinch. While holding the driver with his right hand, Billy cocked his left fist back, then gave the driver a blow to his left upper jaw. The driver slumped over. Billy then reached around the driver's waist and unbuckled the seat belt. The driver regained consciousness and began resisting again. This time, Billy cocked his right arm and punched the driver's left upper jaw again, snapping his head sideways. The driver was now fully unconscious. Billy grabbed him by the collar and pulled him out of the car, allowing his limp body to fall to the street. Some bystanders on the street corner began to scream.

The Tahoe rolled forward. Billy hopped in, shut the door, and hit the accelerator. The back left wheel ran over one of the driver's legs as Billy pulled away. The Tahoe lurched forward into the intersection against the red light. Horns blared, and tires screeched as drivers tried to avoid hitting the Tahoe. As Billy accelerated to the other side of the intersection, he smashed into the left front fender of a cross-traffic small vehicle. The vehicle went into a three-quarter spin. Billy continued driving north, hoping to find his way back to his shelter.

***

Turner had been listening to the radio traffic and knew Billy had escaped. She decided to focus her search efforts on the northern area neighborhoods. A report had been aired describing the red Tahoe with Texas plates now believed to be driven by Billy.

It was 10:58 pm when Turner spotted the stolen Tahoe. She radioed her position and asked for backup. She had to follow close enough so as not to lose him in traffic. Unfortunately, this allowed Billy to see her following him.

Billy sped up and started passing other vehicles by weaving in and out of traffic. Turner turned on her lights and siren and radioed she was in pursuit of the suspect vehicle. Other officers started to respond with lights and sirens.

Billy had been taught how to drive, but he was not experienced operating at high speeds in traffic. Turner kept up as best she could but had to be careful not to hit any innocent drivers. She continued to update dispatch and other officers of her location.

Officers radioed they were waiting ahead of Turner at 43rd Street. If Billy continued, they would cut him off at that intersection.

Turner was driving as fast and safely as possible, but Billy was pulling further ahead. The officers at 43rd Street could see the Tahoe approaching their location. "We are going to ram him!" announced one officer.

Just as Billy was about to enter the intersection, the officer timed it perfectly and accelerated into the intersection. The front of his patrol car hit the right front fender of the Tahoe, causing it to careen to the far left and up onto the sidewalk. Billy was shocked by the impact, and his head hit the driver's side window. The Tahoe hit a trash can and newspaper dispensing machine, sending paper flying into the air. Billy continued to keep his foot on the accelerator and guided the vehicle back onto the street into on-coming traffic. Other drivers had to take evasive action to avoid being hit head-on. The tire on the right front of the Tahoe had been ripped apart. Billy was now driving with one rim on the pavement, sending sparks flying. It made it difficult to control the car.

He could hear sirens right behind him. Billy quickly made a left turn into an alley and ran into a dumpster. He jumped out of the vehicle and ran as fast as he could down the alley and out onto the next street. The officers who had been chasing him were stuck in the alley. There was not enough passage to get around the damaged Tahoe.

Billy ran into a nearby restaurant, pushing people out of his way to get to the back. He ran through the kitchen and storage area, then exited into another alley. Billy ran to the end of the alley and looked for cops. He heard sirens but did not see any officers. Across the street, he saw a wooded park with a drainage ditch. He ran across the park and got into the ditch. He then started running the length of the ditch. His large lungs allowed him to run fast for a long time. He kept running until he no longer heard any sirens. Billy then sat down to rest. His lungs hurt from all the running and his head ached from the accident. He soon laid down in the ditch and fell asleep.

Turner and other officers continued to patrol for Billy with no luck. Turner could not believe he had escaped them again. She had never gone up against anyone like him before.

In all total, another five people had been injured by Billy's actions. The most severe injury was that of the Tahoe driver. He suffered a concussion, a broken leg, and torn knee ligaments. Investigator Chen sustained bruises to her back and sternum but was otherwise okay.

Chapter 9

The following morning, Webster and Velez met with Commander Lopez in her office. Webster shared with her the information he had gotten the night before. She found it hard to believe what they were telling her.

"Where did you get this information?"

"From a confidential informant," advised Webster. "If we reveal who it is, his life will be in danger."

"You can tell me, Jack."

"No, Commander, I can't. We made a promise. You will just have to trust what we are saying or disregard it. But, we are telling you the truth."

"Do you have the conversation recorded?"

"No, he insisted on no wires and had me shut my phone down."

"How did he know you weren't wearing a wire?"

Webster could see Velez trying not to laugh and glanced him a frown. "He told me beforehand not to wear one, so I didn't want to risk losing him as an informant," is all Webster would say.

"It is all hard to believe, but it makes some sense," agreed Lopez. "The question is, what do we do with it?"

"We don't know. That's why we are talking to you."

"I don't know if the chief will believe it," said Lopez.

"We aren't sure we believe it entirely, either. What I can tell you is it came from a source that would know."

"Did this source have a solution on how to deal with Billy?"

Webster and Velez looked at each other. "He said to either shoot him in the head or with a rifle, Commander," stated Webster.

"Shoot him?"

"Yes, ma'am."

"Well, we can't just shoot the boy."

"That's what we told our source, but he said the feds would do it if we didn't."

"We will shoot him if we have to, but we will not commit a homicide just to keep a federal secret."

"We agree," said Webster.

Lopez looked as though she was in deep thought for a few moments. "I'll tell the chief what you found out. Let's see what his advice is."

Both detectives nodded.

"You heard about what happened last night, right?" asked Lopez.

"Yes," answered Webster.

"Stella is distraught over it," said Velez. "She told me they have been so close to arresting him twice, and each time he got away."

The news of Billy's latest episode was all over the Amarillo media. Rumors of his strength and endurance were spreading. Some were referring to him as Superman. Some were calling him Amarillo Billy. The public information officer and chief's office were being inundated with questions and interview requests. News outlets in Dallas had picked up on the story, creating even more attention to the happenings in Amarillo. Interviewed witnesses and concerned citizens were questioning the competence of the Amarillo Police Department. Some were calling for the chief to be fired. Others were in awe of the strength and endurance of this superhuman. The most common name being used by residents and media was Amarillo Billy. He was considered a modern-day Billy the Kid.

Commander Lopez went to the chief's office to give him the latest update. Laura, the chief's assistant, advised she would have to wait a few minutes. The chief was meeting with the patrol commander over the previous night's events. Lopez took a seat just outside the door to the chief's office. It was clear the chief was not happy, as Lopez could hear yelling through the door.

"How the hell can thirteen officers and two federal agents allow one suspect to escape arrest!" yelled the chief. Lopez could not hear the patrol commander's response. "I want a plan in place for tonight," continued the chief in a loud voice.

Lopez could hear the commander say something about needing officers. "I'll give you what you want, but we better get him tonight," yelled the chief. "This has gone on long enough!"

Lopez could hear more conversation but couldn't make out what was being said.

Several minutes later, the chief's door opened and out walked the patrol commander. He looked at Lopez and whispered, "good luck."

Lopez stepped into the office, not knowing what to expect. She provided the confidential information Webster and Velez had obtained.

"Genetic superman, my ass," grumbled Chief Boone. "Where did Webster get that piece of horse crap? I want to know who this source is."

"I don't know, Chief. He couldn't, and wouldn't, tell me."

"So, based on some whacko's theory, we are supposed to shoot our suspect?"

"No, I'm not suggesting we shoot anyone. I'm just telling you what the source said. Webster swore he was a reliable source who knows what he's talking about."

"Well, I don't buy it. We are going to arrest this suspect tonight and put him in jail. Then the feds can do what they want with him. I just want him out of here. Everyone, including the mayor, is all over my back. I'm pulling officers from other assignments and putting them on night patrol starting tonight. I want you to pick six detectives and have them patrol in unmarked cars. I've also asked narcotics to do the same. We are going to flood the streets with cops tonight. If he moves, we'll find him."

"I can do that," assured Lopez. "What time do you want them to start?"

"Just before dark. Have them out by seven pm. Laura! Where's that damn Coca-Cola I asked for?" yelled Boone to his assistant.

She came through the open door quickly. "Sorry, Chief, the machine is all out of Coke."

"Of course it is!" shouted Boone. "Damn it!"

"Is there anything else, Chief?" asked Lopez.

"No," said a dejected Boone.

When she got back to the detective bureau, Lopez told Webster the chief didn't believe the information she had given him.

"No surprise," replied Webster.

The commander then selected six detectives for unmarked patrols that evening. Two of the six were Webster and Velez. She told them they could go home to get some rest until then.

Lopez then met with the Patrol Commander, Adam Brooks. "You took some heat from the chief this morning."

"Nothing I haven't endured before."

"What is your plan tonight?"

"I thought we would saturate the northern half of the city with both uniformed and undercover patrols," said Brooks. "Our plan, should we find him, will be to hang back until we get sufficient officers to surround him and block all escape routes. We will have tasers and K-9s ready to take him down if he resists."

"Have you included the feds?"

"Yes, they will have four unmarked units out with two agents in each car. I've spoken to Agent Rucker about it."

"It sounds like a good plan," agreed Lopez. "Are you going to be out tonight?"

"Oh, yes. I'll be coordinating everything. You're welcome to join me."

"I think I will. I'm going to leave this afternoon to get some rest, and then I'll be back by six-thirty."

"Thank you, Martina. I'll see you then."

***

Billy woke up that morning and was not sure where he was. He was hungry and angry that he had lost all the food he had stolen. With all the driving and running to get away, he had not paid attention to the route he took. All he knew was that he was in a residential area. His shirt had new bloodstains on it. One of the gunshot wounds had reopened and had bled out onto his shirt. He hadn't noticed any pain during all the excitement, but now his abdomen was hurting.

Billy walked the culvert looking into the backyards of bordering homes. He came upon one with no lights on inside and seemingly quiet. There was no activity in the kitchen or dining room. Billy watched it for a while to see if anyone was home. After thirty minutes of seeing nobody around, he entered the home. The sliding back door presented no problem for Billy. He lifted the door off the track and quickly jerked it, breaking the lock. Once inside, he checked all the rooms. No one was home.

Having a house to himself provided Billy a place to hide for the day. He found a refrigerator full of many goodies. Billy ate until he had no more room in his stomach. He then went into the bathroom and took his first hot shower since leaving the facility. He stood in the shower until the hot water turned cold. He dried himself off with a towel, then threw it onto the floor. In the medicine cabinet, Billy found some first aid supplies. He applied some antiseptic to his wounds, then re-bandaged them.

Billy looked for a fresh shirt to wear but could not find any that fit in the closet. In one of the dresser drawers, Billy found an extra-large t-shirt. The shirt did not fit comfortably, but he could squeeze into it. It made his muscles look bigger than they were.

Billy was feeling angry and sad at the same time. Life outside the facility was not what he envisioned. He was not adapted to a life of complete freedom to do what he wanted whenever he wanted. It was hard work just to survive. He wondered if anyone would accept him for who he was. *Maybe I should go back to the simple life in the facility,* he pondered. However, he left because he wanted to see what it was like outside the facility's fences. He also had desires and urges he could not satisfy inside. Yet, would he always be on the run outside the facility?

Billy tried to watch some TV but had difficulty figuring out how to use the multiple remotes in the home. He got the TV to come on but could not figure out how to use the on-screen menu. In frustration, Billy kicked the TV and knocked it over. He explored other areas of the home, occasionally finding tools or gadgets not familiar to him. After several hours, Billy was feeling tired again. In one bedroom was a large king-size bed. Billy liked the size, so he laid down and fell asleep.

Chapter 10

At 6:20 pm, Billy was awakened from the sound of the garage door opening. Billy jumped up to look out the window. He saw a beige Toyota Highlander pulling into the driveway. Billy quickly hid around the corner in the living room, just off the dining room. The homeowner, a pretty woman in her forties, with shoulder-length, soft brown hair, and beautiful brown eyes, walked into the kitchen and stopped.

"What in the hell happened here?" she said out loud. "Chris, are you home?" she shouted. She stared at the mess in the kitchen. She called again, "CHRIS!"

The woman walked into the dining room and set her purse on the table, still in shock at the mess. Just then, Billy walked into the dining room. The woman screamed. "What are you doing in my house?! Oh, my god, you are that man everyone is looking for!"

Suddenly, Billy's desire for sex surged. He was usually more attracted to blond women, but he found this woman beautiful and sexual. Billy walked over to the woman and grabbed her arm.

"Let go of me!" she screamed as she kicked at Billy's legs.

"Stop it. I will not harm you."

The woman began yelling for help and continued to struggle against Billy's tight grip. He pulled her toward the bedroom as she continued to yell, kick, and punch at Billy. Having had enough, Billy took his other hand and grabbed the hair on the back of her head, pulling it tightly. Her head snapped backward.

"I told you to stop. I'm not going to harm you."

With her head pulled back and one arm immobilized, the woman realized it was no use fighting. Billy walked her to the bedroom with the king-sized bed and pushed her onto the bed. She was lying on her back, looking up at Billy with fear in her eyes. She could not stop shaking.

"I'm only going to have sex with you. Take off your clothes."

"Please don't. Take whatever you want, just don't rape me, please."

"Rape you? I'm just going to have sex with you."

"That's rape!" yelled the woman. "I don't want to have sex with you. I want you to leave."

"Why don't any of you women want to have sex? I thought women liked sex. Do you want me to pay you?"

"No! Just leave me alone. Would you want someone to do this to your mother?"

"I don't have a mother."

"Well, I'm a mother, and I don't want you to do this."

Billy stopped to think a moment about what to do. He could see the woman was frightened. He sat down beside the woman. "Tell me then, how do I find someone who wants to have sex with me?"

The woman thought Billy had to be joking. Was this some game he was playing with her? It didn't matter. So long as he was talking, he wasn't attacking her. She decided to play along. She swallowed and took a deep breath to calm herself.

"Sex is between two people who care for each other. You must first become friends and develop a loving relationship. It is wrong just to pick someone and force them to have sex with you."

Billy thought about what the woman had just said.

"If you rape me, I will hate it, and it will hurt me. You said you didn't want to hurt me, remember?"

This had never been explained to Billy. He had no experience with women, and no one had ever talked to him this way.

"I'm sorry," said Billy. "I have these strong desires inside of me that are hard to control, but I never want to hurt anyone unless they try to hurt me or make me angry."

"I will not hurt you," she said softly.

Billy looked at her. "I know. I will leave if you give me your car."

"Yes, yes, of course. The keys are on the dining room table."

Billy got up and left the bedroom. He grabbed the keys, went out into the garage, and drove away in the woman's Toyota Highlander. As soon as Billy left, the woman called the police.

Back at the police station, Commander Brooks was holding a briefing with officers to go over the plan for the evening when Sergeant Anderson stepped into the room.

"Commander, we've just gotten a report of a burglary and attempted rape in the Applewood neighborhood. The suspect description fits Billy. He left the scene in a beige Toyota Highlander."

"Alright, everyone," announced the commander, "let's hit the street and flood the area. Tonight, we find and arrest Amarillo Billy."

Webster and Velez grabbed their equipment and headed to their car. "Is Stella working tonight?" asked Webster.

"Yes, she started at three o'clock. She is probably already in the area looking for him."

In a matter of minutes, officers had flooded the Applewood neighborhood and surrounding area looking for the stolen Highlander. Federal agents, including Rucker and Chen, were out in their black SUVs monitoring the police radio traffic. Commanders Brooks and Lopez were riding together, listening as well.

It wasn't long before an officer reported seeing the stolen vehicle traveling northbound in the 2400 block of Lawrence Boulevard. Webster and Velez headed in that direction, as well as Turner and the Commanders. Commander Brooks radioed for K-9 officers to respond. Thus far, the plan was working.

Billy saw several patrol cars following him. He also saw a few patrol cars at intersections as he passed by. *There are cops everywhere*, thought Billy. He could sense the adrenalin building up inside of him. No one had tried to stop him yet, so he simply kept driving.

Commander Brooks continued to coordinate responding officers. He had set up a coordinated moving roadblock. No matter what direction Billy took, officers were there waiting to intercept him. Soon, there was a helicopter circling overhead. Billy could hear the constant beat of the rotors. Billy turned right, heading east. He could see patrol cars still following him. Several vehicles were not marked, but he suspected they were with the police. Billy eventually came to highway 87 and turned north, heading out of the city.

"Suspect is now heading north on eighty-seven," announced Turner.

"Once he gets out of the city, we will attempt to stop him," radioed Commander Brooks.

Several officers passed Billy to get in front of him.

Billy continued to drive northbound until he was several miles outside the city limits. He could see the police had created a rolling roadblock in front of him and were slowing down. Billy had to think quickly. He noticed a dirt road off to the east. Maybe he could take that and get lost in the high desert. As he came to the intersection, he made a sharp right turn and hit the accelerator. Dust and rocks went flying as he fishtailed onto the road.

Officer Turner and several other officers immediately pursued Billy down the road. The lack of daylight and flying dust made it difficult for officers to see. Webster and Velez followed the pursuit. The helicopter overhead was keeping an eye on the suspect vehicle. Commander Brooks wondered who had ordered a helicopter.

Billy continued with police now in full pursuit. After about a mile, Billy hit the brakes and spun the steering wheel, causing the Highlander to skid in a half-circle, throwing rocks and dirt into the night air. He was now facing the on-coming army of police. He pushed the accelerator to the floor. The tires spun rapidly, throwing more debris into the air.

Officer Turner quickly radioed that the suspect vehicle was now heading straight at them.

"Set up a roadblock!" ordered Commander Brooks.

Several officers behind Turner set their vehicles at an angle, blocking the roadway. Turner shined her spotlight into the windshield of the oncoming Highlander, hoping to blind the driver. It did not stop Billy. He drove straight for the light. Seeing this, Turner quickly got out of her vehicle and ran off to the side. Seconds later, the Highlander smashed into the left front of the patrol car, sending it spinning. Turner could hardly see anything because of dirt in the air. The dust stung her eyes.

Six patrol cars, a detective car, and two black SUVs were arranged along the roadway to form a roadblock. Two patrol cars parked nose to nose, a secondary roadblock of four patrol cars, and then the SUVs and Webster/Velez's car behind that. A K-9 officer was waiting behind the roadblock.

Billy's adrenalin was as high as it had ever been. He was in full combat mode as he drove straight toward the two patrol cars. The officers had gotten out and were pointing their guns at the oncoming Highlander. Billy was traveling at about 70 miles per hour when he hit the two cars in front. Both patrol cars spun wildly, and the front of the Highlander was smashed on both front fenders. Debris went flying everywhere. One officer was unable to get out from behind the patrol car fast enough. The spinning car struck him, injuring his hip and knocking him to the ground. Another officer was hit in the leg with a flying piece of metal, cutting it to the bone. A third officer was hit in the face with flying rocks and dirt, dropping him to his knees.

The Highlander continued until striking the second row of vehicles. The double impact disabled the Highlander and brought it to a stop. Billy quickly jumped out of the car and was blinded by spotlights. As he stood contemplating his next move, Officer Turner, still squinting and blinking from the dust, moved toward Billy. She hoped she could get close enough to try the taser again. Commander Brooks directed his K-9 officer to be ready to release the dog. Using his loudspeaker, Brooks ordered Billy to get down on the ground.

Just then, a loud booming shot rang out, echoing off the hills. The back of Billy's head exploded from the exit of the high-velocity bullet. Billy dropped to the ground.

Commander Brooks quickly turned around to see where the shot came from. He observed a federal agent lying on top of one of the black SUVs with a high-powered scoped rifle pointed toward Billy. Webster and Velez also looked in the direction of the shot.

"Can you believe it?" said Webster. "They actually shot him."

After the shot, everyone's attention was drawn to the large helicopter descending from the sky, throwing dirt and debris in every direction. Officers shielded their eyes from the dust. Officer Turner protected her face with her hand and ran to Billy to check on his status. The large hole in the back of his head left no doubt he was dead.

Once the helicopter landed and the dust settled, everyone could see it was a military helicopter. Six fully equipped military operatives jumped out of the helicopter with assault rifles. They surrounded Billy's body as though they were protecting it.

Agent Rucker and Investigator Chen walked up to Commanders Brooks and Lopez.

"Why did your agent shoot Billy like that?" asked Brooks. "He might have been surrendering."

"He almost killed one of your officers, Commander," answered Rucker. "He rammed four police cars with no regard for the safety of us or your officers. We could not take the chance anyone else would get hurt. Based on his behavior this past week and tonight, he presented a deadly threat. We had no choice but to take him out."

"He was dangerous," agreed Brooks. "But we might have been able to subdue him. You know there will be an investigation, right?"

"Yes, but it will be done by the FBI and Homeland Security. Billy was a dangerous military risk. These soldiers are taking his body for an autopsy."

"No, our coroner will do that," said Brooks.

Rucker just smiled and shook his head. He then looked at the soldiers and nodded his head. Two more soldiers with medical crosses on their sleeves lowered a gurney out of the helicopter. Billy's body was quickly picked up and put on the gurney.

Brooks continued to protest, but it was useless. There was nothing he could do to stop the military. Once Billy was loaded, the soldiers got on the helicopter, and it took off, disappearing into the night.

Two of the injured officers were taken to the hospital by ambulance. Several other officers were treated for minor injuries from flying debris. It then took several tow trucks a couple of hours to clean up the mess of damaged vehicles.

Back at the station, the officers involved all met for a debriefing. Chief Boone was also present. Many officers were curious as to what just happened.

"From what we know," explained the chief, "Billy was an escaped federal prisoner, someone the military had an interest in. We don't know if he was a spy, an agent who turned on the United States, gave away military secrets, or what. They wouldn't tell us much, other than he was a threat to national security."

Webster and Velez listened to the chief's explanation in silence. There wasn't much they could say.

After the meeting, Webster, Velez, and Commander Lopez met in her office.

"Our source said they would kill Billy, and they did," said Webster. "They didn't give him a chance to surrender."

"Do you want to go public with what you know?" asked Lopez.

"No, that would be professional suicide and put my family in danger. Our source warned us the government would cover this up, and he would never back up anything we said. We have no proof he even talked to us. He made sure of that."

"I didn't think they would do it," said Velez. "Stella is upset about it, and I can't explain a thing to her. I just have to play dumb."

"You two did a great job following up on this. In the end, it was out of our hands. Go home and reflect on it, then forget about it. You still have a homicide to solve. Focus on what's important to us now."

Turner spent that night at Velez's apartment. They stayed up all night and talked about what happened while sharing a bottle of red wine.

"I don't understand it, Alec," questioned Turner. "Why did they have to shoot him immediately? I was moving closer to get a taser on him if he refused to surrender."

"We'll probably never know, Stella. It seems they believed this person was a threat to our national security, and they didn't want to take any chances he might escape again."

"I'm just so curious. Who was this guy? Where did he come from?"

"All good questions, Stella. Unfortunately, we will never know."

The next day, the FBI released a press statement thanking the Amarillo Police Department and Chief Anson Boone for their assistance in capturing a dangerous federal escapee. The release described Billy Jones as extremely dangerous and a threat to national security. According to the release, Jones was shot by an agent after attacking officers by attempting to run them over, seriously injuring two officers and causing minor injuries to several others. They promised that a full investigation of the incident would be conducted and procedures to prevent such an escape in the future would be implemented.

In the days after the shooting of Billy, the chief was still getting criticized. Some blamed him for not stopping Billy sooner. Others were upset Billy was shot. Some were upset the chief allowed the federal government to take control. There was even a small group that created a memorial for Amarillo Billy in Cottonwood Park, holding a candlelight vigil.

Seven days after the shooting, Chief Boone called all his commanders and supervisors together for a meeting. "I've had a long, successful, fulfilling career," announced the chief. "Including my time in Lubbock, I've been in policing for thirty years. These last couple of weeks have been stressful for me, and it caused me to reflect on everything I've accomplished. Daisy and I would like to have more time doing things we love while we are still young and healthy enough to do so. Therefore, I am announcing my retirement as of the end of this month. I appreciate all of you and the work you've done to make this city a better place to live. Thank you for your support and loyalty. I know I could be hard on you sometimes, but it was only because I cared about the safety of this community and our officers. Thank you for your service."

At that, the room exploded into applause, and everyone stood. The site and sound brought tears to the chief's eyes. He spent the next hour shaking hands and individually thanking everyone.

Speculation in the news media was that the chief was forced to resign. He denied it, but the rumors persisted. The mayor would not address the rumors but publicly thanked the chief for his service and wished him a great retirement.

Epilogue

Ten days after Billy's death, Dr. Darren Bradford entered the conference room for his regularly scheduled meeting with Steve and David. He would hold these meetings after reading the reports on their development, education, and training.

He used these meetings to question them about their feelings, any concerns they had, and assess their development. Since Billy's departure, protocols had been changed to ensure both were regularly taking the prescribed hormones and other required drugs for their continued well-being.

Steve was the oldest at eight years old. David was six years old. Both were progressing well in the program. From his looks, Steve still appeared youthful, but he was already almost six feet tall. He could pass for someone much older than eight. Steve could already lift more weight than most full-grown men. David was showing similar growth and appeared to be eight to ten years old. Overall, Dr. Bradford believed they had made improvements over Billy. However, whenever hormone treatments were reduced, Steve still displayed some violent tendencies similar to Billy. Dr. Bradford knew they would have to keep a close eye on both boys moving forward.

ABOUT THE AUTHOR

Mark Beckner is known in Colorado from his time with the Boulder Police Department from 1978 to 2014. He rose through the ranks to become Boulder's Police Chief in 1998 and remained in that position until his retirement in 2014. Chief Beckner is best known for his leadership in turning around a department in turmoil and taking command of the JonBenet Ramsey murder investigation in late 1997. While the case has never been solved, Chief Beckner was able to bring order to the investigation and played a role in getting the case to a grand jury.

He now enjoys retirement and has turned his attention toward writing fictional crime dramas. He uses his unique experience and insights to add realism to his crime stories. Feedback and reviews from his first book, **Behind The Lies**, a book of three separate crime thrillers, have been very positive.

Mark still resides in Colorado with his wife Sally, but they become snowbirds in winter, living in Surprise, Arizona. They have two children, Kimberlee and Chad, as well as five grandchildren. When he is not writing crime thrillers, Mark spends time enjoying his family, traveling, bicycling, and playing softball and pickleball. He also finds joy in taking and collecting photographs of scenery and wildlife.

Thank You

I would like to thank my readers for supporting me in my book writing endeavors. I hope you enjoyed these two stories as much as I enjoyed writing them. It would be greatly appreciated if you would leave an online review of my book. Thank you.

And if you haven't yet read my first book, please check it out. It is called **Behind The Lies,** a book of three novellas full of action and drama. It is available from various vendors, both online and through bookstores.

What's next?

Please look for additional future releases of crime thrillers.

For further information, please visit my webpage at:

Becknerbooks.com

Email: becknerbooks@gmail.com

You can sign up for notifications of new releases and offers. I also display some of my scenery and wildlife photography on the website.

Thanks again.

Made in the USA
Columbia, SC
12 October 2021